F   c.2
BAN
                4.95
Banning, Margaret Culkin
   I took my love to the
country

I TOOK
MY LOVE
TO THE
COUNTRY

Books by Margaret Culkin Banning

Margaret Culkin Banning

I TOOK MY LOVE TO THE COUNTRY

Harper & Row, Publishers

New York, Evanston, and London

To
my neighbors in North Carolina
with great affection

None of the characters in this book ever lived. None of the events ever happened except in the imagination of the author. But the background of the story, some localities, ways of life, and contemporary tendencies are faithful to what the writer has seen and tried to interpret.

FIRST EDITION

LIBRARY OF CONGRESS CATALOG CARD NUMBER: 66–20749

H-Q

I TOOK
MY LOVE
TO THE
COUNTRY

C. 2

1

DeSoto, North Carolina, is a village which looks from the air as if it had been carelessly dropped into several small valleys and plateaus between the foothills of the Blue Ridge and the sharp beak of Bald Eagle Mountain. It seems to have spattered as it fell, for bits of it have clung to places at quite a distance from the central town. There are vineyards here and there on clean slopes, an inn on the top of a rather remote hill, and stables at the farthest turn of the Branch which idles through the lowlands. The stream is snaky and a dull green color in contrast to the vividly blue, symmetrical swimming pools which dot the local estates.

The place is always being discovered by someone. Travelers from the North have been falling in love with it on sight for a hundred years and the loyalty of the mountain people has amounted to love for longer than that in its silent, undemonstrative way. The original outline of the old town has never changed and a row of wooden business blocks which have always housed drugs, hardware—and dentists and lawyers on the second floor— prove that in time crude ugliness can become quaintness. The main street, now paved, still sags unpretentiously along the side of the railroad tracks, following the route of the dirt road which used to be the only way in and out of town. But a great deal of money is spent along that street, especially during the spring and autumn seasons.

There are fifteen churches to bear aloft the aspirations, fears and demands of Negroes and whites. There is a package liquor store, clean as a whistle, with printed statements on its walls that no bottles will be sold to habitual drunkards. Whether that is true or not, the alcoholic consumption of DeSoto is astonishing. The grocery store and spreading supermarkets flourish too, and their managers have learned that it is profitable to stock imported caviar and asparagus and pomegranates out of season, for there are many resident epicures.

It is a proud if not a vain village, as a place which is given so much praise and admiration inevitably would become. Proud of its riot of flowering shrubs, its magnificent shocking-pink sunrises, the soft mildness of many of its winter days when the rest of the country may be shivering or broiling. A little superstitious too, for traditionally it never rains on the day of the Horse and Hound Show—if it does rain, most people ignore it. Also at times it is a name-dropper of a town, conscious almost to snobbery of the famous and rich people who come there, many of whom have built fine houses or set up expensive gentlemen's farms on acreages in the vicinity.

Certainly it is curiously well-known for a village which can claim hardly more than two thousand citizens. Of course it has not pleased or satisfied everyone. Hernando de Soto, from whom it takes its name, was disappointed because the Indians told him that the surrounding mountains were gold-bearing and they turned out to be only surfaced here and there with mica. Since his visit four hundred and twenty-three years ago, others have come with high hopes and have also been let down. But there are always new enthusiasts.

"Life in DeSoto is like English country life. I mean like English country life used to be," Sara Bayard often told people when she invited them to visit her, half warning them, half boasting. She was in a position to know about that for her sister had married into the British aristocracy.

For a while Sara herself had lived on that increasingly unstable social level, but since her last divorce and remarriage to Tom Bayard—against Lady Sukeforth's will—she invariably made a point of saying that her home was in DeSoto. To a number of people the place was synonymous with Sara. Her American address was in the books of many travelers whom she had once known well or lightly and the word went around that it was better than comfortable at Sara's place in North Carolina and, if you liked it, it was even fun. Lady Sukeforth herself occasionally suggested DeSoto to friends who did not deserve or could not afford an introduction to Palm Beach. Theatrical people—during Sara's second marriage she had touched that set—who were trying to get into motion pictures or television, visited her occasionally. Usually there were horsemen, for that was Tom Bayard's world. And there were neighbors for, as Sara said in the enchanting and beguiling way she had, "There are more nice people in DeSoto than anywhere else."

Miles Halliday was the cynic who remarked that it was a colony of refugees, that everyone who came to DeSoto to live was running away from something. Of course he was not talking about the Wills or the Altons or the bona fide North Carolinians like them who ran the shops and the politics and the schools, nor did he mean the mountain people who swept their clay front yards to keep them clean of trash and grass, who bred good hounds and tolerated curs and were wise about changes in the weather. Miles was referring to the people who might ask him to dinner. He was a man who was not resident in DeSoto, but he came back almost every year to spend a month at the Inn.

Carver Jones, apt to be sitting on the front porch of the deliberately rustic country club, rejoicing in slovenly golf clothes and his very solvent retirement, loved to explain DeSoto to any newcomer with whom he could strike up a conversation. "What gives this little place its special flavor, sir, is the variety of people you'll meet here. And they go their own way, that's the thing about this town. It's horsy of course, but our little Hunt doesn't dominate the place. Nor the people who raise prize Herefords here, they don't run the show either. You can call your own tune in DeSoto. And another thing—your age bracket doesn't matter much here, not the way it does in most places."

Talk, usually affectionate, about DeSoto might be heard almost anywhere—at the captain's table of the *France*, at the Dublin Horse Show, very frequently in Cincinnati because of the Leighs, in Detroit because the Davis family usually sent some of their horses to DeSoto for the steeplechase races, in Palm Beach, for the Cranes often said that they liked their little place in DeSoto (that cottage of sixteen rooms) better than any of their other residences. In Vietnam a soldier, hating the lushness of the jungle and its fierce color, might tell his buddies that what they ought to see was DeSoto in the spring. The town is mentioned in book reviews and literary circles. Hammond King, the best-selling Negro novelist, lived there until he was sixteen. It is a village that might be spoken of almost anywhere, as it was in the apartment of the Stephen Coopers in New York on one February evening.

"Why don't we go down to DeSoto?" asked Jennifer.

Stephen Cooper did not answer. The question did not seem to get through to him at once. He was wrapped in one of the silences which he used to cover and control disappointment these days. He had already been home when Jennifer came in from work. That in itself was bad news. And one glance—actually she did not even have to glance—had told her that her husband had been frustrated again.

She had put away her coat and paused before the long, unframed mirror between two silk-hung windows to gain time. It reflected her faultlessly, as well as the artificial magnolia which was espaliered on the opposite wall and looked so natural that it might be growing. A beautiful room, people had said so often.

Jennifer touched the sides of her hair as if it needed attention though it did not. Her image was not cleverly deceitful like that of the magnolia but of a young woman as real as she was lovely. A quite tall, very slim figure dressed in dark wool cut for city wear, an untrimmed figure except for the fair hair that seemed to lift from her forehead of its own accord. She had the bearing of a girl but the gray-blue eyes held no childishness. She looked well cared for but not fussed over, thoughtful and yet as if she were not thinking of what she saw in the mirror.

She was not looking in the glass to reassure herself of attractiveness. She was feeling for the right thing to say and to do, searching for the right expression. She must show no trace of personal achievement or success, for that would be hard on Stephen tonight. Nor show any worry, which probably would be even worse.

He had opened the bar at the end of the room, which could be smoothly retired behind teak panels when it was not in use, and had mixed a drink which was almost finished. It was quite a long bar and not so well supplied with decanters and bottles as it used to be. Jennifer noticed the gaps as she crossed the room to give him a light, undramatized kiss. She turned on a couple of low lamps, flipped one off that seemed to make the room too big, moved a chair as if that mattered. She was sick with pity. She had come in with the alertness of the city and the pleasure of an interesting day's work still clinging to her, as well as stray bits of amusement. The hard-faced taxi driver had looked her over admiringly as she gave him his fare and said, "Good night, Miss. Have yourself a good evening."

Amusement had quite faded out. She picked up a newspaper that Stephen had tossed on a table, read the headlines and put it down again. She said, as if she had just thought of it, "Why don't we go down to DeSoto?" But it was not a sudden idea. It had been in the back of her mind for weeks, a possible impossibility, a last resort, something that they wouldn't do of course, but could do if they had to.

When he did not answer, she went on, "It might be the best thing to do. It would be good for you right now."

The last phrase seemed to sting him. He said, "What would be good for me right now is to get a job, make a new connection."

"When you've been pretty much top-flight in your field, there aren't too many openings," said Jennifer. "Most of them are already filled."

"That's what they tell me. And then the interview is over," he said in the cynical way that was new to him.

So many interviews were over, each one more defeating than the one before it. She could not bear what they were doing to Stephen. He wasn't the same person who used to come home in the evening, sometimes tired, perhaps pleased with himself, possibly angry about something, but always glad to see her. "How's my bride?" "How's the most beautiful female editor in New York?" "How's the poor working girl?" "Let me tell you what happened today—"

Now he didn't tell her what had happened today.

She sent up the trial balloon again. "If we went down to DeSoto—"

"For God's sake, Jenny! I can't take a vacation now!"

"I wasn't thinking about a vacation. I meant to go there for good. To live."

"Live where?" he asked, turning toward her as if he didn't think he had heard right.

"In your house. You still own your father's house."

"If I could only sell that old ark— I wrote Joe Harris about it again last week but apparently he hasn't had even a nibble of an offer for it."

"Then why don't we go down and live in it? Here we pay this fantastic rent—"

"I know you paid it this month," he said coldly. "It wasn't at all necessary. They could have waited. They wouldn't have put us out on the sidewalk."

"Of course not. But I thought I might as well."

"I'll make it up to you," said Stephen.

This was a dangerous subject, bruising from any angle. Jennifer moved away from it mentally and physically, going toward the silvered doors which opened into the dining room. The doors could be folded back and the two rooms made into a single enormous one on the occasion of a large party. It was now almost a year since they had been folded back.

She asked, "Lamb chops and a salad enough? There's an avocado."

"You can skip that tonight," said Stephen. "Corinne called up before you came in. She wants us to drop in for a drink at her place and then go on somewhere to eat when we feel like it. Spur of the moment thing, she said. Just a few people."

"Tonight?"

"Yes. You don't have to hurry. But I suppose they'll be getting under way before too long."

Every nerve in Jennifer protested the casual plan. She knew the pattern of that kind of party. It would begin carelessly in Corinne Miller's penthouse. The white greyhounds that were her present showpieces would be stalking the rooms, the flirtation would be open and deliberate and exaggerated, and the obvious cost of Corinne's clothes and jewels and surroundings would be a kind of excuse for her egotism and lapses into lust. She would be wearing some fantastic hostess gown when guests arrived and after a few drinks she would change into something black and backless and the party would move on to a restaurant and end up no doubt at a discothèque.

Corinne Miller was not beautiful but she was always so superbly decorated that she drew the attention she craved and lived for. She had run through a couple of marriages and was marking time now, amusing herself with other women's husbands. She joked and boasted about the alimony her lawyers managed to get for her, which she did not need because she had so much money of her own, none of it either earned or deserved. Her grandfather had been shrewd or hard working enough to make a fortune and when his only son was killed in a car wreck, all the money flowed into the hands of a woman who often was not sure of what she would want next but had no doubt that she could get it when she made up her mind.

All of this they both knew. Stephen had known Corinne before he was married, from the days of debutante parties. Jennifer had not liked Corinne when she met her nor ever been dazzled by her equipment, but their paths did not often cross. And Stephen used to speak of her slightingly, or laugh at her tricks with men and her boldness. It was only lately that he had been seeing her and her friends quite often. One reason for that, though Jennifer hated to admit it even to herself, was that since he had left the Atlantis Corporation a good many substantial social connections had loosened or been quite cut off. He had become a little defensive about Corinne and her frequent invitations and Jennifer had been conscious of that in his tone as he proposed this party tonight.

She said quickly—the horrid flash of imagining what the evening would be like had not taken a moment—"I'm sorry, Steve, but I can't do that tonight. I brought home some manuscripts that have to be read. Did you want to go? Did you tell her we'd come?"

"I said we didn't have anything else on. I thought it would be something to do," said Stephen restlessly.

It was obvious that he did want to go.

"Well, since I have to work, why don't you go by yourself?"

He stood by the bar, moodily considering that. Even in depression he was a very handsome man. But his tall body was made for action and his features for good temper, success and happiness. The withdrawn look was not right for him. Jennifer crossed to where he was standing. Her hand was almost fearful as she laid it on his arm for she never knew how he would react these days. She said, "Listen, Steve—I want to say something in dead earnest—we have to face up to a change—"

8

He did not move away from her hand. But she felt his muscles tighten.

"Do you want to get rid of me?" he asked quietly.

"Oh no! You know better than to say a thing like that!"

"It would be fair enough," said Stephen. "I wouldn't blame you for not wanting to be married to a failure and that's what you may be up against. If I were a professional man, a lawyer or a doctor or a teacher, I'd have something to stand on, a base. I could build up a living even if I had to start from scratch. But when a corporation that has been your life—your master anyway—for twelve years lets you out, when you're thirty-six, it's something else again."

"I hate them," she said. "It was utterly unfair, disloyal—"

"They don't think in those sentimental terms," he said, impatient with her sympathy. "After the merger they had orders from the top to cut down the number of executives in the company and they had to do it. There was nothing personal about it but there were others who had the inside track. Or owned stock in the company. And a public relations department can be pruned more easily than most other departments because it doesn't seem so essential. A man in my kind of job can't prove his results even if he knows they exist. The thing is that I've been pushed off the ladder when I was halfway to the top. I can't begin on the bottom rung again. Corporations are looking for bright boys fresh out of Harvard Business School or for men that other companies don't want to let go. I've been trying to break in somewhere for nearly a year. I've been trying to keep up this show—"

"It is a show. There are other ways to live, Steve, that's what I've been thinking lately. We've got ourselves trapped in a lot of habits and useless expense. When you figure how much of your salary went down the drain—entertaining—"

"Practically all of it. But that's part of the game. That's the way you have to play it."

"You don't have to any more. That's why I thought of going to DeSoto."

"What in hell would I do in DeSoto?"

"Live. Other people live there."

"When they have to retire. When they throw in the sponge. Old people."

"Young ones too. When we went down there the first time I met some who were about our age."

"That's the hunting set. Sara Bayard's crowd. But they come and go. They can afford to."

"Your father stayed there."

"He wasn't well. He retired when he was not much more than fifty. And he was obsessed with the place."

"A good many healthy men are retiring now before they're fifty. Or changing jobs completely. You hear about it all the time. There was a column in the *Wall Street Journal* about it the other day. They get out of business and teach. Or go off to be ministers."

He laughed.

She said, unheeding that, "I've heard you say more than once that it's a rat race here. I think it would be wonderful to live in the country. I remember how beautiful it is. And on the practical side there is the house. You own it—it's all furnished—you told me that the taxes are nominal—there wouldn't be much overhead expense."

"Jenny, you're dreaming."

"Maybe I'm waking up."

"How about your own job?" he asked. "You couldn't move *Portfolio Magazine* to DeSoto. And you've always been determined to hang on to that job even when it wasn't in the least necessary."

"I had to have something to do."

She didn't tell him again that she would have stopped working if they had had children. They had agreed on that long ago. She did not argue that she had no training for idleness. She did not tell him—this she never had and never would—that his work, the business of promotion, making useful connections and entertaining, had never given her the sense of security that her own job did.

She said, "Maybe I'm just a job addict. It could be that I need

10

to get off the hook. What's happened might be a break for me if we change the way we live completely."

"Sounds of courage in the night," he said, and laughed again, but this time in a fond way. "You're a great heroine, Jenny. Straight out of one of those stories you print." He lifted her chin and kissed her.

"Please don't brush it off like that. Think about DeSoto seriously. You'd find things to do. There's business in little towns. You could get a lot of exercise and you are always saying you need more—"

"We have to eat, you know."

"We'd eat without worrying if we were down there. We'd be in clover. No rent, no need to buy new clothes for ages, if ever. And after all we aren't completely destitute. You have at least five hundred a month from the trust fund."

"We've been spending five or six times that."

"But in the country we wouldn't have to. And I've saved something. I have—"

"You hang on to what you've got. And I'm not ready to be put out to pasture yet. Relax, Jenny. Stop worrying. Something will break for me, if I give it time. I'm seeing the Isthmus Oil people this week. They're expanding and they may have a spot for me in their public relations department. They're a good outfit. Now how about our both looking in on Corinne?"

"I honestly have to do this reading. But you go—I really wish you would."

"Well, maybe I will if you're going to work. I'll get out of your way."

The frank talk or the expressed hope about Isthmus Oil had raised his spirits. He went into his bedroom to change and shave and when he reappeared he looked a very handsome man on his way to a good time.

"Corinne's in luck tonight," said Jennifer, who was again trying to read the paper.

"Sure you won't change your mind?"

She shook her head.

"Don't forget to eat."

"I won't."

"And don't work too hard. I won't be late."

After he had gone Jennifer mixed herself a martini at the lonely bar and closed it up. In the aristocratic refrigerator in the kitchen that gleamed with stainless steel she found milk, a banana and a rather dry biscuit to nullify the gin. She did not unwrap the chops. Then she went back to the living room to turn off the lights. No matter what he said or intended, Steve would undoubtedly be late, for spur of the moment parties always lost track of time.

This room used to delight her when she came back to it in the evenings. She was continually surprised at finding herself living so luxuriously, and that had been part of the delight. The apartment was a handsome background for Stephen's position. A stream of business associates and out-of-town customers moved through it and that justified and made necessary what it cost to maintain it. There were a couple of competent servants so Jennifer's house-keeping duties were minimal. If the butler and cook were both off duty and by some chance she and Stephen had no engagement, she would pile leftovers on a couple of trays, but that was about all the housework she had to do. Now that the servants were gone and she had only a woman who came in to clean, Jennifer had made attempts in the last year to create or capture an atmosphere of home. They always failed. She had so much to do in the office that the attempts were hurried and sporadic, and Stephen didn't like to see her working in the kitchen. It humiliated him. He missed the servants more than Jennifer did but she had never been used to service before she married.

He would have plenty of it tonight. From Corinne's place they would go to some smart, expensive restaurant. Jennifer winced at another thought. How much would this evening cost Stephen? He was not a man to let someone else pick up the checks. She did not know how much money he actually had in hand now and she could not ask him, for it might seem like criticism or nagging or even insult. He had cashed in most of his insurance. She knew

12

that. The trust fund was his only sure income now. And he was not going to be able to make a new connection.

Jennifer had known that after the first few months of his hopeful, boastful idleness, when he was still getting severance pay and often saying that leaving Atlantis would probably be the best thing that had ever happened to him. Tonight he had been franker and more realistic in admitting that he had been pushed off the ladder. But she had sometimes wondered how he had managed to stay on it as long as he had. Perceptions of the attitude of his firm toward Stephen had sometimes filtered through to Jennifer, a word or lack of one that was a small signal that he was liked but not taken too seriously as a businessman. Stephen had never been driven by ambition. In the public relations department of the aluminum products corporation he had been useful because he made contacts easily and handled people well. Charm and good manners had been bred into him. But if there was an important deal to be made, someone who was harder or sharper than Steve usually took over. Jennifer had observed that even before the ax fell.

Charm was not enough. He had not made himself indispensable. Because he never had to battle for things, thought Jennifer for the uncounted time. His family had money and assured position and he took a fortunate life for granted. Things had always come his way without too much effort on his part, like the easy opening with Atlantis after he left college, given him because of one of his father's business connections. He had been established in a groove of the business world with practically no effort on his part. The kind of work he was given might not have been what he would have chosen for himself but it was interesting, not monotonous, and the salary was upgraded several times. Atlantis had prestige as a corporation and there was dignity, both of a social and business sort, in being connected with it.

Jennifer felt the twinge of pain which came so often now as she imagined what Stephen must have gone through during these months of being rejected. Gone through alone because her sympathy seemed to be an added blow to his pride. He was not a man to weep on any shoulder, especially not a woman's shoulder. The fact that she had a good job now while he was out of work was becoming a thing he resented, a barrier between them. He lets me pay the rent, she said to herself, but it sours him on me. The idea of going down to DeSoto may be as crazy as he says it is, but the reason I thought of it was that there we would live under his roof. And there would be no expensive, impromptu evenings like this one tonight which he can't afford. No Corinne. Is that why it seemed to me like a possible escape? It doesn't matter. He won't even consider it.

She took the manuscripts from her briefcase and went to her bedroom to put on a robe and settle down to reading. By the time a piece of fiction submitted to *Portfolio Magazine* came to Jennifer's desk it had reached almost final judgment as to its publication. Geoffrey Clark, who was editor-in-chief, usually backed her decisions without question.

She was young for her job at thirty-two because it carried a great deal of authority. But the job needed youth to keep the magazine in the running with other publications. It also called for sophistication. Jenny was mentally sophisticated. The brazen, savage pieces of writing that flowed across her desk would have effected that even without ten years of living in New York. But the sophistication stopped with what she knew. She had never put it into practice. It had not penetrated her emotions or her personal life. She was still a woman who earned her way, preferred decency and loved in a straight and steady line. She never used the vocabulary with which fiction had made her familiar. She couldn't say the words aloud.

She tried to concentrate on the story of passion and adultery in the typed pages she held. A note a reader had attached read, *I don't know whether we can publish this but it has vitality. It would arouse discussion.* That of course was what the magazine wanted to do. But it's always the same discussion, thought Jenny. It's gloating over the violence and cruelty of sex. There's more to the relations between men and women than that. There's money to consider, and hunger and beauty and happiness outside of beds.

14

And where to live. Her mind slipped back to her own situation and she thought, I should have gone with Steve tonight. I'm a fool. I can almost hear Steve telling Corinne, "Jenny couldn't come. She's at home with her career." And Corinne would say, "Jenny's too wonderful!" as if she were saying that Steve was the wonderful one.

Steve thought it was all right for me to have a job when it could be written off as decorative, as just my little hobby. He even used to show it off sometimes—he took a kind of pride in being married to someone who wasn't just a housewife or party girl. But now my job demeans him because it's necessary. Reasonably he should be very glad that I have a pay check to bring home. But it doesn't work that way. It never does. I see all the time that it doesn't work with other people. I've seen it in the office. She thought of May Fox.

May Fox was the woman whom Jennifer had replaced as fiction editor on *Portfolio* several years ago. May had been in love with Geoffrey Clark—everyone knew that—and he probably had been in love with her in the beginning. But it didn't last with him. He didn't want his mistress to be an editor in his office. And May tried to hold on to both jobs. She fought for them and with Geoffrey until the breakdown.

Geoffrey and I make a good safe team, thought Jennifer, because I'm in love with my husband. Sally fits in because she would never want Geoffrey to take her out to dinner. She has to hurry home to get dinner for Mark. The picture came of Sally Lord, her young assistant, rushing for that suburban train every night because the man to whom she was married disliked New York and wouldn't live in the city. On the joggling trains Sally read manuscripts, but never at home. "Mark hates to have me read at home," she had told Jennifer.

Jennifer thought, there's so much gabble in print about mystiques and fulfillment, but what it gets down to is that if women have to work it doesn't make them desirable. But what would Steve and I do if I didn't have my job? We'd have to get out of this place—and fast. The manuscripts fell to the floor as she followed that thought to a conclusion. There was one thing she could do. If she dared to take the risk.

At the table in the restaurant Stephen picked up the check.

"This was my party," said Corinne, but not trying to stop him.

"Up to a point," said Stephen.

The other two men at the table made no protest. Addison Williams was so very rich that he always took great care not to be exploited. It was a principle with him and he had not arranged this party but only gone along with it. Harry Bates never paid for anything. He provided the company of an extra man and felt that was contribution enough. Zelda Merrill paid no attention. She never carried money anyway.

The check was for sixty-four dollars. Stephen took a credit card out of his pocket and handed it to the waiter. It was a considerable addition to what he already owed the Banquet Club, but he intended to pay the whole thing when his money came in from the trust fund in a few days. The amount of sixty-four dollars made him wince inwardly though no trace of that showed in his manner. Why had he let himself in for this tonight?

Corinne leaned closer. Her dress was black, backless and slung low with a sequin halter. Her eyes were greedy.

"Where do we go now?"

Oh no, you don't, said Stephen to himself.

"I'm due home. I told Jenny I'd be back early. And it's later than that, by a long shot."

"Jenny's always on your mind, isn't she?" Corinne pouted. "Of course I know she's a wonderful brain—"

She sounded slightly contemptuous. Stephen pushed his chair back from the table and Corinne. Jennifer was very much on his mind at the moment. He had planned to give her back that three hundred and fifty dollars she had paid for the rent when he got his check from the trust fund. But now there wouldn't be enough left to do it.

2

THE VICE-PRESIDENT of Isthmus Oil who, several days of hopes later, took a few minutes to talk to Stephen Cooper, could not have been more courteous. Nor more final. As Steve walked up Park Avenue toward their apartment house, he wished to God he had not told Jennifer that he believed he might get a position with the oil corporation. She'd be sorry for him. She would try not to show it. She would be very tactful. He was angered by her tact and by having to report failures. The world was haywire when a girl could have a twelve-thousand-dollar-a-year job and a man couldn't find one. He tried to figure out what his next move would be, and found his mind blank and hopeless. Except for the basic knowledge that Jennifer could do all right without him. He would go back to the apartment and have a drink. Fortunately Jenny wouldn't be there for a couple of hours.

He went up to the tenth floor, unlocked the doors and walked through the foyer where a mirror-top table held two very modern lamps. The big room was still and unlit but he had an immediate sense of occupancy. Then he saw that Jennifer was standing by one of the long windows looking down at the snow-trimmed traffic. She did not turn or speak, though she must have heard him come in.

"Why hello," he said. "I didn't expect to find you home so early."

"I've been here since noon," she said.

"Not sick are you? Feeling badly?"

"No, I'm not sick."

"Well, it's a good idea to get away from that office early once in a while."

She gave a flat laugh. "That's one thing I won't have to worry about from now on."

"What's wrong, Jenny? You don't sound like yourself."

Now she turned and spoke quickly as if she were trying to get it over with.

"I'm out," she said. "I'm no longer on *Portfolio*. Sally Lord is going to take over my job at least temporarily. She'll give it a try."

"Sally Lord? What happened? Why, Clark has always thought you were indispensable. I've heard him say so."

"Everyone is dispensable."

"There must have been a reason—tell me."

"I have told you. I'm out of a job," said Jennifer, "and I don't want to talk about it. Not now or ever."

"You poor kid," said Steve. "They haven't any right to do this to you."

"These things happen," she said vaguely.

"I'd like to knock that fellow's block off!"

"Geoffrey's not to blame. He would have kept me if he could."

"A reorganization? Is that it?"

"I suppose you could call it that."

He came to her, his voice warm and sympathetic as he said,

"Don't you worry, beautiful." He took her chin, lifted it and smiled at her. "You're a good editor—one of the best. You'll get something else—something better."

"Steve, don't say that! Don't believe it! I'm not fooling myself. There isn't an editorial job at my level open on any good magazine. Most of them are cutting down staff. And I can't go back to opening manuscripts and throwing out the junk."

"Then the hell with the magazines," said Stephen. "I never wanted you to keep that job anyway."

"But what are we going to do?"

He heard the fear in her voice. He felt it himself. Things had been bad enough up to now but at least there had been money coming in. Now her twelve thousand a year had gone out the window. And Isthmus had turned him down. I must get some kind of job right away, he said to himself, and was taunted with the usual questions—what kind, where?

As he put his arm over Jennifer's shoulders he was conscious that she had become thinner. She felt fragile, helpless, which wasn't like her. She must have had a bad shock today and he knew what this kind of shock was like. Or had she known that this was going to happen? He remembered that she had said something unlike her the other night, about being a job addict, and then she had talked about going down to DeSoto. Perhaps she had a warning or a fear that there was going to be a shake-up on the magazine. This would be tough on her. She would get a little wad of unemployment insurance but when that ran out—he tried to realize that she might not be able to take care of herself. Corinne had said, "I think it must be wonderful to be Jenny and not need anyone." And she had said another time, "There are different kinds of needs, Steve—"

Those were the things that had been at the very bottom of his mind, sticking there. Jenny was well able to take care of herself. He was giving her a very hard time. Corinne—even if it didn't last and it wouldn't, you know Corinne too well, he would think cynically—might take him on and like it.

"It may be a good thing, darling," he said.

Jennifer trembled under his arm. He hadn't called her that in months, nor spoken in that kind of voice.

"We can't stay here," she said.

"There are plenty of other places in the world besides this joint," said Steve. "This is no old homestead. It hasn't any claim on us. I'm sick of it myself. We could sell most of our stuff and have quite a little stake."

He went to the bar and made a couple of martinis before he spoke again. He brought her one ceremoniously, went back for his own and lifted it.

"The other night," he said, "you suggested making a complete break of it. Getting out of New York. Going down to DeSoto to live for a while."

"But you thought that was a fantastic idea."

"I'm not so sure that it was. It might be just the thing. I think it would do you good," said Steve, unconscious of quotation.

Chestnut Hill, the old Cooper place, which was about all that Henry Cooper had been able to leave his son except a modest trust fund, had been a show place in its early days. It had been built in 1927, when Henry Cooper was very rich and steadily becoming more wealthy. He had come upon the site when he was riding by himself one day and had pressed his horse to the top of a wooded hill, following a snarled trail which had probably been hacked out by moonshiners and later abandoned.

At its crest the hill flattened out to a spread of almost an acre, and there was a grove of chestnut trees, symmetrical even in the tangle of undergrowth and now in full bloom. Admiring the lilac-like flowers that almost stood upright on the branches, and the formality of the leaves, each one facing the outside of the tree, Henry Cooper was reminded that the original home of the chestnut tree was Greece. Everything about Greece had intrigued him since his student days when he had majored in the classics. He had visited that country and the surrounding islands several times and each journey increased his interest. Now he tied his horse and walked through the brush to get the views from the hilltop from all angles. The dignity of the location pleased and excited him.

He was the president of an investment company in New York and times were booming. But not long before he had been told by his doctor that he was overworking and must allow himself more relaxation. Rather reluctantly, he was taking a motor trip through the South because of that advice. With his chauffeur he had stopped by chance at the Tulip Inn in DeSoto and found the place so pleasant that he decided to spend two weeks there, resting and riding horseback. His wife was in Europe on her customary spring trip.

Before he mounted his horse again he was planning to buy the hill and build a villa of Grecian type upon it. *We'll come down for a month every spring and again in the fall,* he wrote his wife after he was committed to the purchase, *and when we get old we can hole up here for good.*

There was no prospect that Marguerite Cooper, who was fifteen years younger than her husband, could have liked less than spending two months of her gay and brilliant life every year in a mountain village. She did not conceal her lack of enthusiasm. But Henry went ahead with his plans none the less. He could afford more than one establishment at that time, and he was confident that when the place was finished she too would fall in love with it.

The mansion was well designed and very solidly built. The New York architect whom Henry Cooper employed was one who favored the Greek Revival in its best and most honest forms. He used columns proportioned like those of a Greek temple, yet somehow subdued the whole structure to purposes of living. Instead of being pretentious, it retained the general scheme of a fine and noble plantation house. Local carpenters who worked on the job, able to use splendid timbers and not having to spare expense or workmanship, were immensely proud of the place. And because its style was classic it looked unusual but not old-fashioned thirty-seven years later, although by that time houses which cost as much usually spread their glassed areas and patios on a single level.

Marguerite Cooper took little interest in the development of the new estate. While it was being built she became pregnant for the first and only time and that gave her both excuse and reason for staying in New York and other familiar places where she was happy. Chestnut Hill was her husband's personal project. At a distance she could tolerate it.

The depression which riddled the country when his son was not quite two years old did not ruin Henry Cooper, for he was one of the few who had seen it coming, and he managed to get his investments well diversified so that some of them were saved. But the crash melted down his assets and they never regained their former size. As he saw so many men in reduced circumstances or completely bankrupt, it gave Henry the greatest satisfaction to know that his house in Carolina was finished, furnished and all paid for. His architect had recommended a decorator who, he said, would appreciate the style of the house and choose furnishings in keeping with it. Henry gave the decorator a free hand. He did the house completely on the inside, occasionally consulting Henry courteously about bidding on a piece of furniture that would be available at an auction sale in some gallery, or with the same deference asking Marguerite to make a choice of colors.

But, with less money to spend, the Carolina place soon became a bone of contention between Henry and his wife. There was competition between the costs of keeping up Chestnut Hill— Henry had quite a stable there in the beginning and that meant paying grooms—and the expense of running the city house in New York where Marguerite wanted to live. There were discussions and refusals and compromises. The pattern of their life for some years was that Henry would go down to DeSoto for a month in both the spring and autumn. His wife might put in an appearance there for a week. She agreed at length to sell the big New York house but on condition that they rented a smaller and even more elegant one in the city. The conflict of outlook and desires might have destroyed their marriage. But it did not because Marguerite Cooper died of a cruel and incurable leukemia during Stephen's first year at preparatory school.

She was spared the holing up in DeSoto that she would have hated. But it soon became necessary for her widowed husband. The condition of his heart grew too treacherous for him to meet the strains of business life, and he retired when he was little more than fifty. His wife's death left many hopes and plans forever unfinished but the place in DeSoto held him even in loneliness. He made it his permanent home.

Warned and chastened by the depression, Henry Cooper had created an irrevocable trust, while he still had the money to do it. He reserved the income for himself for his lifetime, and his will named his son as beneficiary, the same terms of monthly payments which he had established for himself to be continued. When he set up the trust he regarded it as a small backlog. But most of his other sources of income disappeared during his years of retirement. It was the untouchable trust which gave him enough to live on fairly comfortably at Chestnut Hill, though he was forced to sell his horses even before it became unsafe for him to ride. He kept a colored couple, who grew as fond of him as he was of them, and they did all the inside and outside work on his place. He took a small part in the activities of the town and badgered the little local library into buying expensive books on Greece. When Stephen Cooper and his wife found themselves both out of jobs, he had been dead for nearly four years. He had died with the comfortable delusion that his son was rising to affluence in New York as he himself had in the nineteen twenties.

3

THEY DROVE AROUND another curl in the road and came deeper into spring. New York City had only begun to kick off its dirty blanket of snow when they left there but here the roadside bushes were glossy green, and purple and red flowers were blossoming on slender trees in the woods. A clear little stream was leaping down the side of the mountain that bordered the highway.

Jennifer looked at a road sign and again at her map.

"We must be almost there," she said.

"A few more miles," said Stephen. "I told you that we'd get here between five and six. It's just five thirty now."

"Heavenly time to arrive. And it looks like heaven."

He took another curve. "You can see the town over there to the right if you look."

She rolled down her window to see more clearly. "The village is just the kernel of quite a big settlement, isn't it? There are lots of houses in the outskirts. Big ones too."

"It's certainly built up. All the property on the left is the hunting country."

"What's the place with all the endless white fences?"

"That's the Bayard place. You must have met Sara Bayard when you were here before."

"No, she wasn't here then. But people were always talking about her."

"They would. She's the queen bee. They are both well-connected but she is the one who has the money. Corinne spoke about Sara when I told her that I was coming down here to live. She knew Sara somewhere or other when she was married to one of the others, not Tom Bayard."

They were still driving past white fencing but Corinne Miller's name sent Jennifer's thoughts off at another angle. Stephen had not mentioned Corinne in a long time, but that did not mean he might not think of her. Might miss her and the kind of sharp gaiety she lived in and provided. This will be a terrific adjustment for him, Jennifer said to herself. I've tried not to think about that. I haven't had time to think about it—we were too busy selling and packing and telling people what we were going to do, nailing it down that way. We were putting up a convinced front. Not looking behind the front ourselves. I still feel as if I should apologize to something or to somebody because I'm not holding down a job.

"On that second hill," said Stephen, "the one where you see the long building and the cottages, that's the Inn. On the next hill—there's the house."

"It looks enormous! I'd forgotten it was so imposing but both times I've been here I was in kind of a daze."

He had slowed the car to study the view of the white-columned structure on its height. He said, "You can easily see why it would be hard to sell it. Not many people would fall for a place like that."

"I like it because it's so different."

"Different all right. Look—there are the horse show grounds. I used to perform there sometimes. I had a horse called Cherokee. My father gave him to me on my seventeenth birthday when I came down for spring vacation from St. Mark's. I showed him in the Junior Hunter class and got a blue ribbon."

When he was seventeen he was being given horses— What do horses cost, Jennifer wondered, hundreds or thousands? I was thirteen then and doing baby-sitting. The Horne kids. The Davises. Frightened to death when I had to walk down the Horne driveway to the bus stop after that girl who was baby-sitting a few blocks away was kidnaped and raped and killed. But I had to have the money. I didn't know Steve's kind of life existed and he couldn't possibly imagine what mine was like when I was in my teens.

"It must have been wonderful to come to a place like this for your vacation."

"Until my mother died there was always a row about my coming here for them. She hated DeSoto."

"You never told me that."

"Didn't I? I suppose there was no reason to go into it. I don't mean that there was a fighting row—my mother wasn't that kind of person. But she would want to have me go off with her some place and my father wanted me to come here. A kid knows it when he's pulled in different directions."

"Why didn't your mother like it?"

"It just wasn't her sort of thing. She didn't like country life— not the DeSoto kind anyway. She didn't care about riding or hunting. And if my father did get her on a horse, something always seemed to happen. I remember once, when they were riding on the trails, a branch snapped across her face and cut her cheek. It was quite a gash and there was a great to-do. She thought it was going to leave a scar and my father took her back to New York to a plastic surgeon. She was quite a beauty, you know."

"From the pictures of her I've seen, she must have been very much of a beauty. I hope there wasn't a scar?"

"No—but I suppose it made the place seem dangerous. And the

mountains seemed to depress her—once Mother told me that they shut her in and shut her out. I couldn't quite figure that but what she said stuck in my mind. She was trying to explain to me—I was just a boy—why she didn't come down here more often. Later on I understood it better. She was much younger than my father, very gay and social. She liked city life. And when she wasn't in New York she liked the fashionable resorts where she would see more or less the same kind of people that she saw at home. Easthampton, Cannes, Deauville—that sort of thing. She was very much admired. But don't get the idea that she was just silly or trivial. She was a very sweet person. Only for her DeSoto didn't click. I think she probably felt lost here and maybe frightened. She was afraid of lightning for one thing and this place has bad electrical storms. Are you?"

"Afraid of lightning? Not a bit."

"Scared of scorpions?"

"I've never met any personally."

"There are little ones around here. And chameleons. They aren't dangerous but they can sting. They terrified my mother."

"Are you trying to terrify me by any chance?"

"I don't believe I could."

"It must have been hard on your father not to have his wife like it."

"I suppose it was. I was too young to get the whole picture. But I'm sure he hoped he could get her to go along with him."

"I wish I hadn't been such a dope when we came here on our wedding trip and I met your father," said Jennifer.

"He liked you. He thought I'd done very well for myself."

"Did he really?"

"But I knew that anyway," he told her with a grin.

She thanked him with a swift touch. She said, "We should have come down here more often before he died."

"I didn't realize he was so close to the edge." Now that Stephen had opened up his memories he suddenly pulled out another one. "I remember his telling my mother once that she would be happy here after a while. He was probably waiting for other things to play out on her— I can see that now. And she said— she had a lovely voice—" He paused as if he were hearing it.

"What did she say?"

"She said, 'Don't make me,' or something like that. Not in a mean way. They just couldn't get together on the way to live. And that was the last time she came down here. After that she wouldn't. Or maybe couldn't."

"Do you feel like your mother or your father did about DeSoto?"

"I don't know yet. But I'll soon find out. I used to like it a lot when I was a kid," said Stephen. "Oldtown Street—that's the main drag—is over in that direction. But we turn off here"— He swung the car into a quiet road and accelerated it. "And there are the old gates!"

It was almost six o'clock and their guests were invited for eight. In her dining room Sara Bayard was arranging place cards, choosing the positions that men and women would have at her table, thinking of their ages, interests, estrangements, favorites, importance. Each person was completely dimensioned in her mind as she put down a silver-edged card with a name on it. It was a first name in every case, except for the man who was staying at the Cranes's house, the one that Molly Crane was playing around with. His card read formally Mr. Harrison. Sara put him as far away from Molly as possible, to serve them right. She had little sympathy with liaisons. Sara married her men. She heard her husband come into the hall and, as he glanced into the dining room, she looked up at him and said, "I'm giving you Bee Loomis and Kit tonight."

"Kit's a big treat," said Tom Bayard.

"Somebody has to take care of her. Sam's not here. And you like Bee."

"Who doesn't?" he said. Like his wife he was still in riding clothes and together they made a composite picture of leisure and elegance. Tom Bayard had always been able to live well on his amateur skills and good looks. Sara's beauty was only secondary to the magnetism of her voice.

"By the way," he said, "I hear the Cooper place is being opened up."

"Did they finally manage to sell it?"

"No, Stephen Cooper and his wife are coming down themselves."

"What fun—I always adored Steve when we were in the gymkhana stage and he came down from prep school. I haven't seen him in years—I always miss him when he's here. Someone in New York when I was there last year—I think it was Corinne Miller—was talking about him, said he was madly attractive. How long are they going to be here, do you know?"

"I heard they are going to live here."

"But why on earth? I always thought he didn't like it much."

"Could be that he's broke," said Tom.

"He'd be a great addition. We need men here so terribly."

"You don't need men," said Tom, "you've got one." He said it possessively.

It was very quiet in the little white-steepled Catholic church. From five to six on Saturday afternoons Father Aberdeen heard confessions. An hour was long enough to shrive those of his congregation who desired it, except at Easter time when he listened to more sinners, including the husky drawl of Kit Piper on the other side of the grating.

Father Aberdeen knew most of the sins of his parishioners and, although of course he would never admit it, most of their voices. He knew that it was William Klatch accusing himself of intemperance and smelling of it, that it was Mrs. Joe Smith whispering again defensively that she had been practicing birth control. Mrs. Vaughan would quaver that she had been inattentive at her prayers five times—perhaps six—Mrs. Vaughan was very scrupulous. And there was no mistaking the satirical edge in Mrs. Dusen's voice. When he heard it he always remembered that once she had said impatiently through the grating, "All my sins are venial, Father. I hardly know what to say when I go to confession for it is almost impossible to commit a mortal sin when you are a woman past sixty." He had told her, "Then repent again the sins of your past life," feeling that it was probable that there had been plenty of them before she was sixty.

He was always severe before he was gentle with the boys who, in terrible embarrassment, would stumble through accounts of their physical experiments. He was a good confessor and it always made him happy to give absolution and know that someone went in peace that was at least temporary out of the darkened box. He loved the serenity of the village and wanted all those who lived within it to match the beauty God had given it.

But this afternoon he did not recognize the voice of a penitent who had come in as the priest was looking at his watch and thinking that it was almost time to leave the confessional and concern himself with the roses in the garden of the rectory. As the curtain lifted he had settled himself to listen again and had known from the first words that this was not a familiar parishioner. It was a Southern voice but not that of a gentleman. He began correctly, "Bless me Father," then hesitated, as if uncertain of the ritual.

"How long since your last confession?" Father Aberdeen asked, reminding him of what was necessary.

"About thirty years ago," said the voice.

"Ah," sighed Father Aberdeen. "Thirty mortal sins in failing to make your Easter duty for all those years."

"I want to come back to the Church, Father."

"With the help of God you may," said the priest gently. "There was a welcome for the prodigal son. And now, as well as you can, and asking God to aid your recollection, try to recall the commandments you have broken and the number of times."

The confession shocked and depressed the priest. This had been a very wicked man. Adultery, living in sin—

"And I picked up a car now and then—"

"You mean you stole cars?"

"It was a kind of a game. There was a time I was pretty up against it."

"Did you make restitution?"

"I sure tried to, Father—it wasn't always possible. If I could have—"

Father Aberdeen did not like this confession at all. There were overtones of falsity, too many excuses. He did not hear the note of true contrition and he knew that when he heard it. Yet here was this man, on his knees, of his own volition pouring out the ugly facts of his evil behavior. Why? pondered the priest, as he listened with distaste. Perhaps he is tired of sinning. He wants to put all this behind him, free himself of it. Or does he? Will he? Can he?

"That's about it, Father. That's all I can remember."

The priest hesitated. He was reluctant to absolve the man. But he had come here, confessed perhaps as well as he could and he claimed that he had tried to make restitution. I cannot refuse him absolution, Father Aberdeen decided. And God will know if this man is adding sacrilege to his other sins.

He began a sharp homily.

A mile away, in his room at the Tulip Inn, which was the best of the local hostelries and always spoken of as "the Inn," Miles Halliday was writing a letter. Rapidly and fluently. He always enjoyed writing to Maud Patton because she was so intelligent. And there were side benefits of which Miles was aware. She would quote him and he liked the thought of his comments spreading in her fashionable circle and calling him to mind. Also it would remind her to invite him to her place on the Cape when she came back from Palm Beach. He would take the letter to the post office in time for the airmail connection at six o'clock and it would reach her before she left Philadelphia. There would be time to return to the Inn, change into dinner clothes, put on the dark red coat he affected in the country, mix a drink to his own taste and be just late enough at the Bayard party.

He wrote:

You will be surprised to hear that I decided against Palermo, partly because so many diligent tourists decided for it, and surprised that the address on this sheet is mine for the next month. But not so surprised as I am. I am always quite astonished to find myself here again. Drawn by what, you'll wonder, and I don't know the answer. Dear Maud, you must come one day and see this place. Life is not complete—one is not really a worldling—without knowing DeSoto. It is *sui generis*, not a resort, not a hillbilly town. It is an extraordinary collection of individuals and pursuits in a setting so beautiful that it shows off anyone to advantage. Here it is credible that at any moment the mountains may skip like rams and the little hills like lambs. This place can and has soaked up a little flavor of everything. By it something is proved.

In the late morning the old ladies and old colonels come out of their boardinghouses as if someone had lit a smudge and forced them out. They hobble and limp or walk very straight, according to their arthritis. The old ladies are adorable. They walk in pairs and wear forgotten hats. Their thoughts can be seen streaming out of them as they do in the comics; that the doctor doesn't pay them enough attention, that lunch is not far off, that they must change their wills again—the Edwardian hats top some old ladies of considerable wealth—that the check from John is late—some are poor. It doesn't matter in this climate when the camellias are rioting. I always greet the old ladies as I pass and never feel so male as when they flutter a response.

But they are only one scene in the revue. It's extremely varied. There are people here who have deliberately left the great world. DeSoto is a retreat, a refuge and a pet. There are Petit Trianons which are opened up only in the season. Others who could afford to live anywhere make it home. Money is never flaunted, and around the village it is chic to wear clothes that should be discarded. But an original Dior or Balenciaga at a party is no surprise.

I dine tonight with Sara Bayard and her husband—the third one, she was Sara Langley—and we shall lay claim to simple country life but probably have quail and a good French wine. I forget whether you know Sara though how you could have missed her I don't know. She is such a beautiful, fascinating if demanding creature—always trying out new horses and new men.

I have never known any place which so completely lacks a

common denominator. The houses and estates don't imitate each other as they do in most colonies. From my window here at the Inn I can look across a valley and see a mansion of Greek Doric design. No one lives there now and if I had the money I would buy it. It is completely out of place in the North Carolina mountains and it is where it belongs. Do come and solve that enigma for me.

He signed and sealed his letter and as he looked up from his desk his glance sharpened with surprise and curiosity. The house on the hill had suddenly come to life. He had never seen lights in its windows before.

The house seemed very impressive as they drove up a length of gravel that stretched from open iron gates that were rather rusty to the broad space in front of the portico. It also looked deserted, as if neither they nor anyone else was expected.

Stephen said, frowning, "I wired Joe Harris that we'd get here sometime today. He was supposed to get in touch with Aga and his wife and have them open it up. But apparently nobody's here."

"We are anyway," said Jennifer rather breathlessly. She felt as if she had been running.

"And here comes Aga!" Stephen got out of the car quickly, opened her door and went across the drive.

A Negro came slowly around the back of the house and approached them. He was indefinably old. Age had bent his height and sharpened his fine features. He bore himself with dignity and as he came closer the welcome grew in his face.

"Well, Aga, it's good to see you—how are you?"

"Not so bad for ol' man—how you, Mr. Stephen?"

"Fine—you remember Mrs. Cooper?"

"I recall her as a bride," said Aga.

He lifted his worn felt hat and Jennifer moved into the greetings with a smile and outstretched hand.

"That's almost the way I feel right now," she said.

"Mr. Harris say you folks come down here to live, Mr. Stephen —Mrs. Stephen?"

"It's true as gospel, Aga."

Aga said, "This ol' house be glad to have life in it. It been pretty lonesome since Mr. Henry passed." He shook his head warningly. "But it need a lot done to it, this big house."

"We'll take it as it is," said Steve.

Agamemnon turned to Jennifer again. "Ma'am, the house all clean. Susie and I clean it top and bottom. But Susie not so capable she used to be. She got high blood. Today she force' stay at home in her bed. She can't work steady no more."

Jennifer said, "I'm sorry. But I expect to do most of my own work, Aga. And I do appreciate your getting it all clean for us."

"We help you and Mr. Stephen all we able," said Aga courteously.

"Is the front door unlocked, Aga?" asked Stephen.

"Your house am all unlock' and waitin'," Aga answered with the ceremoniousness that seemed natural to him.

"All right, then we'll unload the car. Not you, Jenny—Aga and I will do that. You go straight in, unless you insist on being carried over the threshold."

She took her cue. This was the way he wanted their arrival to be, undramatized and underplayed. So that if it were disappointing there wouldn't be so far to fall. But Stephen was not able to keep the excitement out of his own voice and Jennifer heard it. She went up the broad low steps to the stone terrace which surrounded the house. The door was oak and massive, but for all its size it swung open easily as she turned the knob and pushed without effort.

The hall was square, high and formal. Its floor of inlaid wood was bare except for a single small rug laid before a console with a marble top. That faced the doorway and held a pair of graceful alabaster lamps. Two chairs of polished, uncushioned wood stood on either side of the console and on either side of the room were closed double doors with oval tops. For a moment or two Jennifer stood there, admiring the simplicity and dignity. The paint on the doors had obviously dulled from white to cream color but otherwise it must be as it had been from the time the architect and decorator had finished their work.

She opened one of the double doors and was in a room that she remembered now that she saw it again. She had seen it first on their wedding trip when Stephen brought her here to meet his father. They had stayed only a few days before going farther south, and she had been in such a mood of awakening ecstasy at the time that the surroundings made little impression. No one she met seemed very real except Stephen. His father was a courteous stranger who hoped they would often come to stay with him. But when they had come to DeSoto again it was because Mr. Cooper had left instructions to bury him in the local cemetery.

That funeral visit had been for Jennifer a few days of pity and some regret though she had not known her father-in-law well enough for true grief. She had tried to make herself useful in the unfamiliar surroundings but there was little for her to do. She had not stayed long because she was needed on her job and soon went back to the city, leaving Stephen to make the arrangements for putting the property up for sale. There had been no question about doing anything else. They had left it furnished, for the furniture was not suited to their New York apartment, and Stephen had said that it would be easier to sell if it were not stripped and empty. During the last weeks they had often said how lucky it was that they had not auctioned off the things in this house, for the cost of moving what they had in New York or of refurnishing Chestnut Hill would have been almost prohibitive.

What they had not said to each other was that the house might be in bad shape after four years. Jennifer was glad that Stephen had let her come in alone. She had been afraid that she might have to pretend if she met a shabby or neglected sight. But it was not like that at all. Agamemnon had said that the house was waiting and that was the way it felt.

There was a thin Persian carpet in this room and more accurately placed chairs. Two matched sofas with curving arms. The white satin upholstery on them was frail and worn but had been carefully brushed. Everything was clean and in order and Jennifer, as she looked about her, was grateful to the half-ill woman who had conscientiously done all this. But the room was stiff with unuse. She saw the backgammon table, an antique piece with large wooden discs for playing, and was reminded.

"Do you enjoy backgammon?" Steve's father had asked her. She had felt rather diminished because she played no games.

"Would you like to ride over the trails tomorrow?" he had inquired later. "I have no stable now but one of my friends would be glad to mount you and Steve."

Jennifer did not ride. I didn't feel that I was much of a credit to Steve. And here I am again and I still don't play backgammon or ride.

The fireplace was faced with white marble and a bas-relief with Grecian figures was set into each side of it. She remembered that her father-in-law had called her attention to it and to the inscription on top of the figures. She had been out of her depth again. Dropping the coats and thermos case she was still carrying on one of the sofas, she opened a corner door. This room was easier in mood, with many books and a chair angled for reading. He must have been a very lonely man, thought Jennifer, with no one to share his love for this place. He would be glad if he could know that we are here, that the house wasn't sold to strangers. I shall love this house. Dear God, I only pray that Steve will like it.

There was another door—she opened it and gave a gasp of delight. Beyond the row of flagstones a riot of azaleas blazed, brilliant even in the twilight, red, pink and mauve. As she stood, trying to believe that this belonged to them, her husband came up behind her.

"We put the suitcases in the upstairs hall," he said. "You'll have to decide which bedrooms to use."

"Yes, I will," she said, not turning.

"Are you all right? Not sorry already? What were you thinking?"

She laughed. "I was thinking that in New York even a small azalea plant costs six dollars. And look what we have!"

A telephone bell rang suddenly.

"A telephone? I didn't know there was one still in the house."

"The insurance people make you keep it hooked up. I don't know who that can be. Maybe Joe Harris is checking."

He went in the direction of the bell that was ringing and Jenny heard his end of the conversation without really listening.

"Yes, this is Steve Cooper. Well—how are you! Yes, we just arrived. I don't really know—more or less indefinitely—we got tired of the rat race and I'm a pretty old man. . . . No, not you Sara, I'll bet on that. Yes, I'll look forward to meeting your husband. Oh—that's very nice of you but we've just come, hardly oriented yet. . . . I don't think we could tonight but it's certainly neighborly of you, Sara. . . . No, but we have a thermos or two and some sandwiches. . . . Well, I can ask Jenny. . . . She wants very much to meet you, I guess she missed you when she was here before. . . . This makes us feel right at home. . . . All right, if we can leave it that way and if we can get squared around here."

He came back to Jenny looking very cheerful.

"What do you know—that was Sara Langley—Sara Bayard—we were speaking about her on the way down, you remember— What a girl, she sounds just as full of beans as she always was. Evidently the word's got around already about our coming to DeSoto. She says she's having a few people for dinner and wanted to know if we'd join them. I said we'd just got here and she said that was all the more reason, that we probably weren't stocked up with food—"

"There are sandwiches left—"

"It was pretty cordial of her, don't you think?"

"Very—but—"

"That's the way people are in the country. She said she wants to meet you. There's time to change and we don't have to unpack tonight—we have the rest of our lives to unpack—I'd like to see Sara— What do you say? Let's take her up on it."

Jenny wanted to protest—no—not tonight. But she saw his face, happier than she had seen it in a long while, full of anticipation. She said, "If you'd like to—"

4

Now that the day was gone, the mountains became aloof. They were no longer merely beautiful views for people in the valleys to admire. They reverted to their beginnings as dangerous, untrodden heights where rattlesnakes bred, rabbits squealed and hawks soared, looking for prey. No lights showed along the crests of the mountains, yet their outlines were unmistakable, black against a slightly less dark sky spread lavishly tonight with stars.

But the road which bordered the Bayard estate was aglow with small red reflectors which picked up the glare of headlights and indicated the way to the open wooden gates. The inside driveway to the house itself was a quarter of a mile long and it had been landscaped and hedge-clipped though never paved of course because of the horses. White sasanquas, for which the gardens had been renowned long before the Bayards bought them, bloomed like flower ghosts under a long row of old gas lamps on standards that had been restored to use.

It was a country house which had never had to take cost as a deterrent to anything that might make it more satisfactory to its owners, more correct to its designers, or more beautiful to anyone who was privileged to see it. Every elevation had been planned to exhibit some splendid vista or long view. When the weather was good everyone came out on the terrace to look, or at least to be with those who enjoyed looking. Tonight most of the guests were there already with their first drinks in their hands. Miles Halliday and Tom Bayard were both taking pleasure in the moment. In Bayard the scene stirred a sense of proprietorship and landowning which was as close as he ever came to nobility. Miles Halliday felt personally justified at this moment, an aristocrat instead of a snob. Few places were better done than this one. They could ask anyone here, he thought.

"Sara," he said, "Marry me next time. I want this place."

"You can get a place more cheaply than that," she told him, with the laugh that never interrupted what she was saying but played along with her words. "Plenty of houses are for sale without impediments."

"Not good ones. By the way, I saw lights in the Acropolis tonight."

"The what?"

"The Greek job on the hill across from the Inn. Has that been sold?"

"Oh, the Cooper place. Chestnut Hill. Steve Cooper's come down. Tom told me that he'd heard they were coming and just on the chance I called the house and got Steve himself. So I asked them to come over tonight—I thought it would be such fun to see them. They may be a little late."

"I've never met him," said Miles. "His father was somewhat of a recluse, wasn't he? Is the son a shut-in too?"

"Oh heavens no, unless he's changed. I haven't seen him in eight or nine years. Not since his marriage."

"Whom did he marry?" asked Miles. Such things were the warp

of his interest in life and he was always weaving figures into it.

"Some girl he met in New York. She worked, I think. I have a vague impression that she was literary. Right up your street."

"I go to great pains not to be considered literary, dear. Literary people are poisonous."

"You write books."

"Only two books. And if I ever write another it will be a book on why not to write books. So the mistress of the Acropolis is literary?"

"I don't know that for a fact."

"Are they here for long?"

"Indefinitely, so Steve told me on the phone. Something about being fed up and getting old. Of course he was kidding. He's only my age. He was at Saint Mark's when I was at Miss Hall's. We used to be in the gymkhana down here—in the potato races on ponies—and once he took me to a hideous prom. I know he's not much older than I am."

"That's very young to retire. You're just getting into the swing of things."

"Tom said that perhaps Steve is broke. That house has been on the market for a long while. The stables have been boarded up for years. It's not really a very livable place. It's so sort of—"

"Classic?"

"Yes, that's what I mean. It has always looked odd down here— I mean it doesn't fit in."

"Dear Sara, does anything need to fit in here?"

"I do."

"You and the old ladies on High Street?"

"What do you mean?"

"That I would like another drink. Then I'll be only three behind Kit."

Sara looked quickly at Kit Piper. "She's all right so far. Why don't you be nicer about people?"

"Me? Who's nicer? If I keep track of her drinks I can testify at the inquest."

"You're dreadful. But I don't really care what you say about people unless I should hear what you say about me."

"I'll make a point of arranging that—you might be pleased."

They went inside together, into the largest and most beautiful room of the house, a yellow and cream room without a flaw or stupidity. There were branches of forsythia in black porcelain floor vases, a light bright fire against marble, a servant in a red jacket that was not very unlike the dinner coat Miles wore, and twelve other people, all in the early stages of middle life. Six of them, including the Bayards, Bee Loomis, both Molly Crane and her current Mr. Harrison, and Miles himself from some angles, were extremely handsome. Most of them were still talking about the bad manners of a man who had joined the Hunt this morning.

"I saw the whole thing. He was cantering ahead of the Master right after we started."

"Who is he anyway?" asked Tom Bayard, who was Master of the Hunt. "He made a proper request—there wasn't any reason to turn him down—the field's too small as it is— His name, I believe, was Delaney but I never saw him before."

"I think he's staying at the Inn."

"You know him, Miles?"

"No, but it's common knowledge that we are an unmannerly bunch at the Inn."

"If he's Irish, and his name sounds as if he is, he should have good manners. When we go over to hunt in Ireland I always notice that no matter how shabby they are they have wonderful form."

"We're getting some queer people down here."

"The place is getting too large."

Sara interrupted with, "Here they are! Steve, this is wonderful!" She went swiftly with both hands out toward Stephen Cooper, who was standing in the doorway, slightly preceding his wife as if to take the burden of entrance. Sara gave him a light kiss of old friendship.

"And I'm so glad, Mrs. Cooper—"

"It's Jennifer, Sara," said Steve. "Let's get off on the right foot."

"You're such angels to come! Steve, you haven't changed at all! I don't know how many of these people you know. You must remember Bee Loomis—Bee Fairweather—"

A round of introductions began and Miles Halliday, waiting his turn, watched the newcomers with interest. What he had said to Sara was quite true. He had written a clever book or two but writing was not his chief preoccupation. Basically Miles Halliday was social. That was his talent and his avocation. It was people on whom he sharpened his extraordinary powers of observation and his wit. People who gave him what he wanted, a place in the social sun. It was his work and his sport to place each person where he belonged, to use each one who could be useful, to sort the chaff from the wheat, to add them all up to make his own life.

He had long been too selfish and cynical to love a woman. But he liked women—as *objets d'art*, as specimens to dissect, when they surprised him or were purely comic, and a very few with affection. Of the women here tonight, Sara Bayard was the only one for whom he felt any warmth, though he was aware of the lure which Molly Crane could exercise. Bee Loomis was too worthy for his taste, Kit Piper so loosely controlled that she could become a responsibility and one had to watch out for that, and Anne Bennett, with all that money, a zombie. But Sara, tonight in white lace that did not wave or droop but frosted her brown skin, was all he liked best in a woman. She was an original and not a copy. She was confident to her bones, and carried her fortune and her beauty as if they did not weigh on her.

"She never comes into a room dragging problems by the hand," Miles had said once of Sara.

He saw that the Cooper girl—she was younger than most of the women in the room—was not completely at ease, though she was calm enough. She had undramatized beauty—brown-gold hair that had been well styled and a slim, fluid figure. The pale yellow silk sheath that she was wearing was fortunate with the forsythia. She's a young woman who has been about, decided Miles, but she hasn't always been about. She's rather tense, not sure of us—no, not sure of herself.

"And this is Miles Halliday, Jennifer. Miles, you know this is Steve Cooper's wife who—"

"Who lives in the Acropolis," said Miles, over her hand.

"It's called Chestnut Hill. But I know what you mean."

"Beautiful structure, your house. Don't you think so?"

"Mr. Halliday, I'm just getting acquainted with it."

"You haven't been here before?"

"Under different circumstances. Once marriage. Once death."

I shall like to talk to her, he thought with pleasure.

"And the circumstances now?" he asked.

"Life," said Jennifer, with a smile that opened a door to him for a second.

"You mean you are going to live here?"

"Oh yes."

"What an experience that will be!"

"It's an experience to live anywhere, isn't it?"

"This is an especially unusual community."

"That's enough to prejudice me in its favor from the start. We've been living in New York so long that it got rather too usual. Both Steve and I think we'll like the country better."

"Country," he repeated. "Well, don't expect to find it too rural here. It's not exactly pastoral."

"No—this is hardly a farmhouse."

"Though there aren't many houses like this one. This is the pride of the hunting set. Are you going to join it? You ride?"

"I knew I'd be caught out about that," said Jennifer. "No, I've never been on a horse. Steve rides, of course."

"Is he bringing you here or are you bringing him?"

I touched a nerve that time, Miles said to himself. She didn't think that remark was at all funny. I wonder why they did come. Neither of them looks alcoholic. It probably wasn't that.

"We came hand in hand," answered Jennifer.

She did not think she would like this man, yet she was glad he was here. She thought as he had of her, here's someone to talk to. Articulate, though probably merciless. Geoffrey Clark was like that too. Miles Halliday reminded her of Geoffrey and suddenly, in the midst of the gaiety of these strangers, nostalgia for the life that had been wiped out last February rushed over Jennifer.

She heard Steve, who was standing close by, explaining to Sara, being partly frank, but not completely so of course.

". . . and you wake up one day and wonder what it's all about and why . . . tired of the squirrel cage . . . and my girl was working too hard. . . ."

"What were you working too hard at?" Sara asked Jennifer.

"It wasn't too hard . . . but I was one of the editors on *Portfolio*."

"Were you? I adore that magazine—I always see it at my hairdresser's."

Jennifer laughed inwardly for that was an office joke, the people who said in a rather superior way that they saw *Portfolio* at the hairdresser's, or in a dentist's office—or borrowed it from the cook. It was such a popular woman's magazine that it was not considered chic.

"We amuse you, I think," said Miles, not missing the smile in her eyes.

"I wouldn't be so insolent. But I wish you'd tell me what it is that makes DeSoto so unusual. Why do you say that living here will be different from settling in any other small place?"

"Because this is a synthetic community. It's made of a new social fabric—wrinkle-proof, drip-dry—just what so many people want today—you know what I mean?"

"No, I don't," she said. "I'm sorry."

"Look at it this way. Why did small towns used to exist? Because they served a practical use. There was a mine in the offing—it was a good site for a mill—it was a natural market center for farmers."

"And DeSoto doesn't serve any practical use?" ·

"It serves a lot of people who have nothing to do by making

them feel that they have something to do. It serves modern leisure—that awful strung-out leisure of people who live too long—and it serves the indestructible widows whose tribe constantly increases, and—" he shrugged—"our friends here."

"But the town is a hundred years old. It was here before there was such a thing as modern leisure."

"I suppose it's always attracted people with soaring thoughts and rhymes in their heads. And nature lovers."

"Don't they still come?"

"The nature lovers and poets? Yes—but they're rather outnumbered by those who think they had damned well better love nature—that it's the only cure for what ails them."

"Is that why you come?"

"I come because it's cheap. Money can go a long way here."

"What good news," said Jennifer.

Sara Bayard said to the red-coated servant, "Thank you, Benjamin," and they went in to dinner.

Jennifer sat between her host and Mr. Harrison. Sara had rearranged the place cards at the table after inviting the Coopers. Tom Bayard wanted to know if Jennifer would be hunting, and after her discouraging answer he did not brighten up until the talk drifted around to the perils of government controls. Mr. Harrison was absent-minded. Jennifer had noticed before dinner that he was preoccupied with a lovely lilylike woman who was at a distance from him at the table. His glance would go toward Molly Crane as if he could not help it, as if he were tossing his thoughts to her and getting hers in return. They are in the middle of a love affair, thought Jennifer. They try to be careful and make it obvious. There must be some obstacle or they wouldn't be so guarded.

She was quick and experienced in analyzing people and trained to remember names. Already the guests were individuals in her mind. Mrs. Piper—that was Kit—was drinking too much, asking for renewed cocktails though there were wineglasses at her elbow.

She was annoying Miles Halliday who was next to her. He would be impatient with incoherence.

The couple called Bee and Archer Loomis were tall and handsome and apparently well liked. They looked happy, as if they deserved affection. Directly opposite her was a not old but not young man whose face was interesting. She liked the way he glanced at her now and then, with a friendliness that was almost encouragement. His last name was Bennett—they called him Gavin—and his wife was Anne, the woman who looked slovenly even in her beautiful dress. Sara Bayard was obviously, as Steve had said to Jennifer, the queen bee. And Tom Bayard certainly thought so. His wife's opinions were constantly on his lips.

How strange to be here, Jennifer said to herself. I wish we hadn't come—it broke the thread. I want to go back to the house—to our house. Those old rooms have more character than these. And there are the azaleas. I must unpack and see about food in the morning. We live here now. We've burned our bridges. But not for this kind of thing. We must make our own pattern. Steve will surely realize that these people are not for us. We can't be part of a group like this on our income.

The man across the table was telling Tom Bayard that he was flying back to New York tonight.

"It's only a couple of hours from that cow pasture here where I park the plane."

"Flying yourself?"

"Yes. In all ways it's simpler."

"Anne going with you?"

"No, she's staying here. She still has to take it easy. We were lucky to be able to rent the Weston place again this year. If they ever decide to sell, I might buy it. There's plenty of land to raise some quail and pheasant. Anne used to like to go after birds."

So the slovenly woman in the chiffon dress was recovering from something. Anne saw that as Gavin Bennett mentioned his wife's name he had glanced at her with a trace of apprehension. The talk flowed on, now concerned with the best cover for quail, a conversation of sport and wealth. And Mr. Harrison was looking at his love and wishing that the dinner would end. So did Jennifer.

They were in the cream and yellow room again and cordials were being served when Gavin Bennett sought her out in a quietly deliberate way.

"I think you deserve an apology," he said, "for our rather inbred talk at dinner. It must have bored you."

"No, it was interesting. But a bit over my head."

"I doubt that very much. We probably sounded adolescent. Your husband tells me that you are going to make DeSoto your home. I often wish I could do that instead of coming and going. I wish even more that I could have done it at his age."

She could see that he was older than Stephen, perhaps by as much as five years.

"We had no choice," she said, and was glad to be frank with someone.

"That can make it easier. I hope you're going to like living in the country."

"I'll have to. But this doesn't seem like country."

"This? Oh, I see what you mean. Don't take this seriously—our little comforts and snacks are superficial—they don't affect the real country. You mustn't let Sara's luxuries disappoint you. What did you think you were going to find here?"

"I wasn't sure. But I thought that living here would be very simple—completely different from city life."

"It can be."

"But everyone seems so sophisticated—"

"Keeping each other warm," he said, "that's all. There are all kinds of people around here who live very differently."

"Unhorsed people?"

He laughed. "Go down to the post office when the mail comes in and you'll find out—and if you want simplicity, ride up the mountains on one of the old trails."

"But I don't ride—"

"You can take your car if it's a small one. Or even walk. You will feel the peace underfoot if you walk. You'll feel it when you pass the mountain cabins and see those quiet, weather-beaten people sitting on their porches, never in a hurry, just soaking up life. Watching the mountains can be the most peaceful activity in the world. And the birds in the early morning are extremely exciting."

"Of course—there will be birds. I hadn't thought of that."

"Are you interested in them?"

She said, "I know nothing about them. There was a robin's nest in our back yard when I was a small child that fascinated me. But during most of my life I've only seen city sparrows and pigeons."

"See if you can find a hummingbird's nest. There must be one on that hill where you live."

"I like to hear you say 'where you live.' "

"I like to say it, with the hope that I may see you here now and then when I get down."

"Tell me what is so special about a hummingbird's nest?"

"It's beautiful architecture."

"You know a great deal about birds?"

"No, I'm no bird watcher," he said. "I've never had time. But there are hummingbirds on this place we leased here so I've found out something about them. Read up on them a little. I like the dynamics of flight. I do some flying myself. The hummingbird is a living helicopter. It's also the most beautiful of animated beings. And with all that, the female is a dedicated homemaker. A perfectionist. Wait until you see that nest of hers. And by the way you have to find it yourself. There's a tradition down here that no one is supposed to show one to anyone else."

"You're telling me the kind of thing I want to know about this place."

"You don't need anyone to tell you anything. You'll soon find out what the DeSoto atmosphere and habits are like. But there's one thing to bear in mind. The people here tonight—and most of the others hereabouts who are not indigenous—have come here not for show and not because it's a place to make a living but because it seems to offer a solution. To their difficulties and disappointments or needs. Or desires."

"Like us," she said simply.

"Like Anne and myself. My wife," he said, his voice softening with tenderness or pity, "has been ill. Inexplicably ill. That was what brought us here first several years ago. For a while I thought we might make our permanent home here—in due time. But—I don't know," he finished, riding his unspoken thoughts out of sight and hearing.

"Where is your home now?"

"In New York. Out of the zones where the most satisfactory homes are found. Or built."

"No hummingbirds' nests there certainly," she said, smiling at him.

Stephen Cooper's sense of well-being tonight amounted almost to exhilaration. He had not felt like this in a long time, not since he had been let out of the corporation. Ever since that happened he had been less than himself, only part of the person he had always been. For that person was not only an individual but a place in life.

There was no snobbishness in him. Stephen did not think he was better than anyone else nor as able as many others. He respected those who were more intellectual, admired those who had special skills. Stephen had never dwelt with self-satisfaction on his personal advantages or thought much about status. He accepted what he had and took it for granted that it was his to keep.

Suddenly, without warning, he had had to face dismissal, lack of money and the revelation of his own incapacities. Though he had refused to complain to Jennifer or anyone else about it, he knew he had been badly treated by the executives of Atlantis. The merger which had been the basic cause of the loss of his job had been one which he had not only approved but promoted. When there had not been enough room for everyone after the consolidation he had been squeezed out, not for any fault or failure in himself but because other men were more tenacious.

For almost a year Stephen had been trying to make himself into a harder and sharper character than he was, putting up false fronts and knowing that they were false. Looking for work had been a defeating experience. He couldn't sell himself for he had no real confidence in what he had to sell. As the months rolled on without results he felt less capable with each rebuff.

The decision to come to DeSoto had been impulsive. Once made, he could not go back on it. There was no other place to which he could retreat. But he had never been sure that the venture made sense or would work out. It was not until this afternoon when they came over the mountains and he saw his father's house on the hill that he realized that the place meant something to him. A sense of belonging somewhere—the first stir of that kind he had felt since Atlantis had released him—came over him.

He did not tell Jennifer about that, nor about the satisfaction he felt as she opened the door of the house which he owned and could offer her as home. These reactions had surprised him, caught him off guard, and he didn't trust them. They might not last—perhaps they were purely corny. He did not want to force anything on Jennifer and would not tell her that he was glad they had come until he was sure of how she felt about it. He was not at all confident that she would be happy here. She had liked her work in New York and would never have given it up willingly. But they had tossed her out, and though it was rough on her at the time it looked tonight as if it might turn out to be the best thing that could have happened.

Bee Loomis was talking to Mr. Harrison and Molly Crane chose Stephen as the next most attractive man in the room.

"I think your wife is charming," she said.

"I'm glad that you like her."

"Who was she before you were married?"

She asked that pleasantly. He knew it was not insolence but

only the usual attempt to fit a new piece into the jigsaw puzzle of society and mutual acquaintance.

"For my money she was the loveliest girl in New York," he answered. And that was the way he had felt when, on a public relations errand to the offices of *Portfolio*, he had first seen Jennifer.

"I'm sure you still think so."

"With more conviction all the time." Stephen looked across the room at his wife, deep in conversation with Gavin Bennett. He was doing most of the talking. Jennifer never made speeches. He loved that about her. It struck Stephen humorously, and a little ironically, that he wouldn't have been able to get an interview with Bennett in New York while he was looking for a new business connection all those months. Now they were at an intimate dinner party together. Also, now he didn't have to ask for interviews.

"She must be terribly brilliant to have been the editor of a magazine."

"Jennifer didn't run the whole show. But they seemed to think highly of her."

He said that as he used to say it, with some pride that Jennifer was not like the run of idle women, the shoppers and the man hunters. It was only lately that her job had humiliated him, because she had a position and earning capacity and his was gone.

The lovely femininity which had drawn him to Jennifer in the beginning no longer had seemed to him to exist in the last few months. She seemed too strong for a woman, too sure and competent. It was worse because she didn't scold or reproach—because she tried to hold him up—and began to pay the rent. He fell into love in reverse—love that was continually ashamed because it couldn't back up its desires with a livelihood. A love that took the worst out on her.

Only when Jennifer failed, when he saw her frightened and helpless, had tenderness crept back. He couldn't let her go on the streets of New York looking for a job. So he had gambled on this move to DeSoto, knowing that if it failed their situation would be worse than before, wishing sometimes in these last weeks that Jennifer would back out, refuse to come, let him off the hook.

But she hadn't wavered. She had sold and packed, been delighted with a good bargain even if she was losing some pieces of furniture she had treasured. She had been gay and amusing at the farewell parties—and a number of these had sprung up when it was known that the Coopers were leaving the city and were apparently enthusiastic about their new plans. Stephen had been surprised and rather resentful that *Portfolio* did not arrange any farewell celebration in Jennifer's honor but of course he did not mention that to her.

"Are you really going to live here? All year round?" Molly was asking.

"We plan to."

"I hope your wife won't find it too dull for her. She must be used to very interesting people."

"She's in the midst of them tonight," said Stephen. "I don't think she'll find it dull at all. It was Jennifer who first suggested that we come down here to live."

"It did seem too bad to have that big house empty."

"That's what we thought."

"Tony Harrison adores DeSoto. This is the first time he's been down here. We had a grand hunt this morning. Oh—excuse me—" Molly saw that Bee had relinquished Mr. Harrison—"I have to ask Tony about something."

Stephen found Sara. "It's a wonderful party," he said.

"Are you having fun?"

"Better than that." It was better because this was a party with no business motive hidden in it. Better because he felt that he was among friends instead of customers or competitors.

"I'm glad," Sara said. "Isn't it strange, Steve, that we both have come to roost down here?"

"Do you live here all the time?"

"Pretty much. More and more. We go to Camden now and

then—once in a while to Virginia. And if it gets too beastly hot we go up to Rolling Rock and cool off. Are you really going to settle in?"

He told her what he wouldn't have told Molly Crane.

"We just about have to, Sara. Things weren't going too well for me in New York. I couldn't carry on there any longer."

"Who wants to?"

"When you're there you think you want to. Or have to. But this afternoon I began to wonder if I hadn't been fooling myself."

"We have a good time. It's quite a good Hunt. You'll like it."

He looked very noncommittal.

"Of course you will hunt with us?"

"I probably can't afford it right now. I haven't any horses—"

"Oh, that can be arranged— We can fix that."

She was still talking about arranging that when Gavin Bennett came to say good night to her.

He told Stephen, "I'll look forward very much to seeing you and your wife when I get down again."

Stephen thanked him and said, "I'd better see how my Jenny is getting on."

As he came up to her Jennifer said softly and a little eagerly, "Ready to go?"

"Do you want to?"

"Our house is probably beginning to think we ran out on it."

"All right, darling, let's go home."

But it took half an hour and another drink for Stephen before Sara let them leave, with promises of seeing them again very soon. Tom Bayard repeated what Sara said. Bee and Archer Loomis echoed it and Kit Piper, not quite so coherently, told them to keep a week from Thursday and that she would call them about it. Miles Halliday bowed in his mannered way and asked Jennifer, "One day may I see the inside of the Acropolis?"

"Of course. I'd be very glad."

"That was a whole lot of fun," Stephen said as they drove toward the gates. "You enjoyed yourself, didn't you?"

"I really did. After I got over feeling strange. I like Gavin Bennett enormously and the Halliday man is sort of spicy. Gavin Bennett is very easy to talk to. Who is he?"

"Just one of the most important men in New York. He has his finger in any number of big things. He began with steel, I think, but he has plenty of other interests. A big chain of hotels and motels for one thing, both in this country and all over the Caribbean— We sold them a big order of aluminum for one of them. I happen to know about that. I have never met him until tonight. He's a real tycoon."

"He doesn't seem like one when you talk to him. He's not a bit pompous. He knows about hummingbirds. And he likes the mountain people."

"He certainly seemed to take a shine to you."

"I think perhaps he realized I felt a little lost."

"There wasn't the slightest reason for that. They all were singing your praises. We certainly got off to a good start."

"But we can't keep up with those people, Steve."

"There's no question of keeping up. They took us right in. I like the friendliness. That's the way people should be. And are down here."

"The ones there tonight all seemed very rich."

"Don't hold that against them," he said with a cheerful laugh.

"I don't—but it makes a difference."

"Not very much in DeSoto."

"Maybe not," said Jennifer rather doubtfully, "I wouldn't know. But I've never lived in a place like DeSoto."

Most of the places where Jennifer had lived would have made a chain of dreary memories if she had looked back at them. She almost never did that, unless an incident or a person seen on the street excited a sharp and almost always unpleasant association. At the beginning—as far back as she could remember—there had been the house with the robin's nest in the back yard. The dim image of her mother was in that setting and since she could faintly recall kindness and fun, she must have had an early taste of them.

Her mother had been killed in a car accident when Jennifer was only five years old and her father had married again, soon and disastrously. He was a frail man, whom she remembered as invalided, and Jennifer knew now that he must have been ineffectual in many ways. But he was always gentle, and by example he showed his daughter what dignity was. He was well born—his own father had been a judge of considerable standing and Philip had a college degree. But the family had petered out to end in Philip Walton's incapacities. If there were scattered relatives on her mother's side, Jennifer did not know who or where they were. She guessed that they might have broken any family connection after Philip's marriage to his second wife, Selma. Certainly they had taken no responsibility for Jennifer, and Selma made that a favorite taunt.

His second wife resented Philip Walton's breeding almost more than she came to hate his ailments and incompetence. But it was her scornful comments that made Jennifer aware that she was cut from a different cloth than the children whom Selma brought from a previous broken marriage into her third one.

"I suppose you think you're better than my boys because your grandfather was a judge!" "All right, princess—just get out and scrub the kitchen floor!"

That was the sort of talk, more frequent as Jennifer's father's health worsened and his doctor sent him to a tuberculosis sanatorium. Jennifer was only nine and there was a regulation against having children visit in that hospital, but for some reason it was relaxed in Jennifer's case—perhaps it was pity for both her and her father. She was warned not to get close to the bed. But she knew the hours for visiting and the number of the bus that went by the hospital and went there by herself as often as she could. It hurt and frightened her to see him grow thinner and more waxy white, but she would sit quietly and smile at him and listen to what he told her. He was the only person she had to love and she learned to love at a distance. Philip told her to be a good girl and to mind her mother—meaning Selma—and Jennifer promised that she would. He said she must study hard and go to college.

Once he said, "If your mind is well furnished you will be happy." And for a time Jennifer thought of her mind as a room with soft chairs and clean white curtains.

After Philip Walton died, Selma took over the mortgaged house and property and took over Jennifer too, perhaps to eliminate any small claim that the child might have had. Before long the house was sold and they moved from the wooded outskirts of the city into a succession of flats that were as Selma said, "in the middle of things." She went back to work in a shop. She went back to other tastes and occupations as well. She was a coarsely handsome, hard-drinking woman who needed men, cajoled them and fought with them. Sometimes she brought them to the flat and Jennifer, sent into the kitchen, would hear the brawls.

She lived with her father's second family because she had no place else to go and Selma kept her because she was so useful. Jennifer did not forget that her father had told her to mind her mother, but she never forgot for a moment that Selma was not her mother nor the two boys her own brothers. She did most of the housework in the flats and by the time she was thirteen she began to earn money by baby-sitting, as other girls in her school were doing. Selma did not object though the work that Jenny was expected to do in the flats was not lessened. But the girl's life became easier. She could watch children and study her lessons. The baby-sitting gave her some freedom and independence. And there was the money.

The life with her stepmother did not harden Jenny and her father's example had given her a kind of amulet against hate. She was a curiously sanguine child who was far more competent and self-reliant than her years should have demanded. Somehow she managed to keep Selma's doings and the street life of the boys at a distance. They did not belong to her. But school did—with its order and constant change and its praise—for she was quick to learn and a favorite with her teachers. Also there were the homes where she took care of children so that she came to know house-holds that were quite different from Selma's tawdry lodgings.

Because she was earning she was able to get through high

school, paying for her books and clothes and lunches. She was discussed in teachers' meetings and small encouragements were offered her. By that time ambition was alive in her and, although she was still docile with her stepmother, she had made up her mind to be on her own as soon as possible. Meager scholarships for further study were rather plentiful in the city and Jennifer had little trouble in being awarded one. She had to endure some subsequent abuse and talk of her ingratitude from Selma when she said that she was going to the university two hundred miles away, but Jennifer knew that to mind her stepmother any longer would soon defeat her father's other injunction: to be a good girl.

At the university, the self-help department arranged a medley of jobs for her. She worked in the cafeteria and typed papers and theses, for she had mastered that skill in high school and become very proficient. She had learned to drive Selma's battered old car, and during one vacation she drove a woman, who advertised for a companion, to Florida. She read everything she could lay her hands on, from the classics to the advice columns in the newspapers. The printed word became a passion. She developed the always original, commonplace plan of going to New York, getting a job on a magazine or in a publishing house, and ultimately becoming a writer.

Every cent she earned was important. She had only two pairs of stockings so she browned her legs in the sun as she studied and went bare-legged. She figured on the price of everything, on the length of time a bottle of liquid shampoo would last, on pencils, paper and shoes. Because her earnings did not allow her to experiment with clothes or to make mistakes, she had a sure taste in selecting them. Because she had no leisure for the follies and small dissipations of the teens, the charm of her manner was not tampered with. She was not ignorant or gullible—life with Selma had been informing even when it was disgusting—but a kind of brave innocence carried her along to the time when she actually arrived in New York by bus, found a room at the YWCA, and only a week later was given a job as a kind of literary scullery maid on *Portfolio.* The brave innocence was still apparent when three years later—by that time she was assistant fiction editor and had a small apartment of her own—Stephen Cooper met her in the business office of the magazine and found her unforgettable.

Now they had passed the red reflectors that marked the boundaries of the Bayard estate, still known locally as the Langley place. The mountains loomed up grandly and among the stars the taillight of an airplane swung for a minute. Jennifer wondered if that was Gavin Bennett touring the sky, still surprised at that bit of penetrating, almost intimate talk she had had with him tonight.

Steve was speaking again. He was full of talk tonight, as if released from tension.

"Sara's quite a girl, isn't she? Didn't you like her?"

"I hardly had a chance to speak to her. She's certainly very beautiful. It was rather hard going at the table with her husband. Probably my fault."

"He's not so bad. He's the best one she's had. The first husband she had couldn't be tolerated—I met him once and I knew she wouldn't keep him around. I don't know what happened to the second one, he was an Englishman, I think. Tom Bayard's a gentleman anyway."

"But no scholar—"

"That wouldn't bother Sara much. They like the same things. She and Tom are Joint Masters."

"Masters?"

"Of the Hunt. They want me to join that by the way. And I do need exercise. I've been getting soft since I gave up squash."

He had given it up because he had had to resign from the club in New York when he was let out. The company had always paid the club bills.

"But you'd have to have a horse. Wouldn't that cost a lot?"

She was thinking, we have about seven thousand three hundred dollars left in the bank, and that five hundred coming in regularly every month. That's all there is except my bonds—worth six thousand fifty in this market—and they must be kept for a reserve. A horse?

"That's not going to be a problem, due to the Bayards. I told Sara frankly when she brought it up that I didn't think I could afford to hunt and she said she'd mount me."

"Give you a horse?"

"Not give me one. I wouldn't let her do that. But it's this way. They have trouble getting their horses exercised. Of course they can't let anyone who comes along ride them, that could ruin a good horse. And grooms and trainers can be overworked in a stable as large as theirs. She said it would be a favor actually if I'd come over and have a look and see if one of their hunters would suit me. She meant it. You know that was one thing I was afraid of— though I didn't dare mention it after we decided to take the plunge—I was afraid that we might be bored to death down here. Or go to seed."

"We won't—"

"No, I don't think that will happen. This place is growing—I don't mean just the town but the whole area. Archer Loomis was telling me about new plants—textiles, hosiery, a lot of products. They locate beside the highways, comb the region for labor and transport their employees by bus every day—the old company towns are a thing of the past. It's a completely new, modern setup."

"Could you get into something like that?"

"I don't know. I might. The first thing anyhow is to get acquainted. Look the ground over. Make friends. These hunting people have a lot of interests—that's why they can afford to hunt."

"I suppose so." Jennifer went on irrelevantly, "Has Sara Bayard any children?"

"Two boys. Twins. She was talking about them tonight. They were by the first husband. I hope they don't take after that bum. I remember hearing—or maybe I read it in the newspapers at the time—that there was quite a battle over the custody of those kids. I suppose he tried to hold her up. But she has them part of the time, she told me tonight, and seems crazy about them."

Jennifer wondered why Sara Bayard hadn't been given full custody. But she did not ask about that.

"Does she spend much time here?"

"Most of the year, she told me."

"Why, I wonder? I mean—anyone so beautiful and obviously rich as she is—I should think this might be too small a setting for her."

"Apparently she doesn't think so. But everyone has a personal reason for coming to DeSoto," said Stephen.

"Yes, Miles Halliday and Gavin Bennett were both telling me that tonight—from very different points of view. It was fascinating. The Bennetts came because his wife was ill. He said that he envied you for intending to live here all the time."

"I'm not sorry so far."

"I don't believe we ever will be, Steve—let's never be! Look, there's our house, waiting for us. Isn't it incredible? Doesn't it make you proud? It's a very proud house."

"As a matter of fact it does make me feel pretty damned good. If you're going to like it."

"I'm already in love with it."

"Not just with the house?" he asked, reaching one hand toward her for a quick caress. "Jenny, I've been pretty much of a mess this last year. Don't think I don't know it—"

"You had a very rough time—"

"So have you. We both took a beating. But I wasn't going to have my wife on the streets of New York looking for a job, that was one sure thing. Here you're going to have a home and a lot of friends—you were where you belong tonight, right in your element with those people."

She did not contradict him, not say—I was out of my element. I knew it, Gavin Bennett knew it and I think that the Halliday man did too. The life that had been her element for years flashed through Jennifer's mind—a kaleidoscope of her pale gray steel desk, the constant flood of manuscripts, the business luncheons at Pierre's with authors who had to be guided or encouraged or persuaded, the race to deadlines, the problems that Geoffrey, her brilliant boss, created with his hangovers and his women, the competition, the achievement—that had been the element she had earned for herself in New York. And for eight years—not quite that but the last months didn't count—there had been Steve also, the other element in life for her, her husband, her escort, the man whose business game she helped to play as hostess—the lover who came to her at night or on a rainy Sunday. There had been two elements in Jennifer's life, each separate from the other. They had never blended—she hadn't tried to blend them—there was no reason for that. Now both were gone. Now there was only Stephen, who would be different in this atmosphere and place, and this strange untested adventure must be made into a new element suitable for them both.

This time they went into the house together.

"Back home," he said. "Feels familiar already. I think a night-cap is in order—how about you?"

"No, thanks—I have to go upstairs and straighten things around —we went off in such a rush that I left everything in a mess. It won't take me long."

"Which rooms did you decide to use for us?"

"Oh, the front one that was your father's is a natural for you. I looked in there before dinner and it's a fine, substantial man's room. The bed in there is made up, God bless Susie. I don't know about the others—"

"One bed is plenty."

"As you will—have it your way tonight. But Steve, can I have the small room, the one next to yours, for my own? There are mountains from both windows, and there is a door to the hall as well as the one to your room, so I could come and go without being a nuisance. I didn't realize that room was there when I was here before or I didn't remember it—"

"There are so many doors in that white paneling that you probably thought it was a closet. That was my mother's room. She never used it very much."

"I'll use it—that's what it needs—use and being liked. It's a little forlorn, that poor room, and it twisted my heart for some reason. Steve, there isn't any mortgage on this house, is there?"

"Not a cent. I thought of putting one on it more than once but it meant taking a trip down here to arrange it—appraisals and all that—and there would be interest to pay on a mortgage and—why?—were you worrying about that?"

"No, but I'm glad that there isn't one. In the only other place I ever lived in that wasn't rented—when I was small and my father owned a house—I used to hear them talk about the mortgage on the house. I thought it was something like a chimney but I knew it meant trouble."

"Well, this place is in the clear—"

"Oh lovely house," she said in a dreamy voice, and turned to the stairs. She went up slowly and lightly, here and there stroking the banister. She was thinking, I won't wear that shortie I put in my dressing case for tonight. I'll take the long white satin one that Steve gave me for Christmas out of the big case. He will like to have me wear that tonight. For a while—

Steve watched her until she turned the corner on the landing, delaying the nightcap, forgetting it for the moment. He had not dared to hope this was going to be so good.

5

THE POST OFFICE in DeSoto was not merely a place where stamps were sold, mail sorted and pictures of criminals displayed. It was a meeting place, a hopper into which all the various elements of the town and the vicinity were poured every day, including Sunday. There had been an effort once or twice to establish mail deliveries throughout the area, but so few people wanted it that the proposition had never been carried through. Servants from the inns picked up the mail for their guests. But from the shops and business offices, from the elegant residences and the cottages, people themselves came to get the day's supply of letters, papers and packages. Not just for that. It was a place to linger in greetings and conversations, to congratulate each other about the weather or complain about it, or just to kill a little time.

Ranks of private mailboxes covered the walls. The smaller ones had combination locks, the larger ones were dignified with keys.

Into some of the boxes only an occasional letter or card was inserted by the sorters but most of them were stuffed full twice a day. Every weekly and every national newspaper and magazine passed through the DeSoto post office. Little envelopes containing invitations for cocktails or dinner were put in and taken out by the hundreds every month. Acceptances. Regrets. Thank-you notes and messages of sympathy. At the tables high against two walls those people who couldn't wait until they got home opened and read their mail.

But whether the mail from the outside world was light or heavy for a DeSoto resident, one thing would almost certainly be in his box every day and that was the local newspaper, so properly called the *Town Crier*. For its purpose was to call people together, to tell them when and where to mourn, to rejoice, to contribute and to buy.

The *Crier* was a small sheet, now of six pages and again of perhaps eight or ten, depending on the volume of its advertisements. But it was the amalgam which held all the diverse interests and incomes and backgrounds of DeSoto together, an amazing feat which had been successful for almost fifty years. Nearly everyone read it, finding out about the arrivals and departures of people whom they often did not know by sight, informing themselves about local events, local charities, the times of all church services, as well as who was dead, just born or just out of the hospital.

Now and then there would be a few leading paragraphs about national events—a great flood or an act of war would not be ignored. The paper also reflected local politics without bias or opinion. Occasionally, when there was space or the editor had time, a gentle short editorial would appear, usually to remind people how fortunate they were to live in or near DeSoto.

The editor, Maury Wright, gray-haired but with the amble of a boy as he walked along the streets, not exactly looking for news but somehow absorbing it, had preserved a simplicity in both himself and his paper which was certainly not naïveté for he knew too well what went on in the town and the world. It was rather a factual directness, an impersonality which was not cold but completely realistic. Reporting the arrival of the Duke and Duchess of Windsor in New York (and he reported it only because the Langley family had so many British visitors that the item had local interest) he had written:

> The Duke and Duchess of Windsor have arrived in New York. The Duchess was formerly Miss Wallis Warfield of Baltimore. The Duke was formerly King of England. They are visiting friends and relatives.

This was a thoroughly democratic statement, not meant in the least to be funny, though many readers laughed with delight over it. It was especially notable because it intimated that to be a Southerner, like Miss Warfield, was more important than to be a king. For the *Crier* was always a Southern paper in mood, although so many subscribers came from Northern states. In fact, the *Crier*, as Maury Wright knew, was sent to most of the states in the Union and often drifted abroad. He knew the affection with which it was held and how to preserve that, by complete lack of snobbishness and the intimate touch.

He printed news of the sort which is exchanged on street corners, about a bad car wreck and what the damage in dollars would amount to, about the man who got a hole in one on the ninth, about the pair who won the bridge tournament. His paper had been desegregated before the Supreme Court put the word into common use. Only when the tax lists were printed, and of course had to be copied from the rolls as they stood, was one list of names identified as Colored and the other as White. Cocktail parties and dinners were never reported, but the pleasant weddings of local girls might be given a half column.

"You want what the bride's mother wore, Mr. Wright?" a girl might ask, bringing the news into his scrambled office.

"Sure do, honey. That always makes an interesting item for our older women readers," he would tell her.

"It's the one restful paper in the world," said Carver Jones. He had not yet thrown away the issue which a week ago had printed his name twice, once telling that he was going to speak to the Rotary at the Inn, and in another column that he had given several acres for a boys' football field in DeSoto. Mr. Jones had been international president of Rotary some years ago but he had transferred his membership to the local chapter.

But it was not the variety of mail or the almost blanket coverage of the *Crier* which gave the DeSoto post office its special character. It was the diversity of faces, figures, ages and clothes. Bill Long, artist and bridge expert, with his untidy blond hair and madly bright shirts that never were clean. Mrs. Olds, now using two canes and never managing to get the combination of her box right the first time. John Pepper with his unlit cigar. Men who used to employ hundreds of others and then wore handsomely tailored suits, now in faded slacks and old golf caps, others in the vests and boots prescribed for formal riding. Old men who did not do anything after the last heart attack shuffling along in fear of a fall. Village girls wearing stretch pants and balloons of hair—dark skins, white skins—they all came to pick up their mail. The semisocial function went on all day, reaching its peak in the morning when the sorters "put up" the first batch of incoming mail and at five in the evening when the last airmail load would be in the boxes.

It was a fine, bright April day. The air was clean, almost liquid, as if it could be taken in as an intoxicant or restorative. The "pretty day," the "real DeSoto weather," was the topic with everyone this morning. Lucia Jones, one of the governors of the Garden Club, whose smile could be almost a weapon of attack, came into the post office brandishing the smile from right to left. Then she saw a woman with a face and figure straight out of mountain living, who was peddling branches of pink dogwood, and the smile became a different exposed weapon, a frown. She looked with reproof also at Jennifer Cooper, the person who was buying some of the branches, and approached the pair.

Jennifer was thinking of how beautiful the dogwood would be in the tall marble urns on either side of her doorway.

"Mrs. Valiant, I have explained to you that it is wrong to cut pink dogwood!" said Mrs. Jones. "It grows very slowly and we must not strip our mountains of their natural beauty!"

"Grows on my own property," said Mrs. Valiant in a disobedient mutter, knowing well that it couldn't be proved that it did not. This was her best source of income in the spring. She looked away so that Mrs. Jones was forced to talk to a head scarf patterned with dogs, and Jennifer wanted to laugh. She knew that the disapproval included her, but she liked the defiant little woman better than the righteous one with the sharp voice.

Mrs. Valiant gave Jennifer a smile of conspiracy. "Not her mountains nohow," she said, just loud enough so that Mrs. Jones would surely hear.

"When you buy from them you encourage vandalism," said Mrs. Jones to Jennifer in a platform voice.

Jennifer said, "I'm afraid I've already bought it," and gave Mrs. Valiant a dollar. Carrying the branches she went to open the box they had rented. A man was turning the key in the lock of one just below her own and she waited for him to finish, watching the people as they milled around and talked to one another. Gavin Bennett had told her that the post office would reveal the community and so it did. She thought that she would like to know the woman whose olive sweater and pink skirt were such a good combination—and that tolerant-looking man who could have posed as a senator or ambassador—and the fat woman with the cordial, almost chuckling expression. She hoped she would not have to know the authoritative woman who was probably so right about not cutting dogwood.

The man straightened up from his mailbox and gave her a swift glance. It surprised her because she read caution in it for just a second before it became bland. He said almost overpleasantly that he hoped he hadn't kept her waiting.

"Not at all."

"Beautiful day," he said and with his letters folded inside a newspaper he went out of the post office.

All kinds, thought Jennifer. But there was something about that man that seemed strange, even though you never know whom you'll see next. He didn't fit even into this medley. Because one thing you don't see here is people who are on guard. I can imagine him on a city street, reminding you that there are dangerous people in the world.

Dave Delaney got into his car unhurriedly, pausing to speak to someone in another car—the man to whom he had paid his fee for the Hunt. He did not go back to the Inn when he drove off but took the highway that went through the main valley, up and over Bald Eagle Mountain and rolled on to Portal City sixty miles away. When he was well out of the village limits he pulled up by the roadside and opened one of the letters inside the folds of the newspaper. It would have been unintelligible to anyone except himself, but none the less he tore it into very small pieces when he finished reading and threw them into the next trash barrel that he passed. His drive took him ten miles up the mountain and then he turned off on a tar-paved spur that took him over to the old winding road that had been used before the highway was constructed. It was rutted and out of repair but Delaney knew where he was going. He jolted along until he came to an abandoned roadside stand still bearing a melancholy rotted sign with the lettering COLD CIDER.

Delaney drove with skill and observantly, as if he were carefully inspecting the territory but not as if it was unfamiliar. Near the roadside stand he turned off again, and now his car crunched through long grass and sparsely grown saplings. There had been a narrow drive here once and it was a long one, perhaps an eighth of a mile before it came to an open space where there was a big old barn, several sheds and the remnant of a burned house that must have been a large one. Delaney stopped his car and got out. This was the place. It had been isolated even when he worked here as a boy and now it was completely deserted and probably forgotten.

He studied the location and was sure that this side of the

mountain was not visible from the town and there was also sheltering timber all around the open patch. The barn and sheds could be used after some reboarding and cleaning. The necessary equipment could be moved in here at night and then, thought Delaney, we're in business. According to the letter he had destroyed, Todd and Dennis were ready to come down, though they were not sure that he had made a good choice of the place for their operation. Delaney was sure he had. He had been getting the feel of the town and the people here during the last two weeks. It had grown a lot and was much more stylish than it used to be, he had found, but it was still full of freaks and loners. Newcomers were taken for granted and a person could establish himself pretty much at his own rating. Also, Delaney had a soft spot for this place. He told himself now, these damned mountains get in your blood. If everything goes all right I might even call it a day and settle down here, live like a lord.

Memories rustled around him as he stood there. When he had run away from that farm in Georgia where he had been bound out as an orphan, he had trudged up this way, worked in a livery stable in DeSoto and then, after Mrs. Prentiss built this place in the woods, he had worked for her, taken care of her horses. He used to drink with her too. She got so she didn't care what she did. Everyone shied away from her, no one came near the house unless to sell or deliver something. She was a crazy old widow and she burned the house down with herself inside it. Delaney wasn't clear himself how it had happened.

The sunlight struck through the woods finding bright color, and he thought, flaming wild azaleas, haven't seen those in a long while. He returned to his car and went back to the village, stopping this time at an office in a weather-beaten building whose front window was lettered JOSEPH L. HARRIS REAL ESTATE AND DEVELOPMENTS.

The man behind the desk inside was burly and commercially hearty. Delaney introduced himself.

"I tell you, Mr. Harris," he said, "I've sort of fallen in love with this place. I came down for a rest and vacation—doctor's orders to go slow—that's what they tell you after a while—"

"When the doc says that, it's what you have to do," said Joe Harris, "and if you want to take life easy, sir, you came to the right place."

"I sort of sensed that. I guess it attracts a great many people."

"No end of them. Can hardly keep up with the newcomers any more. People like to get away from the cities these days. You thinking of settling down here, Mr. Delaney?"

"I don't know yet. But I'm interested. It's got what I want. I went out with the Hunt the other day."

Joe Harris looked at his client again. He thought of the Bayards and the Loomises. This fellow didn't seem quite the type but you never knew.

"That's one of our attractions," he said. "Where are you from, Mr. Delaney?"

"New York," said Delaney. Sometimes he was. Sometimes from Philadelphia and they had also operated for a while outside of Minneapolis.

"Is your idea to build or buy?"

"Buy. Or rent. I'd like to rent furnished if I could find a place to suit me. I'm a widower."

"What type of house have you in mind?"

"I don't want anything junky. I like space. And privacy. Something presentable."

Joe Harris said, "Too bad, you should have come in a few months ago. I had one of the finest properties around here on my list and it might have been just what you're after. You may have seen it. The square house with the columns on the hill opposite the Inn."

"I've driven by the place. The gates were closed, I noticed. It was for rent?"

"Preferably for sale but the owner might have rented it. It was completely furnished too. But the owner decided to come down here himself. He's from New York like yourself. Had enough of it, he told me, though he's still a young man. Stephen Cooper's father built that place and lived there until he died a few years ago."

"What were you asking for it? Just for curiosity."

"Sixty thousand and, believe me, at that price it was a give-away."

"You say the father died some years ago. Why didn't it sell?"

"Well, a lot of people prefer to build to suit themselves. And they bring their furnishings from their other homes."

"I got rid of mine," said Delaney, thinking that the blackmailing bitch got all that good stuff, more than ten thousand dollars worth.

"That house is off your list definitely?"

"Steve seems to want to keep it for himself."

"If he changes his mind I just might be interested. Not at sixty thousand. Forty thousand is as high as I'd want to go."

Harris thought with sadness of the lost commission. Steve Cooper would have taken forty a few months ago.

"What else is available?"

The real estate agent meditated, talked aloud.

"One beautiful estate—sixty acres more or less between DeSoto and Cranston. In the hunting country. But that is rented right now to the Gavin Bennetts— He's a big shot in New York, comes down here by plane, his own plane, whenever he can. There are a lot of moneyed people around here now."

Delaney knew that. It had been a major consideration.

"Let's get on with something that's available, Harris."

"You want something in its own grounds?"

"Yes, I want privacy. I'm here to be quiet."

"There's the Henderson house. It's at the foot of old Bald Eagle. Not too far out. You take the main road out past the Roman Catholic church. You know where that is?"

"Yes. I'm a Roman Catholic. I attend that church."

He had made a point not only of attendance but of being noticed at the altar rail, where he had a right to be. He had made his confession. He had dropped a five dollar bill in the collection box. It was all part of building up a personality that would fit into DeSoto and be trusted—a Catholic and a churchgoer—a man who liked to ride horses—a gentleman looking for a good house and inclined to settle down—

"Some of my very good friends are Catholics," said the agent automatically. "This house I'm speaking of is an old house but they don't build them like that any more, not so solid— After you pass the church, you go over the bridge and when you get to the foot of the mountain you turn left. The place has a splendid view and it's just possible that the estate it belongs to might be willing to rent it though they'd prefer to sell outright."

"I think I'd like to see that place," said Dave Delaney. This sounded as if it would do for now. It would make him accessible to the operation on the mountain—no one to mark his goings and comings. Not that he'd want to be stuck with a house that even a real estate agent couldn't boast about. But for the time being it might be the thing, and later on when he sold out, if he really became this character he was building up, he could go on from there. "I'll look it over," he repeated and added, "If at any time anything should break on that other house—Cooper was the name?—you might keep me in mind."

6

Jennifer clipped the ends of the dogwood branches and put them in the marble urns on the terrace which flanked either side of the front door. The urns had browned and yellowed with weather, but in all the years they had stood there they had never been broken or even chipped. She took a minute to enjoy the effect. Each thing she did like this gave her a sense of growing possession and made life at Chestnut Hill more natural.

It had been fascinating to unstiffen the house without destroying its dignity, to scribble her own signature on the rooms. The changes she had made were careful because she did not want to do anything that would incur much expense. But now in the hall and drawing room there was more sense of ease. The furniture was not so rigidly symmetrical against the walls as it had been, chairs were conversational, tables useful for gloves and opened packs of cigarettes. Jennifer had found a storeroom where stray pieces of

74

furniture had been put away and shrouded with old sheets, and had brought out from their dusty coverings a red-covered footstool embroidered in petit point, and a scarred but still beautiful piecrust table with circles carved around its edge where individual teacups could be placed. It was just as handy for highball glasses.

She had also come upon some delicate furnishings that had almost certainly been made long ago in France. There was a gilded rocking chair with a rose brocade seat. It was a gay and frivolous chair with painted figures of bewigged ladies and gentlemen on its curved back. Matching it was a cabinet with doors decorated in the same gallant mood that opened with smooth elegance, and a small glass-topped tea table. Jennifer transferred these things to the small neglected bedroom which she had claimed for her own special use.

Stephen said that he did not know where the French furniture had come from but he remembered the piecrust table.

"That was in the old New York house," he said. "I used to count the circles. It was probably sent down here when Father retired. Might be a fairly valuable piece. After the house was sold they had an apartment over by the East River for a very short time—before Mother became sick—and she may have rigged it up with the gilt stuff. It doesn't look like my father."

Jennifer had no doubt that Henry Cooper had kept it because it looked like his wife.

She said, "It certainly doesn't look like me either. But it enchants me. Maybe living with it will teach me how to be a leisured lady."

They had been in residence almost a month and the pattern of their days had begun to take shape. The Hunt, Jennifer found, had its useful points. It meant that Steve was up early on at least three mornings a week, for he must be at the meet by ten o'clock. Jennifer would drive him to the Bayard stables to get his mount and leave him there to hack over with the other riders to the location of the meet. The Town Crier always printed information as to whether it would be at the Burnt Cottage, Red Fox Hill or in the Fieldstone Meadow, the usual places where the fox hunts started from, and several times Jennifer had driven over in the car to see them take off.

The formal drama of it had fascinated her when she saw it first. The scarlet coats, the careful protocol observed by the Master, the First Whip and the Huntsman. She was proud to see how easily and naturally Stephen fitted into the picture.

On that first day he rode over to her car, reined in his horse.

"Quite a sight, isn't it? Like me in a pink coat?"

"But it's scarlet—why do you call it pink?"

"Because of the name of the London tailor who once made them. His name was Pink," explained Stephen. "Now look—if you drive the car to the top of the far ridge—then take the Old Arrow Road—you can see the whole thing—the action—the hounds—maybe even the fox."

"I'll do that. I can't get over Tom Bayard! He's so different."

"He's an excellent Master."

"Master is the word," said Jennifer. Tom Bayard, feeling for conversation ineptly at a dinner party, was not the same man who was Master of the Hunt. Gracious but not casual as the others saluted him, superbly at ease on his black horse, Jennifer gave him a respect that she felt was due to him in this character. When he noticed her and lifted his cap, she felt like a peasant girl being honored by her betters. And that was so absurd that she almost laughed aloud.

After a couple of times she did not follow the hunt, driving to some distant hilltop to get a glimpse of galloping horses and baying hounds. She would go back to her own house, to put away the breakfast dishes, make up the bedrooms and fix the flowers. Susie rarely came to help before noon and Jennifer enjoyed those morning hours of complete possession of the house. Then she would go to the markets in the village, push a food cart around thoughtfully, survey the fruits and vegetables and consider the prices.

On the days when there was no hunt, Stephen would have

colloquies with Agamemnon, see that a start was made in mending a fence or pruning a tree. He always had errands and objectives for himself. He would prowl the hardware store. He would drive thirty miles to look over a pack of hounds or in another direction to find the right kind of crushed stone to repair the driveway. He made plans and reviewed them with Jennifer. He had said nothing more about the possibility of making some connection with the regional industries after that first night. His plan might be to clear the south slope of the hill and set out thousands of everbearing strawberries. Someone had made a lot of money out of that, he told her. Or the plan might be to buy a good piece of bottom land on mortgage and get a herd of Angus. These were ideas, not ventures. Jennifer did not know if he had ever made any attempt to make a business connection at any mill or plant. She did not ask him and she almost hoped he would not. For if such an effort ended in his being turned down, it might sour and spoil what they had.

"You were cut out to be a country squire, Steve," she told him one evening.

"Nothing to the squire act," he said, "but people are friendly. And you know everyone is glad to see this place come to life. I hear that all around town. By the way, I stopped in at the town hall the other day and registered to vote."

"I must do that."

"Yes, they appreciate it. I was talking to Clint Allen, the contractor. He's the political boss around here, the one who can give the nod to anyone who wants to run for office. Nice fellow and a tarheel from away back."

"Do you think he will give you the nod to run for mayor someday?"

Stephen laughed. "It would be a nice little job at that but he could never use a Northerner. From his point of view I'm always a Yankee, even if not a completely damn one."

"Your father settled down here years ago."

"It's still their town," said Stephen. "By the way, Jenny, I suppose we ought to latch on to a church here eventually. Everyone seems to make a thing of that. Don't you think the Episcopal one would be for us?"

"I never thought about it."

"That's the church that Father used to say he absented himself from—his excuse for making a contribution when they came around."

Jennifer was rather astonished. In New York they had never gone to church. She liked the idea of it in a vague way, for it meant that Stephen was putting down a new root or thought that he should recultivate an old one. But she did not think he really meant to do anything about it until, on the following Sunday morning, he said after breakfast, "Nice day—how about taking in Saint Matthew's this morning? I think the *Crier* said it begins at eleven."

She had hunted out a hat—it was the first time she had worn a hat in a very long time, but it was plain enough not to look silly—and they had gone into the village for the service. As Stephen had said, almost everyone in DeSoto seemed to be going to church. Cars were lining up before the Baptist, Methodist and Presbyterian churches, in some places almost moving bumper to bumper.

Kit Piper waved to them from behind the wheel of her open car.

"Kit's a Catholic," said Stephen idly. "She's a fine hunting woman too. Pity she can't behave better."

"She's lovely this morning. Leave it at that, Steve."

Jennifer saw a number of other familiar faces. Women whom she had noticed in blue jeans in the supermarkets were elegant this morning in perfected tailoring and white gloves. Old, untidy ladies she had seen at the post office obviously felt themselves grand in bits and pieces of furs that they did not need on such a warm day. Bee and Archer Loomis passed with a bright greeting and went to a front pew in Saint Matthew's as if that were their habit. And to her complete surprise, Jennifer saw Miles Halliday go down the middle aisle looking like an usher at a fashionable wedding.

She herself had felt slightly self-conscious and intrusive as they entered the church, but Stephen had more or less propelled her along to the front section of pews. He bent his head for a couple of minutes after he sat down, then took the hymnal out of the rack in front of him and began to hunt out the one that was listed first on the bulletin board beside the sanctuary. All this he did quite naturally and slightly reverently.

When the time came, he sang as if he knew the hymns well. Jennifer was again surprised, but she figured that he had probably learned them in the compulsory services at preparatory school. Wherever he had memorized them, he had not forgotten the beat of the tunes. Once he gave Jennifer a little poke as if to remind her that he was there and that she was there and wasn't this all right—and once he gave her a sidelong glance of mixed amusement and pleasure.

There was no doubt about his pleasure. It was there, somewhat beyond satisfaction. Stephen did not analyze it. He had again that sense of taking the place he should take, being where he properly belonged, and he felt the joy of a man joining in a chorus with other men, doing his share of the sturdy, virtuous singing that publicly acknowledged something. The right time, the right place —he and Jennifer both in it—so Stephen sang well. He followed the lesson for the day and read the responses, never mumbling and giving the solemn cadences full value. During the sermon that followed he let the minister's words flow easily around him, not paying much attention to their substance. He hoped irrelevantly that this fine weather would hold through tomorrow for the hunt. Though they needed rain.

Jennifer listened more carefully to the grave words of the young minister. Her critic's training told her that the construction of his talk had taken a good deal of time and effort. There was no cant in what he said, no stolen quotations, no trick appeals to emotion or sentiment. It was a hard task—Jennifer gave him full credit for that—to tell a congregation so dissimilar in their sources and habits and ages that each of them had a place in this church and a right to this hour. He tried very hard to prove that.

Jennifer tried very hard to believe it as he said, "Let us pray." She bent her head to touch the rail of the pew with her forehead. She prayed—it must be that, so intense was her feeling—that he was right. Then they stood again to sing and Steve's voice, quite on key—she thought, he sounds so happy—rolled out again—"Now thank we all our God!"

It was approaching the height of the spring season and every time they went anywhere Jennifer saw new faces and met more people. There were Cranes and Davises and Leighs—habitual part-time residents, opening up their houses, filling their swimming pools. There were the Frasers. In the Fraser house there was no talk of horsemanship or any sport but there were many books and a library of opera recordings. There was the small delightful Bentley house, five rooms which Jerome Bentley had designed and built himself, and where it was a special privilege to be invited. With satisfaction Jennifer was finding that many of the people she liked best were not at all rich. Young men and women came to DeSoto for their spring vacations from college and mingled at cocktail parties with their grandparents.

Miles Halliday had come to Chestnut Hill several times by himself and also to the cocktail party which Jennifer and Steve had given a week ago because they thought it was their turn to be hospitable. It had been very successful. As she saw Steve's pleasure in being host in his own house she realized that he had never enjoyed their semicommercial entertaining in New York as he did this. She had been aware too of his pride in her that day and thought with amusement, he loves having me a pure and simple housewife. Also she had been rather astonished at her own warm pleasure in the party and felt as if the big rooms were delighted too.

They were spending more money than she had thought would be necessary. That worried Jennifer more than it did Steve. She had thought that the chief expense in DeSoto would be for food. That was true but liquor ran a close second. Steve fortunately had riding clothes which he had bought only two years before when an important client had invited him to spend a week on his Virginia estate. So there was no outlay necessary for that equipment, but there were the memberships in the Hunt Club and also in the Country Club. Steve said, "We couldn't live here without belonging to them." There were wages for Agamemnon and a larger bill than was anticipated for the gravel. What they paid Aga and Susie was trifling compared to the wages of the couple they had employed in New York. But money had come so easily then. They were earning nearly forty thousand dollars a year between them, before taxes. Requests for contributions to local projects and funds drifted in almost daily here as they had not in New York. "We'd better send them a little something," Stephen would say. The little somethings mounted up as did the cost of necessary towels and sheets and kitchenware that had to be replaced. And when they bought the second car they had to cut so deeply into their cash reserve that it had dwindled to not much more than five thousand dollars. Not counting the bonds, which Jennifer would not count except as a final reserve.

Stephen had been having their two-year-old Buick greased and oiled at the garage when he had come upon that bargain. It was a compact, with very little mileage on it, priced at eleven hundred dollars.

"I was lucky to happen to be there," he told Jennifer, "when it came in. It's almost like new. They're selling it to settle the estate of some old spinster and that's why it's priced so low. They said they would hold it for me until tomorrow, so we have to decide at once. It really would be a shame to pass up a car like that at the price. And it would save you a lot of time and energy if you don't have to taxi me around."

Before they had the second car Jennifer not only drove Stephen over to the Bayard stables when there was a hunt, but often came back to pick him up and turn the car over to him for the rest of the day. She thought as he told her about the bargain, that will be eleven hundred dollars plus gas and insurance on two cars. But I wouldn't have to wait around the stables until he canters up with Sara. I wouldn't have to see them mount those horses and ride out of my world.

She hated the way she secretly felt at such times. She could hide the feelings but not prevent them. A sense of inferiority would come over her as she saw the others managing their spirited horses. She was jealous, especially of Sara.

It was not the kind of jealousy she had felt when Steve was with Corinne Miller, not a fear of sexual unscrupulousness. Sara was too open and direct for that. Steve was an acquisition to the group she hunted and played with. But Sara was committed to Tom Bayard. Jennifer liked Sara. She was often under the spell of Sara's beauty, her zest. But that did not stop those gusts of envy, the occasional wish that she too was able to gallop over those fields, rise with her horse at a barrier, talk the lingo.

Of course they asked her.

"Why don't you give it a try, Jennifer," Sara had suggested more than once. "You don't know what you're missing. You can begin in our riding ring. On White Star. The kids both began on her."

And Tom—or Steve—would say, "In no time you'd be crazy about it."

She made excuses. "Not today." "Not for a while." "Not until I get settled in better." The important reasons she did not mention. One was that it would mean clothes and equipment and be expensive. The other reason was that she was afraid. She did not want to be ridiculous if she tumbled off a horse. But it went deeper than that, down to actual physical fear, to dread of the height and power of the horses, fear of falling, being trampled on. The fear shamed her, demeaned her to herself. There was something aristocratic about the courage the riders displayed—to whom it was not courage at all. Jennifer lacked it as she lacked skill in games. When she was growing up she had learned endurance, but she had not been taught physical bravery.

If we each had a car, she thought when Steve had suggested and pressed the purchase, I wouldn't have to be a spectator, feeling inferior and out of things and resentful. I could do so many other things. Explore the mountain roads, find out where the colored people live. And I would have so much more time.

She could use more time. Her days were crowded with the errands, the cooking, and limbering and beautifying the big house. Susie was old and arthritic and undependable and, since she was paid by the hour, not having her very often was one way to economize. But the house must function and on as little money as was possible. The mosaic of her early experiences stood Jennifer in good stead now, even though she lacked training in the sport of kings. Ways of making do, remembered from years when Selma had moved from one inadequate flat to another, came back to Jennifer. Gingerbread is quicker to make than cake, and cake took butter and butter is expensive. She made gingerbread. She poured bacon drippings on slices of onion and made potato cakes.

She had tucked away in her mind unwritten recipes picked up in the places where she had done baby-sitting. One employer had taught her how to make omelets for the children's supper and in another house she had learned to prepare Swedish meatballs and veal birds. But after she had come to New York she had done as little cooking as possible and the bits and pieces of household knowledge had been, so she had believed, forgotten. Now they kept cropping up.

Steve said, "Imagine a girl who never did anything but work on a magazine turning out cornbread like the original Aunt Dixie!"

"I did a lot of things in my early days. I had to. And actually the work on *Portfolio* comes in handy now too. For my first two years on *Portfolio* I read copy for the back of the book. That's where the household hints and recipes are printed. Some of it is bound to stick in your mind. They tested all sorts of food—it gives you an idea of what to do—and they had colored pictures and charts of the insides of animals. I could draw you a picture of a corn-fed steer right now and show you where the best cuts are—and the cheapest—"

"My love and a butcher too—"

So many things amused them. The strain of the past months was gone. Why was it, Jennifer wondered at the base of her happiness, that she wasn't completely confident, why did she feel that she had better look out? For what? Why didn't their life seem quite firm? It did not but she couldn't put a mental finger on the reason. Partly it was because of the worry about money. Partly because the house and this way of life in DeSoto seemed to have come to them accidentally, not been earned. Partly because neither of them was earning and that still gave Jennifer a slight sense of guilt. I don't feel that I really have a right to this, she thought this morning, looking at the dogwood in the urns, thinking that it was beautiful, yet feeling that she was putting on an act even to herself.

She heard a car and walked quickly to the end of the terrace, wondering if it was Steve coming home. She didn't expect him at this hour. But it was Miles Halliday getting out of his Jaguar, which went oddly with his occasional claim to poverty. Her first reaction was annoyance—he had no right to come here unannounced in the middle of the morning.

As he instantly admitted, coming up the steps. "I hoped not to disturb you or anyone. I was merely going to lay these things at your door and silently steal away. This is the magazine which has that piece on modern writing—all fun and viciousness. And I brought you the latest Brinn novel—you will hate it but the thing today seems to be not to read books you like but those you hate. How magnificent those branches are in the noble urns. How this house must love you for what you do to it!"

She took the books and papers, also the clatter of words and said, "The dogwood is contraband. I bought it at the post office from a woman who was being scolded because she had cut it. I got my share of black looks for buying it."

"From one of those mounties who go in for professional wildflowers and are always putting up notices, I suppose. It must have been my beloved Mrs. Valiant who was selling it. She is my favorite hitchhiker. I always pick her up. She lives on the mountain and has seven or more sons. One of them is married to a countess, one owns seven newspapers, one is in jail. She shoots the mistletoe from trees that don't belong to her and sells it in the post office at Christmas."

"I don't believe a word of that."

"No, don't. But I do adore her."

"She's your type, Miles. Not afraid of anything."

He laughed and sat down on the top step. "I'm afraid of death and taxes. And a little afraid of you. Waste a few minutes with me. I didn't really want to steal away. Blue jeans suit you."

She did not join him on the step but leaned against the baluster, her annoyance gone. She said, "I've a hundred things to do. But they will keep. And maybe you won't. I'm grateful for the reading matter. I am a bit short on reading. But I don't have much time."

"In this idle place no one has time. There is nothing to do and no time to do it."

"I've plenty to do. I am a housewife and housewifing takes time, my friend. And sweat."

"And blood and tears, I'll bet. Does it give you a sense of triumph?"

"Terrific."

"Of course I've never known why you came here."

"Of course I'll never tell you."

"So obviously you were not meant for this. For the activity that is not productive."

"Why don't you leave me alone, Miles? Why needle me?"

He said ruminatively, "You didn't have to run away. To take refuge. You could manage anywhere. Maybe you're writing a book."

"I wish I could."

"It's your line, isn't it?"

"It was my first ambition. Long since abandoned. I soon found out."

"Why did you give it up?"

"Why did you stop writing?" Jennifer countered.

"I wasn't good enough."

"You were quite good. Last week I got two of your books from the library. I liked *A Page Torn out of Paris*."

"I must go and take those books off the shelves of the library and never return them."

"Wasn't *Rich Boy* a movie?"

"To my eternal shame."

"You must have made money."

"There was that slight comfort. And I had a good broker who knew when and where the splits were coming. So I have enough to live on. If I'm asked out often enough by my friends."

"You will be. Mutton needs curry."

"The best compliment I ever had. So it seems like mutton to you in DeSoto."

"It seems like heaven, to tell you the truth. What bothers me is that I've done nothing to deserve it."

"That remark," said Miles, "should be in cross-stitch and hanging on the wall. Surely you don't believe that deserving exerts the slightest influence on anything. You'll be talking about the wages of sin next."

"I suppose you don't believe those get paid either?"

"If they are, it's almost always to the wrong person. Sara Bayard can tell you all about that."

"Why Sara?"

"Do you know anything about her?"

"I know she was married before. And that she has a sister in England, Lady Something-or-other."

"Lady Sukeforth. She was the older—the much older—of the two Langley girls. Their money came from the Middle West—nuts, bolts or some such things—and when there was a tremendous surplus the father came down here and picked up a little plot of about three thousand acres. He wanted to be a landed gentleman and he was. He grew tobacco. When the bottom dropped out of that market around here, he just enjoyed being landed and the family vibrated between Lake Forest and DeSoto until Joan found herself the heir to an earldom and went to live in England. In great style too. Sara went to Foxcroft and showed horses in Madison Square Garden and met a handsome rascal and married him."

"You don't have to tell me any of this, Miles. It's none of my business. I like Sara."

"You might as well hear about it. It's common knowledge. You'll like her even better if you know the story. This Bernie Desert, husband number one, flung her money around and got her pregnant and then he started in with cheaper girls and began flinging them around. Sara couldn't take that and allowed herself an episode. So she couldn't get full custody of the boys and I believe that Desert is living happily ever after on what she settled on him. He was rotten but she paid the wages, you see."

"It's a horrid story."

"Continues to be horrid in the next installment. Sara went to England to be with her sister. My guess is that Joan Sukeforth didn't like the competition. She married Sara off as quickly as possible to some relative of her husband's who had a pindling little title of his own. Sara told me once that she would have married anyone to get out of Joan's house."

"And she wasn't happy the second time?"

"Or maybe he wasn't. Sara is quite a handful. Anyway, very soon a divorce was quietly arranged. Sara dropped the title like a hot brick, and came back, head up of course, and married Tom Bayard, who hasn't any money and isn't bright but is a fine animal. And I don't think he married Sara for money."

"He's devoted to her. Anyone can see that."

"It's going well now. Better since they spend so much time here. They tried Greenwich and Rye and played around at Palm Beach at first. But they weren't too popular. Sara scares wives right and left. And Tom got to drinking too much. So she made up her mind to settle down. She once said to me, 'I brought my love to the country.'"

Jennifer said in a wondering voice, "She said that?"

Miles had warmed to his gossip. He said, "The thing about Sara is that she can carry off anything. She can take all the hurdles. And you know she's basically puritan in spite of everything. Never a bitch or a tramp. But anything that takes guts—Sara's right there."

"And so she brought Tom to the country."

"There's a lot of that being done around here," Miles said, regarding her with a questioning smile.

"I know—you call them refugees—you told me it's a synthetic society. I'm not sure that I believe that. It's unusual but maybe it's an experiment—one of the waves of the future."

"Don't be trite, dear."

"Being trite never bothers me. There's a kind of integration in DeSoto that fascinates me. Not just between colored and white. But integration of people who are rich with others who have only a pittance, integration between people who have leisure whether they wanted it or not. Maybe that's what we're all headed for, a lot of free time between the cradle and the grave. This place is beautiful but I'm not sure that it's so exceptional—in Florida and California and Arizona—on islands—there are colonies not quite like this one maybe but not so different. And the obvious reason is that life is getting too long or too disappointing or too crowded for everyone to have real work. Maybe people are learning the hard way not to confuse life with earning a living."

"The hard way?" he asked. Meaning the morning and the dogwood and the cardinals hopping about, and their idleness.

"If you have a guilt sense about earning," said Jennifer.

7

THE DAY was warming up and Cicely Martin took off her olive-green sweater before she gathered up her packages and letters from the seat of the car and walked over the pattern of flagstones which fronted the house which was so exactly right for her and Julius now. It was one of three new houses on Redbird Lane, which itself was only three years old, and properly named for the brave cardinals who had not been frightened away by all the pounding and sawing which had gone on during the recent construction on the hillock which used to be the birds' own preserve.

For a year the Julius Martins had been settled into the third house in the new real estate development. Cicely had not, in all that time, spoken a word of criticism of their new home. She had taken a few callers through it—a short journey—and with her lovely smile had agreed when they called it a darling or a sweet house. When they asked her rhetorically if she didn't love it, she always said that she certainly did, with charming enthusiasm. And she didn't fake it. Determinedly she did love this house, as she would have loved anything created by Julius and herself, even a defective or disappointing child.

Anyway they had to leave Cleveland. After the doctors had told them that Julius must stop working, must live in a milder, more equable climate and must be guarded against nervous tension, they had searched memories and maps and considered family and friendly connections to decide what would be the best place for them to settle in permanently. Florida would be too hot and they knew too many people who wintered there. California was impossible on account of his mother, who had a house in Santa Rosa and was a sure source of nervous tension. They played with the idea of Majorca, where they had once spent a delightful week, but it seemed very remote and what about the winters? How about the summers if they chose one of the Caribbean islands? They could not plan to move about with the seasons. Then one day in a casual conversation about the South, a friend spoke of DeSoto with enthusiasm.

"That's the most enchanting place! A resort but not resorty if you know what I mean. John happened to be asked to be a judge in their Horse Show one year and we went down for a few days. I fell in love with it. I honestly would have liked to stay there forever and amen."

"No horsy spot for us," said Cicely.

"But it's not just that. I get awfully tired myself of people who can't like anything that hasn't four feet. DeSoto is sort of a lyric place—all sorts of people go there to retire or who just have a yen for the country. And it's not full of old people sitting on benches and giving you the creeps. You remember the Frasers? Well, that's where they went after he had that row at the university and resigned from the faculty. They just adore it down there. She wrote me that they'd never been so happy. They built themselves a house."

The description stuck in Cicely's mind. "We might drive down there and take a look," she suggested to Julius later, on a desperately indecisive day. "It wouldn't commit us to anything." So they had done that. It was in the autumn and the Smokies and the Blue Ridge were one long grand balcony overlooking peaceful panoramas of farms and tiny settlements. When they first saw DeSoto it seemed almost alight with the yellow leaves of the birch trees. All the other color, the crimson and scarlet and green that dressed the mountains, was splendidly blended. "Nature beats the moderns in its abstracts," said Julius. The village seemed relaxed, but it was not hushed or stupid, and in some subtle way it made them feel welcome without noticing them.

They liked everything about it, including what they heard and tested of its costs. Expense had to be considered. Their income would be almost quartered in another year. Julius' salary and share of the profits in the law firm in which he had been a partner had been maintained during his long illness and convalescence but his self-respect would not allow it to continue much longer. Hospitals and doctors had chewed up their resources. The big house in Cleveland which involved a number of servants and much entertaining was no longer feasible nor in the least necessary for the future they were facing. What they wanted now—Cicely planned it happily—was something utterly simple that she could take care of herself, and all on one floor because of his heart.

That first time they stayed at the Inn for several weeks. They covered the vicinity of the town almost acre by acre, choosing among landscapes, discounting what was obviously not for them. They admired the house of the Eliot Frasers but that was a larger one than they wanted. The Frasers were as contented as had been reported. Alex Fraser was slowly writing a history of ethics and Dolly Fraser was growing roses in a perfectionist way.

None of the houses available for sale was right for the Martins. So they bought a half acre on Redbird Lane and talked to Arthur Fleming, a local architect. Before he had become local he had belonged to a quite famous firm in Chicago and had fled from it. "Fled from building beehives," he told the Martins.

"We're getting rid of sixteen rooms and an ocean of waste space," said Cicely to Fleming. "I never want to see an attic or a back stairs again. All we need is a living room, two bedrooms with baths and a kitchen. And a terrace for the sun and moon. Just a cottage. Only I hope it needn't look like a box."

Fleming was clever and it did not look like a box. The small bones of its timbers gave it delicacy. It was gray-shingled with a house-long living room, two bedrooms clustered on the west, and a kitchen and storeroom to serve them on the east. Sliding doors concealed the wardrobes and the kitchen was a completed picture puzzle of conveniences, each one not taking an inch more space than was necessary. The little house was completely functional—a modern reproach to the Grecian-type mansion which loomed up on a hill nearby.

Unless the weather was bad, Julius could sit or lie on the flagged veranda with its bamboo roof and almost invisible screening. When it rained or was too windy—they hadn't known about the wildness of mountain winds until that first February in the house—the living room was a refuge with an open fire and every comfort. Cicely could prepare food on the built-in stove and counters and then slide back a glass partition and place dinner on the built-in tables at the end of the living room.

"Don't you love it?" she would ask Julius. She asked it so often that sometimes he looked at her a little quizzically, even a little worriedly, before he said again that it was giving him a new lease on life.

He had to have a new lease. He couldn't renew the old one. He couldn't go on working for a nine-hour day clotted with judgments and decisions, broken only by competitive golf or squash, or by obligatory dinners taken or given, or by vacations that were always too short and always harassed by work left unfinished. He could not go on like that and live, but no one was ever more surprised than Julius Martin when he was told that and had to accept it as truth.

Julius wanted to live, even in the hours when he wondered if it would not be a better job to die and allow his fifteen-year younger wife to marry again, more closely in her own age bracket. But would she do that? Or, if he died, would she be a forsaken, helpless woman? Her parents had always been inadequate and selfish, and since he had taken her away from them when she was nineteen, Julius had given her a devotion that was passionate but always somewhat paternal. Even during his long illness he had managed to make her feel surrounded by love that would take care of her.

He couldn't work but he could think. He couldn't help thinking. And in his thoughtfulness he tried to find the constructive angle in this break with their former pattern. Even before his collapse he had sometimes wondered what life was going to be like for Cicely in middle age and during the stretch of time after that. They had lost two children at birth and had not dared to attempt having more. Cicely had no talents that she could develop on her own and no desire for any. She had been a very happy wife, thinking in twos, of what they both would do, what they both liked, always making Julius her frame of reference for everything. That was the result, he knew, of having been married when she was so young and still unformed. And it was delightful to live with.

But more than once, since they had been committed to DeSoto, Julius had hoped that in the country Cicely would find new resources, discover things to interest her and to rely upon. Then, lying on the veranda, he would doubt that. He would ask himself what in hell he was doing—had done—in taking Cicely to a new community, stripping her of the personal service to which she was accustomed and of familiar friends, pulling down the scaffolding of her social life and letting her get his meals. She had never lived in a doll's house like this one. She had been brought up in big houses, although in an atmosphere of turbulent, uncertain wealth which was usually dependent on alimony. When Julius had married Cicely, he had been well enough along in his own profession to install her in a big house where there would be no financial uncertainties as long as he was able to earn.

Now here they were in this cottage. Julius had been prepared for a reaction from her willingness to live like this. He had been ready to soothe and to encourage her when it came. What puzzled him was that it did not come. He suspected her of concealing moods but he could not find disillusion, even when he gently probed for it. Cicely would laugh and say that she couldn't be happier and didn't he love it? Julius did not love it but he liked it in contrast to his long hospitalization. He liked it also because it was reasonably safe for him and so safe for Cicely. But he wondered about her. He had known his wife's charm and gaiety and sweetness. Known her bravery too when the babies came and quickly went. He had not known that she had this consistency. Did she really love this place, this kind of life? The housework was not too exhausting, for a colored girl came in to do the heavy chores, and Julius was able now to take care of all his own needs. But they lived in semi-isolation. Cicely welcomed people who called on them and was cordial and pleasant, but she refused or evaded invitations. She would not go to parties without Julius, and as yet he dared not attempt to mix in even small groups.

She came in now with groceries and mail, kissed him as she gave him his letters and said that the day was heaven.

"How was the big city this morning?"

"Teeming. Swarming. In the post office you almost had to fight your way. Then I went to the liquor store and an old lady of maybe ninety-two was buying gin with a defiant look. Where do all the people come from? I drove by the golf course and the cars were packed in the parking space by dozens."

"Why don't you try that golf course? You used to be good."

"I don't particularly want to."

"You might if you got started. You shouldn't be cooped up here with me all the time."

"What do you mean cooped? I live here."

She went to the kitchen, opened a cupboard and put the box of gingerbread mix beside the pancake mix. It fitted exactly but so tightly that she could not get out the box of cornbread mix that she wanted for lunch. She finally managed to do it, set the box on the counter and then went into her bedroom to leave the sweater in the drawer in the wardrobe where she kept her knitted things.

Cooped. She wished he hadn't said that. She tried never to think that. She could hear Julius opening the newspapers—the tearing of the paper wrapper was audible from here. Everything was audible. Suddenly it all seemed unbearably small and close, stifling. She closed her eyes, let the memory loose. She thought, I would go down the big hall, with doors open, pass the upstairs study, and there was my room. She saw the picture she was trying to erase—the big chaise, the rose-colored armchairs, the desk, the space, the dressing room with all its unnecessary mirrors—Lily coming in with her breakfast tray was always tripled in them. She thought, it was a lovely home, this isn't a home, there isn't enough of it and it's all so horribly new. I mustn't let Julius see how awful it feels sometimes, how lonesome and tight, like prison must be. The doctor said I had to choose—it couldn't be the way it was ever again—it had to be like this—or death. Death, like the children. I could never bear it again. She flung the sweater into the stocking compartment and went back to the veranda where Julius had begun to read the papers. Cicely stood looking at the view until she felt her face was ready to carry a smile. She thought of something casual to say.

She said, "In the post office this morning I saw that woman who lives in the Greek-looking house up there. First time I've placed her. I heard someone call her Mrs. Cooper so she must be the one."

"What is she like?"

"Oh, quite young. Lovely looking really."

"She might be someone you'd enjoy knowing."

"I doubt it. She's one of that ride-to-hounds clique, I'm sure."

"There's a letter here inviting us to be patrons of a steeplechase that's coming up soon."

"Hardly up our street," said Cicely.

"I don't know. Apparently they sell parking places where you can see the show. For twenty bucks. We might subscribe for one and go for a little while. I wouldn't have to get out of the car."

"You think it would be all right? You think you should? You know how we always loved to go to the races!"

He heard the unguarded excitement and nostalgia in her voice.

"Why don't I send them a check anyway," said Julius. "It won't break the bank. Then we can go if we happen to feel like it."

Agamemnon and Susanna Pearl Livingston lived on one of the side roads that tourists hardly noticed as they sped through DeSoto toward the mountains, because after the roads began they almost immediately disappeared around narrow curves and sharp angles. They usually tapered off to end at the edge of a small, irregularly placed group of houses or in front of a church. In these vicinities the colored residents lived, now almost a solidly voting group. They lived quite comfortably, for wages over the years had become more adequate and less seasonal than they used to be when Northerners first began falling in love with DeSoto. There were not many tumbledown houses and very few hiked up at their corners on piles of stones. They looked as if life in them went on easily, with children swarming the yards and something always being nailed onto a house or roofed over as it was needed.

Agamemnon had the largest house in his neighborhood and its porch was grown over with old grapevines that still yielded fruit. It was what Aga called a good board house, which had been a term of pride when tarpaper shacks lined within with old newspapers were common. It was a big, roving, two-story house, with more rooms than the old people needed now, but they never thought of moving. Their extra rooms were family rooms where their children had once been bedded, old aunts had died of cancer and ministers had stayed during revivals. There was a small square front entry with a horned hatrack on one wall, and on the opposite one was a framed motto with letters illuminated in red and gold which read, IN THIS HOUSE EVIL IS NOT SPOKEN.

In the main room the big central table was covered with a fringed red cloth and a Bible dominated it. A smaller table held a television set and on a pedestal in one corner was a statue of a boy. It had come from Greece and had once been part of a fountain at Chestnut Hill. The fountain had been broken by a carelessly driven truck, but Agamemnon had salvaged the statue and with infinite patience glued the damaged parts together so that they hardly showed cracks. Mr. Cooper was dead and nothing could be done about the fountain, so he had brought the marble boy home.

He and his wife were deeply religious. The white painted church, only a stone's throw away from the house, was their other home. They had been prime movers in getting it built and paid for, and all their five children, from babyhood to independence, had sat every Sunday in the second pew from the front.

The children were gone now, all of them: two to California, one in a hotel in Miami, one in the navy, and one child to a kind of eminence in New York. Pictures of the grandchildren in California and Miami flanked the Bible, and on the big table also lay a magazine in which was a full-page picture of the son Mailer in New York, leading a protest parade. Once recently his face had flashed at them from the television screen and they had heard his voice, which was so natural, and his carefully articulated words, which did not seem natural, proclaiming defiance.

That was Mailer's work. His mother and father accepted it as that. They were neither blind nor indifferent to the great upheaval that was rocking their race. They were aware of how subservience was disappearing, saw with satisfaction the improvements in the roads around Negro settlements and with some worry heard of Negro children going to white schools. They read the paid advertisements in local papers in which white men, whose fathers would probably have shot Negroes if they had approached the polls, now besought the vote of "our Colored neighbors." Aga and Susie absorbed all this into their lives without pride or vengeance or vainglory. Their religion forbade such feelings. And in their house they spoke no evil.

"Miss Stephen a very considerate lady," said Susie, taking off her head scarf and putting a covered pan on the kitchen table. "She send you loaf of cornbread that she bake herself. She enjoy that cookin'. And she like that big ol' house like she been born in it."

"Nevah thought Mr. Stephen come back," said Aga. "Nevah had that in my mind at all."

"You figure yet why they come?"

"They feeling for something," said Aga. "They feeling for a place where they be at ease. They got to watch they money—Mr. Steve say so. I don't know. When the horses go out to pasture what Mr. Steve goin' to do with hisself? He nevah make no farmer. He don' study like his pa. I surely regret Mr. Steve got no more money to spend. He spend so easy."

"You think they stay?"

Aga chuckled. "They stay through Steeplechase Day for sure. Mr. Steve love horseflesh."

Sara and Tom Bayard were hacking home. The meet had been called for two o'clock today because it had rained hard this morning, but it was now late afternoon. They took the shortest cut because they were looking forward to a swim, and went past the colored graveyard where the old markers were only fieldstone but the new ones were granite or marble. On the road past Agamemnon's house they slowed the horses because of the pavement.

"When this road was dirt it used to be easier for the horses," said Sara.

Tom said, "Road builders don't care about horses any more."

"We're pigs," she said. "It does look much better through here than it used to. That's old Aga's house. He still works at Steve's place, doesn't he?"

"That must be slim pickings. I don't think Steve's very well fixed."

"He doesn't need to be."

"Not so long as he rides our horses."

"Oh Tom, that's horrid! He's been a great help."

"I prefer paid trainers," Tom said, "like Ross Painter."

She turned her head. "What's got into you all of a sudden?"

"I get tired of seeing you build up Steve Cooper, that's all."

"You mean because he's been asked to be presiding steward at the steeplechase?"

"That was your work, wasn't it?"

"Well, darling, you couldn't be it—not and be Master. And Jim Clark is tied up with the Camden thing and couldn't make it. We're lucky to have someone as competent as Steve. I'm thinking of how the races will be run off, not about him. He gets along with everyone."

"I guess so," said Tom, a little less sulkily, "but you better not feature him too much or you might get that pretty wife of his in your hair."

"She is pretty," said Sara. "And don't worry. Steve thinks the sun rises and sets in her even if she doesn't know one end of a horse from the other. I can't imagine what she does with herself all the time."

"There's always Miles Halliday."

"If she rode, maybe they'd come with us to Dublin in June."

"On what?"

"It doesn't cost so much." She was teasing him deliberately, but Tom was more exciting when he was jealous, more spirited, more fun.

Tom Bayard said before he touched his whip to his horse, "Let the girl have him, Sara. As long as you have me, just let her have him."

8

THERE WERE TIMES in DeSoto when its patchwork composition and disparity of origins and incomes vanished, blended together by some common interest or enthusiasm. This happened if an ice storm knocked out the electricity for a few days. It was apparent when the new arts and crafts building had its opening and those who had given a thousand dollars to the project and those who had given one dollar—or none perhaps—streamed side by side through rooms filled with paintings, weavings and ceramics, all the work of local artists. It was true on a night of national elections when everyone was watching the returns, and of course true on the days of the first journeys into space. But it was especially obvious at the Horse and Hound Show and the steeplechase in April. Important patrons and unimportant spectators were practically indistinguishable at the races. Everyone in the town probably was not in attendance but anyone might be, and it looked as if they all were there. The schools were let out at noon and the shops closed.

Racing had gone on in DeSoto for a long time. In its earliest days the local horsemen used to gather for an afternoon of racing through their own cornfields and meadows. At the time Stephen Cooper's father had kept a stable, an annual steeplechase had been developed, but the riders were mostly neighbors and all nonprofessionals. In recent years, after some pushing by the Hunt Club and some argument over whether it would spoil the ingenuous spirit of the town, the races at DeSoto had been formalized and were on the calendar sanctioned by the national steeplechase association. So they attracted those who made a business of racing as well as those who raced for pleasure.

In spite of that the event had never lost its original family and neighborhood feeling, nor its look of being a huge picnic along the hillsides. A stranger would not have known whether the colorful throngs sitting on the grass slopes or the people in the tightly parked cars had preference of place. Strangers always exclaimed at the rare beauty of the setting. The blue mountains were a backdrop for rows of tall pines and Normandy poplars that seemed groomed for the occasion. The course itself had been laid out by experts who treated it with respect. Where a flowering tree could be left or encouraged, that had been done. There was none of the geometric precision of most race tracks. Only in a broad stretch of flat land between two rises was the formality of a pageant. Here were the starting posts, the judges' high stand, the stewards and patrol judges, gallant in pink coats and riding lightly prancing horses, with lithe grooms leading entries to be weighed in, and the owners and the gamblers watching every move of the animals in whom they had invested love or money.

The course itself was a stiff one. There were some local people, like the Loomises and Cutlers, who would not enter their horses because the hurdles on the hilly terrain could be dangerous for a horse at top speed. There were fences, hedges and a water jump on the two mile course, none of them easy obstacles. But the purses were large for most of the races, and the distinction of winning was often more important to the owners than the money.

Post time was two o'clock and for the previous half hour the announcer had been blaring over the loudspeaker that all those who did not have a right to be in the paddock or judges' stand must find places in the spectators' section. Mrs. Valiant, who was peddling small bunches of wild arbutus, paid no attention, crossing the paddock to find more customers. Miles Halliday, who had no official position, stayed where he was, leaning on the open window of Jennifer's little car, which bore a pasted label giving her a place near the judges' stand since Stephen was the presiding steward. Miles was wearing the plaid jacket he always wore to horse events and a Swiss hat with a tuft of feathers in its band. Mrs. Valiant was in starched pink gingham and topped with her churchgoing black straw sailor hat. Her dress touched her ankles. She never wore anything shorter.

Jennifer had not known what to wear to a steeplechase for she had never been to one until today. But she had guessed right and looked cool and uncrumpled in a blue sweater and matching skirt. Kit Piper, sitting in an open car in the row behind the one where Jennifer was parked, had been very handsome half an hour ago before the flasks were opened and the paper cups filled. She was beginning to look flushed and tangled. Sara Bayard was in riding clothes for she had driven over in the van which brought one of her horses for entry. She was not riding him herself. One glance at Sara had made Jennifer feel dowdy and commonplace. Sara was perfect for this setting. Her hard, rounded black cap, chalk-white stock and gleaming boots made her seem even taller and slimmer than usual.

"Sara is annoyed with Tom," Miles said to Jennifer.

"She doesn't look it."

"Too good manners for that," said Miles, "and Sara is never a shrew. But she didn't want Tom to enter his horse in the Lancaster—much less ride him—and that's apparently what he's going to do. Own Risk—that's Tom's horse. Sara's entered her own Sold Out in that race and she wants him to win, and doesn't want Tom not to win, so she's in a fix. And she knows Tom isn't a steeple-

chase rider. He's fine in the field—a good Master—but not a
gentleman jockey."

"I thought Tom always did what Sara wanted," said Jennifer.

"Usually does. It's rather odd. I suppose the time came when he
wanted to assert himself. Maybe it's a touch of exhibitionism. Or
maybe," Miles went on in the casual way that could be cruel, "he
thinks that your husband is stealing his show. Steve has the center
of the stage today and that may be hard for Tom to take."

"There's nothing Steve wants less than the center of any stage.
It's just a job that was wished on him, he said. He told me there
wasn't anyone else to take it," Jennifer said.

But she could see that Stephen was in authority today, running
the show. She was inwardly proud to see how well he did it. He
was unhurried, perfectly competent and somehow both leading
and controlling the disciplined excitement. She was very careful
not to let her pride show. Very careful too not to expose the
feeling that lay beneath the pride and that became restless as Sara
walked over to Stephen and put her hand on his arm. Jennifer
turned, looking down at the paddock.

"Who is the man down by the horses?" she asked Miles. "That
one with the very rakish green hat. I've seen him around."

"His name is Delaney," said Miles. "He stayed at the Inn for a
while. Now I believe he's rented a house. He hunts now and then
but he seems to be a loner. Probably drifted here accidentally and
stuck. That happens. Fortunately in DeSoto people who don't
belong here usually come unstuck rather quickly. He looks like a
gambler— I suppose he's put some money on a horse. It's not his
first time at a race track, I'd bet money on that."

Delaney had put quite a sum on Dark Shadow, who was
running in the Lancaster today, the big and final race of the
afternoon. At the moment he was critically inspecting Sara Bayard's entry, Sold Out. A beautiful horse, but the jockey who would
ride Dark Shadow was a professional from Atlanta with a record
for wins. Delaney glanced at the crowd with satisfaction, at all the
highway patrolmen directing traffic on the roads. It would be very
quiet in town today, silent on the mountain. The boys would have

no trouble. There were so many strangers around and so many horse vans that one more big van would attract no notice.

A car drove into the empty parking space next to the one occupied by Kit Piper's custom-built sport model. Cicely Martin lined it up neatly and said, "Number eighteen. This is ours. And we're just about in time."

"We have a very good spot here," said Julius.

"You really feel all right?"

"I feel just fine, darling. Stop worrying. This is going to be a lot of fun."

"It's wonderful! Like being in a box at the theater—quite by ourselves and able to see everything. I didn't know that there were this many people in the whole state. There's quite a gay party going on next to us."

"So I noticed when you pulled in. They won't bother us. We'll have a nip ourselves after a while. I'm glad I remembered to bring it. Here's your program. I bought two so each of us can pick our favorites."

Cicely opened the green and white program, thick with local advertising, lists of patrons and subscribers, and with the owners, trainers and riders of the horses in each race printed on successive pages.

"I didn't realize that they had been doing this for seventeen years. There's a lot I haven't found out about this place. It says here that our neighbor, Stephen Cooper, is the presiding steward, evidently the big boss." Her glance went to the judges' stand. "I wonder which one he is—maybe the tall, youngish man talking to that marvelous-looking girl in riding clothes. Isn't she something! If that's Stephen Cooper, it's not his wife. She isn't on the stand. I'd recognize her."

The announcer's voice bounced back from the slopes. "The stewards are requested to clear the course. Ladies and gentlemen, welcome to the eighteenth annual meeting of the Lancaster Cup races at the steeplechase course in DeSoto. The first race will be the Fort Courage race, named for the old fort which used to stand in this location to protect the pioneers from the Indians. Please scratch entry number three in your programs. Number three—Play Around. Please scratch number ten, Silver Boy—"

Pencils and pens were correcting the lists of entries in the programs now, and the horses that were still in the Fort Courage race were being ridden, escorted by stewards, to the starting point.

Miles Halliday, studying the names of owners, told Jennifer, who wasn't actively listening, "Two entries from the Keyneck stables in Atlanta. Chris Keyneck was nearly bankrupt two years go—then he fell on his feet— His wife walked out on him and got a divorce and while everyone was pitying Chris he married this girl with pots of money."

In the high official pavilion Steve Cooper was watching and directing the order of the day. Now he said a word on the walkie-talkie to the announcer, then answered a query of a paddock judge. He heard Sara, who was watching her husband in the paddock talk to their trainer, say, "I hope Ross is persuading Tom to scratch Own Risk in the Lancaster."

Stephen grinned and said, "I doubt that, Sara."

Julius Martin felt the impact of the crowd on his usual solitude. From habit he touched his pulse but he was not disturbed. He was completely and forever the spectator now—today his sense of that was sharp—and he seemed to have a vantage point because of that. He could see the whole thing in its proportions, relate it. He thought, racing is a very special thing, timeless, and classless actually—it's both the sport of kings and the climax at the county fair. It's the privileged going through their paces before the underprivileged, but the groom and the stableboy can place their bets and there's a moment when the skill and nerve of the jockey counts more than the millions of the man who employs him. Nothing is more beautiful or more historic than a man in command of a horse—a continuation of tradition without a break. It's good—keeps personal courage flowing. Cicely is like a child on a holiday—poor Cicely, what have I done to her—

Dave Delaney did not consider this race at all important and was glancing at his watch, thinking that Todd and Denny should have the job done by this time and be well on their way up the mountain.

The huge van which had a horse's head ornamenting one side rolled slowly out of iron gates which stood open at the end of a long private driveway. One of the two men in the driver's box looked back at a hand-carved sign on the entrance post which read GAVIN E. BENNETT. He said in a contemptuous wonder at the easy theft, "Bye-bye, Mr. Bennett. Can you beat it!"

"Dave said it would probably be no trick. Nobody home and nothing locked up. They all go to these races, the hired help and all. Taking candy from a baby is hard work compared to this."

"That Jaguar can't be two months old. Only a thousand miles on it. Custom job. Must have cost ten, twelve thousand."

"Can we crowd another car in the van now, Denny?"

"Sure. Just about do that." Denny was watching the landscape but not for beauty. His eyes sharpened suddenly. "That must be the other place— Dave said there was about a mile of white fence along the road— He said to be sure to look for the main gate and not go in one of those that they can open from the back of a horse. There's a driveway that will take the van, Dave said."

"Same technique, Denny, remember. If anyone shows up and stops us or looks curious, we play dumb and ask the way to the races."

"I know. I got it."

"He said there was a Mercedes to watch for at this joint. He figured that these people might not take that car to the races. They got a horse van and a station wagon and God knows what. The key might be in the Mercedes even."

"I can manage if it ain't unlocked," said Denny.

"We'll drive up around the house. Then locate the garage—"

The van rolled along slowly, as if the driver wanted to be sure of being in the right place. In the distance the men could see a big house fronted by a terrace, with the blue gleam of a swimming pool behind a grove of trees. To the left a sign with an arrow read, DELIVERIES, GARAGE AND STABLES, and pointed to a subsidiary road as wide as the main drive.

The van moved now between high boxwood hedges. Todd and Denny came in sight of a long garage, with two cars under cover in the stalls and several empty places.

"What a setup," muttered Denny. "Hell, they'll never miss one little Mercedes—won't know it's gone."

Todd was scanning every direction. There was a long covered passage from the garage to the house, deserted. There was an unpaved road leading somewhere. They heard a horse neigh and then tensed, figuring on their chances.

"They wouldn't leave horses without nobody," said Todd.

"I'll take a look."

Denny got out, put on an act of being puzzled and looking for someone so he could make inquiries. Then he went closer, down the dirt road, and after a few minutes came back, quick and light-footed.

"God, they could run the Derby down there. One old nigger was all I saw and he had his feet up—asleep, I think. That's the whole damn police force— Back her up real close—we have to move fast."

They were very expert. The van back was lowered without any noise when Dennis pushed a button from the front seat. Cars inside were tied and crowded closely. The white Mercedes started almost silently and Todd guided it up the tailboard, then swung ropes from the side of the van around it, pushed wedges under the tires and made it fast.

"Close her," he said in a whisper and leaped out. In less than a minute he was beside his partner, gawking at the landscape, and the big van moved slowly and as if it had mistaken its way toward the gates of the estate. It lumbered along for a quarter of a mile before Todd, considering a long stretch of road ahead, said, "Better get rid of that horse now. Nobody in sight. I'll watch it."

He braked the machine and Denny leaped out. Standing on the edge of one huge tire he ran a knife under the edge of the picture of a horse, plucked it off neatly, revealing a painted identification of MOORE'S REFRIGERATED FOODS.

Now the van picked up speed. The two men had no need of a road map or signs. They already knew the route through the town—so quiet a village this afternoon with even the post office closed for a half day—and they headed for the mountain road.

"There's Dave's house," said Todd to Denny, who already knew that. He said, after a minute, "Dave's got big ideas. He could pull out of this racket."

"What a guy! He'll be watching those races as if he didn't know about nothing else in the world."

"He's a brain all right. Careful too. Nothing ever rough about Dave's setup. You go into the Atlanta place, you'd think it was run by the Rockefellers. Everything smooth and yes-please-what-can-I-do-for-you."

"He gets rid of most of the parts there, I guess."

"Don't fool yourself—he's got more than that outlet. Some of this stuff goes out of the country— There's a big market in South America—I heard him say that one time."

"He'll like this haul. New Thunderbird out of Raleigh, the three that we took off the delivery truck from the factory last night when those fool guys were eating, and the Jag and the Mercy. Good picking."

"Why don't we stop for a beer?"

"Too much of a chance," said Todd. "We'll have one when we get these under cover."

The great van took the mountain road fast in spite of its size. But it broke no speed limits and never went over a double center line, though the few small cars it passed almost waved in the wind it created. It swung around curve after curve to the point where the old road that had been abandoned cut off, and turned there. The weather had been dry and when the van finally made the turn into the ruts which once had been a driveway it left no deep tracks. It stopped in the open space where the sheds, now repaired, and the broken walls of the old mansion stood.

The tailboard went down again and the stolen cars were taken out and driven into the empty sheds. Each operation left no trace. Delaney's racket dealt in parts taken from new, expensive cars, unmarked parts bearing no numbers that could result in identification. Tonight, after the cars were dismantled, the bodies would be pushed over the edge of the ravine, certain to sink in the lake directly below. Dave Delaney said that Hoodoo Lake had no bottom, and disposal here was far easier than it had been when the car bodies had to be smashed and distributed in lots and fields filled with the carcasses of old automobiles. Tomorrow the van would roll on to Atlanta with a profitable load. There would be a profit of from ten to twelve thousand dollars on the forty thousand or more worth of cars they had on hand today. Todd and Denny could pretty well figure that themselves.

Delaney's big bet was placed on the Lancaster but the other races preceded that one at tantalizing half-hour intervals. The Lancaster was always the last race, for it was not only the most hazardous but the only event that would hold most of the spectators until the end of the afternoon, as the committee in charge of arrangements well knew.

Bored during the long intermission, Delaney leaned against the fender of his car and idly watched the crowd, his glance picking out faces that were familiar and his thoughts circling the people to whom the faces belonged.

His occasional intrusion into the hunting field had given him a surface acquaintance with that group. There were the Loomises—stuffed shirts, he said to himself, recalling their courteous aloofness. Little Sam Piper who couldn't manage that lush of a wife. She was something. Delaney had seen her once or twice in church and had recognized the signs of her hangover. Still not bad-looking, though.

Cooper was all right in his way, always civil enough. Riding the

Bayard hunters, probably up against it for money in spite of his big house. But that Cooper house had every other place around beat. That house, thought Delaney, has class. The Bayard layout was bigger but they could have it. He thought, no one could look down on a man who owned the Cooper house and had the cash to keep it going. He began to add sums mentally—no one but himself knew how much there was in the four banks and nobody was going to find out. He thought, I'd build a fence around the whole hill, not one of those white jobs but something special.

The Cooper woman was always sort of under wraps. She didn't hunt with the crowd though she seemed healthy. She was a beauty in her way. Maybe she and her husband didn't get on. She's nobody's fool, Delaney said to himself. When you get a good look at her— I did one day in the post office and I thought right then, there's a dame that knows what's going on. Halliday is playing her up today, showing off as usual.

The very sight of Miles Halliday made Delaney's mouth ugly. There was something about Halliday— Without being able to exactly analyze it, Delaney felt active resentment. In the Inn, Halliday would nod a good-morning greeting that gave no identity to the one who got it. In a place like the Inn most of the people made casual talk if they could. The men asked what your line was, where you were from. Not that it was anybody's business, and you strung them along when they asked, but it was a natural question. Halliday never asked. He would sit there at his corner table and joke with the waiter, make a monkey out of the nigger all right, but if Delaney was at the next table he wasn't there as far as Halliday was concerned. Halliday would put on that red coat of his and sail out of the place at night as if he were the Duke of Windsor. He's as phony as they come, thought Delaney, watching Halliday wave at someone. Following the direction of the gesture Delaney saw that it was a signal to Sara Bayard. Under the rakish green hat that Jennifer had noticed, the sharp eyes narrowed in admiration. That Sara Bayard could give all the rest of these people cards and spades.

He thought of her in that first-name manner. But it was not disrespect. Most people in DeSoto thought of her as Sara Bayard, unless they had lived in the place long enough to think of her as Sara Langley. There was a kind of tribute to her connections, her money, her beauty and her individuality in singling her out as Sara. The sharper watched her, remembering all the things he had heard about her, the facts he had accumulated from the talk at the garage. This wasn't her first husband. She'd sloughed off a couple before Tom Bayard. It was her money they lived on. She had a sister who was married to a lord. But she didn't need any build-up. She was the real thing.

When he was a green kid, Delaney used to think that Mrs. Prentiss was the real thing, because of the big house on the side of the mountain, all the silver dishes in the dining room, and the oil paintings, and the way she ordered people around. But that was in the beginning when he first went to work for her. He found out that she was just an old lush, an old woman still after anything in pants, who would take on anyone she could get.

Sara Bayard wouldn't be like that, thought Delaney, still believing, curiously enough, after all his years of corruption and in spite of himself, that there was a real thing. He could not hear what Sara was saying and could only imagine the sound of her laugh, but he admired the proud lift of her head and the vitality she released seemed to carry across the field even to him.

As it did to Jennifer, causing the horrid, unjust rise of jealousy in her again. This was worse than seeing Sara and Steve take off on a fox hunt. It made no sense to resent the sight of them talking together, sharing some problem or pleasure—now she was laughing at something Steve had said, that was obvious—they were companionable, almost intimate, such a handsome, well-matched couple. Jennifer warned herself, don't let Miles guess how you feel, he's very sharp and intuitive. Don't look at Sara again. But she saw Sara without even looking at her.

"Would you like to wander?" asked Halliday as if he did guess at her restlessness. "The next race won't start for a while. Let's go calling on people."

For that was part of the steeplechase event, the part Miles Halliday liked best. Walking around, seeing who had come together, accepting a drink beside some station wagon which had set up a bar in the opened back. He would sort out greetings, offer very gallant homage to some elderly woman, give a minimum recognition to someone who would never be of any social use to him.

He asked Jennifer, "Have you met the Martins?"

"I don't think so. Which are they?"

"The people in that car on the other side of Kit's. Why doesn't Kit join AA and go back to God before her kidneys are gone?"

"No, I've not met them," said Jennifer, ignoring the jab at Kit, "but I've seen Mrs. Martin and wondered who she was. I like her looks."

"He's been ill—they don't go out. I met her once, not him. First time I've ever seen them at anything. They have only a little place but they're civilized people. Julius Martin was a very top-flight lawyer. He handled the mediation in one of the steel strikes. The President used him. Let's speak to them."

"Oh Miles, what a snob you are!"

"I should hope so," he said, guiding her to the other car. "How are you, Mrs. Martin? Miles Halliday—I met you at the Frasers'— it must have been when I was down here a year ago."

"I remember very well," said Cicely. "My husband—Julius, this is Mr. Halliday."

"And I want you both to meet Mrs. Cooper."

Cicely's smile was eager. "I'm very glad, Mrs. Cooper. We're neighbors in a way. I can see your house from our cottage in the valley—it's marvellous in the moonlight with its white columns."

"It shows off by moonlight," said Jennifer. "It puts on quite an act. But it impresses me too. I hope you'll come to see it closer— and see us."

"Cicely would love to," said Julius Martin. He went on quietly,

"Excuse me for not getting out of the car. I'm having a dull convalescence, which is hard on my manners and my wife."

Cicely looked at him in surprise. This was not like Julius at all. He was normally reserved with strangers, slow and careful in making up his mind about whether he wanted to know them or not. But he had accepted Jennifer at once, and that casual invitation—he had almost reached out for it.

Jennifer felt something unusual too. It was her immediate flash of sympathy and warm liking for these people, as if she knew much more than she actually did about them, as if she would take friendship with them on trust. Whatever their situation was—was it something more than illness?—Jennifer wanted to go farther with the Martins.

This had happened before to Julius Martin, though not often. Very rarely he was conscious of a clear perception of another person, as if by a mental X-ray. If it occurred with a client he didn't have to press inquiries. He took character for granted. In the minute when he had taken Jennifer's hand and met her glance, he was sure that it would be good for Cicely to know her. And Cicely was in need. He thought, Mrs. Cooper isn't at all like this man with her, she doesn't have that applied and greased social manner. She's natural, good value.

They were all matching impressions of DeSoto, the weather and the day's sport when they were interrupted by a man's voice, someone coming up behind Jennifer.

"I don't believe it—Jule Martin, where did you drop from?"

"Gavin Bennett, as I live and breathe!" Julius exclaimed with the same incredulity, and Jennifer turned quickly. She had not seen him since that night at the Bayard house. She had not forgotten that meeting but it had been overlaid with many other ones and become blurred. Now instantly it was clear and recent again. She picked it up where she had left off, feeling the same ease with him, the same attraction. He seemed younger in his sport clothes.

For the moment his attention was going to the invalid in the car.

"How do you happen to be in DeSoto?"

"We live here," said Martin with a grin.

"Really? We were talking about you the other day in New York and someone said you'd left Cleveland—and you landed here?"

"Yes—Cicely, this is Gavin Bennett from New York—you've heard me speak of him. His firm used to employ us when they had a problem with steel in Cleveland. He's your bread and butter or used to be."

"Your husband was our brains," said Gavin, "and our peace-maker."

"And I'd like to have you meet Mrs. Cooper—"

"I'm lucky enough to have met her already," said Gavin Bennett. "Hi, Miles, how are you?" He turned to Jennifer and said, "I've been looking all over for you. I saw your husband being official and was sure you weren't far off. How are you? Ever find that hummingbird's nest?"

"Not yet."

"Liking it here?"

"It's all delight and astonishment."

"This is turning out to be old home week," said Miles.

"It's turning out to be very pleasant," said Gavin. "I'm very glad you people have found each other. But of course you would."

"It happened only a few minutes ago," said Cicely, "and we have Mr. Halliday to thank for it."

"I have my moments of usefulness," said Miles. "How long are you down for, Gavin?"

"The day," he answered, still looking at Jennifer.

"Just today?"

"I'm afraid that's it." He asked Jennifer, "Will you let me stop by at your house when the show is over? Anne's getting tired or I'd ask you to our place."

"Our house is closer," said Jennifer. "Do come. Both of you."

"I'll have to run Anne home first— They string these races out and it's too long an afternoon for her."

"The Lancaster seems to be coming up at last. Win any money yet Gavin?"

"Maybe I shall. It's my lucky day," said Gavin. "I think I'll watch this race from here."

Excitement had risen in the various groups of spectators. People were leaving their cars, breaking up conversations, putting down drinks, focusing their field glasses. The horses being ridden to their places at the post seemed to have more importance than those in other races today. Looking at her program Jennifer saw that the purse was $2,500 and that the trophy had to be won three times before becoming a permanent possession of any owner.

"It's a big purse."

"There's a lot more money than that on this race. It's the event the gamblers close in on."

None of this meant much to Jennifer but she shared the general rise of interest. Suddenly she was not only an onlooker but a participant. And when the races were over, Steve would come home and they would have drinks with Gavin. Would Steve bring Sara and Tom—why not? Better let Miles come too—there's more of the crabmeat mix in the refrigerator and rye bread and the sharp cheese and plenty of nuts. Gavin has not been in our house—not since we've been living there. I think he will like it— In the late afternoon the sunset mends the rips in the fabric on the old sofas.

She was planning her party instead of concentrating on the horses in the field below when Miles said, "Tom stuck to his guns. But you see what I mean? He doesn't ride like a jockey—he's lean but the wrong build. The jockey on Dark Shadow is a professional, that's the difference. That's one of the horses from the Keyneck stable—the people from Atlanta I told you about."

"Which is Sara's horse?" asked Jennifer.

"Number seven—white and green on the jockey—that's Sold Out."

"She doesn't hunt him, does she?"

"No—saves him for the races. Ross Painter trained him—he's riding him today. Quite a show, isn't it?"

"It's so dramatic that I don't care who wins."

It was a scene of skill and pride. Jennifer looked again toward

Steve, high up on the central stand. She said to herself—he's thinking of nothing else—this is it—he's living this completely and I'm glad. He was alone now—Sara had gone to the paddock evidently. Steve was standing very tall. Watching, missing no smallest detail.

Sara's beautiful horse was full of spirit, dancing a little, but Ross Painter was riding him as if he understood and shared every motion. Tom Bayard did look more awkward—or did she imagine it? She looked at the program—his horse was number 10 and the one called Dark Shadow was 4. *Mr. Thomas Bayard*, the program read, *owner and rider of Own Risk*. And 7 was owned by Sara Bayard, ridden by Ross Painter. Only gentleman riders had Mister before their names on the program.

In that moment Jennifer felt that she knew why this meant so much to some people, why the breeding and training of fine horses could be so deeply important, why Ross Painter was a man to admire if not an educated gentleman, why people gambled— She wished she had a bet on this race. On which horse? Not Sara's— not Tom's—maybe Dark Shadow, number 4.

Only the race counted now—everyone was looking toward the starting point. Mrs. Valiant's pink gingham was motionless and the basket, emptied of arbutus, dangled from her arm—she had picked her favorite as she always did. Miles had ceased to classify people. Gavin Bennett, without taking his glance from the race-course, moved slightly closer to Jennifer as if to watch with her. Cicely had walked to a vantage point in front of the car, forgetting illness and displacement.

They were off—Own Risk immediately in the lead as seven horses flung forward on the green. The first quarter mile was fairly flat, then up the hill, over the four-foot hurdles, on toward the water jump. Now they were out of the spectators' sight though the judges could see them from the high stand. They would come around again in full view in less than a couple of minutes, for in the Lancaster the course was circled twice.

Dark Shadow had gained when the horses were visible to the crowds again—Own Risk only a few lengths behind—Sold Out slightly in the lead now—not now, Dark Shadow had passed him.

"I told you," said Miles Halliday to no one in particular.

"Dark Shadow is trying to make it."

"Tom shouldn't press his horse too far," said Gavin Bennett. "He might bolt—"

Again the horses and riders had mounted the hill and gone out of general view. The loudspeaker kept up with the race from its vantage point in the pavilion. Number 4 was leading now—7 in second place—number 10—there was a sharp break in the stream of information—a pause that shouldn't have come. Almost instantly the tension rose even higher as people guessed that this pause was the result of something unexpected, of trouble, possibly accident. Then in the space of seconds number 4 appeared again, well in the lead—but galloping wildly behind him was a riderless horse— number 10 unguided and in the path of number 7.

Kit Piper shrieked, "My God, something's happened! That's Tom's horse!"

"He'll tangle with seven," came an echo of hysteria, and some-one yelled, "Oh, shut up!"

Miles said in a very deliberate drawl, "Our boy fell off. Someone always does."

All the horses were past the goal posts now—the riderless one was being rounded up by outriders though he still pranced de-fiantly. Guesses and identifications were flying from one person to another—"Bayard's horse bolted"— "Tom took a spill"— "Is he hurt?"— "Look, they've taken the doctor"— "The ambulance is going up the hill"— "It's just a precaution, dear"— "That's Sara Bayard—see her running like mad!"

Jennifer saw her and also saw that Steve was running in the same direction—he surely wouldn't do that unless it was serious.

Gavin Bennett's face was grave as his words were calm. "Don't be alarmed—he's probably not badly hurt."

On the edge of the paddock Dave Delaney said to a stranger, "No matter what, Dark Shadow is the winner—they've got to pay off on him. Number five came in second and six was third. He didn't have any business to place but that fellow had to pull in the

Bayard horse or he sure would have tangled with the runaway."

There was no normal cheering for Dark Shadow and his jockey. A few scattered handclaps were heard and then the amplified voice soared over the field again. "Spectators are requested not to come on the course—we shall bring you the results of the Lancaster race in a few minutes. . . . This is the eighteenth running of . . . Spectators are not permitted on the course. . . . There will be a delay of a few minutes before we bring you the official results of today's final race. . . . Cars leaving the parking spaces and the outer fields are requested to use the north gate. . . . Spectators are not permitted on the course. . . ."

But in spite of that prohibition some were there already. Boys slid under the five-barred fence at the top of the hill, saw and ran back into the crowd with their news. Mrs. Valiant, behind a holly tree, saw and knew all the people surrounding the shape on the ground. She knew Sara Bayard, whom she thought of still as the Langley girl, and lanky Dr. Forbes, and Frank Holmes, who drove the ambulance, and young Cooper, who'd come back here to live. She watched the doctor's gestures and attitude, for she had seen enough of death to know when a doctor gave up.

The words almost rode on the breeze that was tossing the flags about on the judges' pavilion—"dead"—"trampled"— "It's Bayard—"

Julius Martin said gently to Cicely, "Let's go, dear. Let's get out of this."

She started with apprehension. "You're all right?"

"Fine—but it's better to break it up—there's nothing we can do." He waved a hand at Gavin Bennett, who came quickly to grasp it. Julius said, "Good to see you, and when you come down again, look us up."

"I surely will. Take care of yourself. This has been a pleasure, Mrs. Martin. If you'll back out straight, I'll tell you when to cut—"

"Thank you," said Cicely, "and I hope—I wish that—" Her words scattered but she maneuvered the car out of the narrow space with skill. She could do things with her hands even when her mind was set against doing them. She would go back now to the little house and put the casserole in the oven.

"I liked your friend," she said.

Julius had thought the nerve of jealousy in him was dead. But it wasn't. He saw himself, huddled in the corner of the car, letting his wife drive him as if he were a child—saw Gavin Bennett, muscular, healthy, active.

"He's a very smart guy," he answered, "but someone told me once there was some problem with his wife."

Gavin was saying to Jennifer, "I'm afraid I should get back to Anne and take her home. This accident—if it's true—will be a shock. I don't like to leave you like this. Where's Miles gone?"

"He knew the owner of that horse that won and probably went to speak to him," said Jennifer. "He wasn't with me anyway, he just happened around."

"Why don't you go home, Jennifer? This is a grim ending—get away from it—"

"Steve's going to meet me here—and there might be something he'd want me to do."

"Then may I call you later on?"

"I wish you would. Perhaps, you know, this is all exaggerated."

"Perhaps—"

But after Gavin had left her she was sure that it wasn't exaggerated. She took a cigarette for reassurance, crushed it as soon as it was lit and walked swiftly down toward the judges' pavilion. To the two men who told her, "Not this way, ma'am," she answered that she was Mrs. Stephen Cooper and the reply seemed to be a password.

A Negro whom she recognized as one she had seen at the Bayard stables was taking the saddle off a sweating, steaming horse, talking to him in a low-voiced, kindly twaddle—"Pretty boy don' mean no harm you quiet you down pretty boy you don' get blame—"

"Do you know where Mr. Cooper is?"

The voice grew mournful. "He up there on the mount, Mis' Cooper—"

She took the quickest, hardest way, up the bank which separated the straight lower course from the higher level by the water jump, not watching the bushes and tearing her stockings. There was a barrier of mountain laurel, gaily pink and sticky, and she pushed herself through that and saw them, the men hatless, the body still uncovered on the ground.

Someone was bringing a blanket from the ambulance.

"Not yet," said Sara, "not yet. I want another minute. Steve, I have to have another minute."

"Of course," said Stephen, "but take it easy, Sara."

Jennifer was close and unnoticed on a tuft of higher ground. She could see it horribly. Tom Bayard's head was battered—the side toward herself must have been struck by the horse's flying, furious hoof.

"I couldn't stop him," Sara said. "Usually, you know—"

"He was doing something he wanted to do very much, Sara."

The doctor said gently, "It was almost instant, Sara."

"I never lost a man like this," she said, and her voice dragged as she said, "All right—if you have to—take him."

The men from the ambulance covered the body and Stephen took Sara's arm and turned her from the sight. Jennifer saw the blotches on the elegant riding clothes, the grass stains on the knees of Sara's breeches, the red, still undried blood on the white stock where she must have held that cruelly torn head.

"Jenny—you shouldn't have come—"

"I had to. I couldn't stay down there any longer."

Archer Loomis' car swung up the hill. He leaped out of it and after a shocked survey of the scene he went to put a protective arm around Sara. Stephen crossed the trampled turf to where Jennifer was standing.

"Terrible thing for her—"

"Ghastly—poor Tom—and it's awful for you—"

"Oh, I'm all right. I suppose the news of this has gone out?"

"People seem to know—or guess."

"Is the crowd leaving?"

"It's breaking up now—the loudspeaker is giving orders—trying to keep them from coming up here."

"That's right—good work."

Loomis came to speak quietly to Stephen. "We must get Sara home. I'll drive her and Bee will come to stay with her tonight."

"Good."

"Steve," said Sara, and the word was a pitiful demand for him.

"I'm right here, Sara."

"Is Own Risk hurt?"

Archer Loomis said the horse was all right.

"Steve—do we have to shoot Own Risk?"

"Of course not."

"I don't want to have him shot. That horse really loved Tom. And Tom—"

"Come, Sara."

"I will. I just have to know what to do next."

"You're going home and Bee Loomis will stay with you."

"You come too—"

"Sara, the doctor will give you something that will help."

"I don't want any dope. Please come with me, Steve. I have to talk about it. Figure it. Believe it. Stay with me until I believe it."

Stephen looked at Jennifer and her lips said, "Do what she wants. Stay with her."

He said to Archer Loomis, "I'll drive Sara home if I can take your car. And will you get Jenny back to hers? Jenny—there'll be things to do— Don't expect me until I come—"

"I won't—"

Archer Loomis told her what had happened. He explained in horseman's talk and Jennifer did not understand it completely. But it was clear that Tom Bayard had entered the race against the advice of his trainer and the wishes of his wife. No one could be blamed but himself. He had urged the horse beyond its capacity, until the animal became bewildered and bolted. That the accident was fatal was pure chance. Steeplechase riders were often thrown. Perhaps if Tom Bayard had been a professional he would have rolled to safety, shielded his head—but of course, said Loomis, the fall might have stunned him.

Loomis was saddened but not unnerved. They are like that, thought Jennifer. It's part of their breeding and their bravery to accept such a thing as this. Steve will accept it. She thought of the blood on Sara's chalk-white stock, of her saying that she must believe it, that Steve must stay with her until she did believe it. She wanted Steve, not the Loomises. God help her, I'm glad to let her have Steve, glad that she has someone to turn to tonight. It's natural—the riding made the bond—let them have the bond and be glad there is one. Don't think any farther than that—it's not decent. Tom isn't even in his grave.

9

SHE WAS ALONE in the house, still in a state of shock. Jennifer stood for a few minutes watching a pattern of sun moving on the old rug up to the Greek inscriptions on the sides of the fireplace. She knew now what the words meant and often they haunted her mind.

The inscriptions had intrigued her from the first days in the house. Stephen said that he had never known what they meant, that he had never had any Greek. She had tried with the help of a Greek dictionary to translate them, but the words she found seemed unrelated. Then, going over the books one day, she had come upon an inventory. It was in a brown leather notebook and written by hand. Henry Cooper had been a methodical man and he had listed his possessions and their value, perhaps for insurance, or possibly for the information of future owners.

Marble facing for fireplace with inscription and figures. Excellent copies of some found in early Grecian residence. Inscription from Sophocles: *Be it soon or be it late, men find that sweet turns to bitter and again to love,* proving date of originals post-Sophocles. Cost, with freight charges from Athens—no duty because dealer proved more than one hundred years old—$3,459.00. Facings will probably increase in value but would be hard to sell because unsuitable for modern dwellings.

She had shown the inventory to Stephen, who whistled with surprise and pleasure at the value and said that when they were really up against it they could rip out the fireplace. "And maybe get thirty-four dollars and fifty-nine cents for it," he added cheerfully. "My father was more or less of a nut about anything Greek and I suppose he was taken pretty often."

Jennifer loved the inventory. She found the rugs and the sofas and even the French furniture also listed in it. Stephen was probably right that the things would not bring much at a sale, but the descriptions and values fascinated her and gave her a secret pride of possession.

"*Sweet turns to bitter*—" She was thinking of how quickly it had turned for Sara Bayard when the telephone rang.

"You got home all right?" asked Gavin Bennett.

"Oh yes. It's true—he was killed."

"So I heard. Very sad." Like Archer Loomis he understated sadness, accepted it. "Shocking thing for Sara."

"I saw her—it was dreadful!"

"I wonder if I could hold you to that drink I invited myself for. Anne has gone to bed with a couple of tranquilizers and I'm a lonely man."

"Steve had to take Sara home. He said he didn't know when he would get back here."

"Then you're a lonely woman."

"I'm a horrified one. I can't think of anything but that awful tragedy."

"I think I had better come over."

"I do wish you would come."

It meant hurrying to put glasses and plates on a tray, and remixing the crabmeat with mayonnaise, and deciding to slice a little ham because if Anne was in bed he probably wouldn't have had any supper. It meant a glance in the mirror, a combing and fresh lipstick. In spite of what had happened today she felt anticipation and a slight pleasurable excitement.

From the terrace of the cottage in the valley Cicely Martin saw lights go on in the pillared house on the hill. Julius was resting on his long couch. The afternoon had tired him more than had been apparent at the time.

Cicely was bracing herself with a gin and tonic. Dulling herself. She didn't know which it was but she wanted to escape. Not from Julius or from this evening but from all the evenings ahead that would be just like this one.

She imagined the life in the house on the hill—all the people who would be in and out of it tonight—being shocked and sorry about what had happened, of course, but warmed by each other, having each other to talk to— a small sigh slipped out. It was hardly as loud as the chirp of a cricket outside on the lawn but Julius heard it. He was not asleep. He was still contrasting himself with Gavin Bennett, thinking how life could fool a man, how illness was master over plans and ambitions. And death—there was that man today, looking the very symbol of strength and prowess, and half an hour later a horse kicked him to death. With no warning.

And Cicely had sighed.

"Cicely—"

"I thought you were asleep."

"No, just pleasuring myself. That was a lot of fun today—until the accident."

"Except for that it was a wonderful day."

"Lovely here tonight."

"Just divine," she said.

"No place quite like it."

"I adore it."

"I hope you'll manage to see something of that girl—Mrs. Cooper. I'll bet she has a lot to offer. And she'd like to know you."

"Oh, Julius, she was just being polite. She's one of that horsy set. She wouldn't want to bother with me."

They were drinking very slowly and Gavin had been grateful for the ham so Jennifer had cut some more. The room was still flooded with sunset when he arrived, hot on the heels of his own invitation so he said. He had kept away from talk of the accident. Instead he admired the house which he was seeing from the inside for the first time.

"It's not been decorated," he said, "but assembled. It has great dignity."

"But it unbends. It's been very friendly to me," said Jennifer, "and I didn't bring it a thing."

"You brought it yourself. Which was probably what it needed. I don't believe it looked like this until you came here to live."

"The house needed a woman who cared about it. I think it had never had one. I haven't done much to it except try to appreciate it. It's so completely different from the place where we lived in New York. That was decorated—contrived, compared to this."

"You like this better, don't you?"

"The house?"

"The whole setup you've fallen into here."

"Sometimes I think I protest too much about that," she said with a smile that mocked herself a little. "As I told you today, it's full of surprise and delight."

"What don't you like about it?"

"It isn't not liking. Just that sometimes I wonder, in the midst of all its charms, if I belong here. You see, I used to work. I mean I did earning work. I'm busy enough here. But all my life before now I had to earn. I was one more girl earning a living in New

York when by some miracle Steve came along and wanted to marry me."

"Why was that a miracle?"

"Oh, it was. It was the most unexpected, wonderful thing that ever happened to me. I'd been working for three years, getting promoted a little now and then, doing a better job, and—"

"Then came the big promotion," he finished for her. "The miracle, I mean."

"Well, it was!" she insisted, and they both laughed at the argument over a word. He said that he would refill their glasses and Jennifer turned on the lights which Cicely saw from her veranda. As he gave Jennifer her drink, Gavin used her given name questioningly and she laughed and said that it always made for much better communication.

They talked about New York.

"You sound as if you like the big city, Gavin."

"I don't frustrate myself by not liking it. It's where I work. I'm like you—I've had to earn."

"Don't you think earning is exciting?"

"It's always been that for me. At any level."

"But I remember that you said that you envied Steve because he was coming to live here."

"Perhaps I overstated that. This place has been for me a proof—or a hope—that there is peace and safety. It's my investment in those things. I like to know that it is available—here waiting if I need it. Of course Anne needs it now. But my place is still in the city."

"What's wrong with Anne, Gavin?"

"It's mental. It's not going to be any better. She will deteriorate." He said that frankly, almost sharply, and added, "I admit that only to a very few people, whom I trust completely. To the rest I still pretend."

"You can trust me."

"Oh, I know that. I've known it from the first time I looked at you across Sara's dinner table."

"Poor Sara—I wonder how she is now—how she'll get through tonight and the dreadful days ahead."

And I wonder how long Steve has to stay with her. Of couse Bee Loomis will take over. Steve must have gone back to the steeple-chase course to check things, or he'd be here by this time.

Gavin was saying, "She'll get through all right. I'm more sad for Tom than sorry for Sara. He was evidently trying to prove something, maybe to himself, maybe to her, and it wasn't neces-sary. He should have let well enough alone. But Sara's not a person who needs pity. Or wants it. She's never had an easy life but she takes the hurdles before her as she comes to them and she usually clears them. It's not that she's insensitive—she's very emotional. But she's an extrovert—never broods—never has pitied herself when she's been in a difficult or dangerous situation. She knows there'll be another day. Another meet."

Yes, thought Jennifer, today, even in the first shock and horror, she thought of the horse.

"She has a whole lot of courage," Gavin said, "and it's not entirely physical."

"All the physical courage around here makes me so ashamed," said Jennifer.

"What do you mean?"

"Because I don't have it. I wouldn't even tell this to Steve—it would embarrass him to have such a wife—but riding scares me. The horses are so high—and they seem so unreasonable when they get dancing about and trembling with all that vigor. How in God's name people can get on them and gallop through woods and jump rivers to kill some miserable fox is something beyond me. So now you know my dark secret. I'm a coward."

He laughed as she told him. He said, "You've had all this riding pushed at you, that's your trouble. If I could get you on a gentle horse and ride with you on some of the trails you'd feel quite differently about it."

"Perhaps. But that's one of the reasons why I feel that I don't quite belong here. I know that many—most—of the people who live in DeSoto don't ride. Do you remember telling me that I should look around the post office? I do that every day and the variety of people is fascinating. But each of them seems to fit in somewhere—even the ones who want only a pleasant place for dying."

"And you don't think you fit in?"

She said, "I'm not thinking only of the necessary people, who sell the gas and sort the mail and teach in the school and preach in the churches. They're valid—they belong. But most of the others who come here manage to tie into something—if it's not riding, it's golf or bridge or painting or collecting money for good works or just living in a handsome way. And I've been a person who's had a nine-to-five job with a martini and a problem to solve at lunch. And a pay check. I feel sort of undressed and indecent without a pay check. I don't know why I'm telling you all this."

"Because I want to know—that's why," he said quietly. "Is it all right to ask if you need that pay check?"

"We can manage without it. With luck and being careful. But it's Steve's money."

"Why shouldn't it be?"

"He wants it that way. But earning your own is so safe."

"Have you ever trusted anyone to take care of you?"

"I could always do it myself," she said.

"That's not the answer."

"Isn't it?" A silence fell between them, but after a minute she interrupted it, suddenly listening. Her face changed—he thought, she's putting the puzzle out of sight— "There's Steve," she said, "and he must be exhausted. He'll want Scotch."

Gavin took a glass and lifted one of the decanters on the end table.

"A long or short one?"

"Short—and plenty. Steve's really had it today."

He dropped ice cubes into the whiskey. "One thing I want to ask you, Jennifer. Don't you ever come to New York?"

"There's no reason to. And it's expensive. Why?"

"I'd like to see you there if you do come. Show you some of my favorite places."

"I wish it were possible."

"You never know. I'm listed in the phone book. We have an old house in the sixties off Park and there's almost always someone on duty there, though when Anne isn't there and the children are away at school I stay at my club. But you could reach me through a call to the house if I'm in the city."

"You have children? I wondered."

"Two—both teen-agers. Ronny is at Foxcroft and Pete's at Exeter."

Stephen Cooper, in the doorway, heard the names of the schools before he recognized the visitor.

"I wondered whose fine car that was. How are you, Mr. Bennett?"

"Jennifer calls me Gavin," said the other man. "Being neighborly. I hope you don't mind my coming around. I asked her if I might and I've been drinking your whiskey and trying to keep your wife from thinking too much about the tragedy today."

"That was very good of you. I was held up."

"How is Sara?" asked Jennifer.

"She's been wonderful. Very brave."

"Gavin was just talking about her courage."

Stephen took the glass of Scotch. His face was tired and his glance remote, as if other people and places were closer than his guest and his wife.

"I telephoned for her boys. They're coming tomorrow. They sounded like good, sensible kids. She didn't want to get in touch with her sister, said that she didn't want anyone here who didn't like Tom, and I guess Lady Sukeforth didn't. So that was that. She sat there, pale as a ghost, cool as a queen, facing it. Working it out."

"Lady Sukeforth or not," said Gavin, "that was a good marriage. I'll go along now. Thank you, Jennifer. Good night, Steve."

They saw him to the door and came back into the big room. Stephen poured another drink.

"One for you, Jenny?"

"No—I'm way past my quota."

"How did Bennett happen in? I've never seen him except at that dinner Sara gave."

"I hadn't seen him either after that until this afternoon. Then he joined up with Miles and me—Miles introduced me to a couple of attractive people who live in the valley below us—and Gavin suggested that he'd like to come for a drink—his wife couldn't, she is pretty frail—so I thought a little party would be fun. I hoped you'd bring Sara—before it happened, this was—it is so awful about Tom! I'll never forget that sight—"

"I'm sure I won't," said Stephen grimly. "You know Sara wanted me to persuade Tom not to ride, to scratch his horse. But I didn't. I didn't feel I was in a position to do it. I've been riding their horses—he might have thought it was criticism. I felt that he might resent any advice from me. Anyway I didn't interfere. I don't think it would have made any difference." His voice was sad and thoughtful as he added, "But I feel sort of responsible for what happened."

10

MILES HALLIDAY had never come to DeSoto in midsummer before.
Places usually ceased to exist for him when they were out of
season. But he had been cruising on a yacht of a friend off the
coast of the Atlantic in August when a storm, which was also out
of season, had so battered the craft that it put in at Charleston for
minor but tedious repairs. Miles had been bored with the cruise
and his companions before the storm. Corinne Miller had sometimes amused him in New York, as he observed her brazen
shopping for men with the confidence that she could afford
anyone she wanted, but at close range on the yacht he found her
cloying and tiresome. They were hardly in Charleston harbor when
he made excuses to his host for flying north at once by himself.

Though he was routed through Charlotte which was only a
hundred miles from DeSoto, he would never have thought of
stopping for a few days in the village if Corinne Miller had not

told him that Sara Bayard was there. Miles had believed that Sara was in Ireland. He knew that after the accident she had leased a castle in the Irish countryside for the summer and had considered wangling an invitation to visit her there. But Corinne had said very positively that Sara had only stayed in Ireland for a couple of months and then had gone back to that place in Carolina—"It's that place that Steve Cooper went to after he was let out—did you ever know Steve? I adored him but he was stuck with one of those career girls—." Miles had picked up quite a little information from Corinne, and though he discounted most of it, he decided that a few facts were probably true.

This is a fool thing to do, Miles said to himself, superintending the transfer of his luggage from the terminal to the car he had hired. The heat was intense and passive, heat which had been too long in one place and was sour with dust. Even if Sara was in DeSoto, what of it?

He had come because the thought of Sara had been restless in his mind since spring, since he had last seen her, tearless and beautiful, at the funeral service of her husband. She had not worn black nor been veiled. She was controlled but not composed. Her eyes held shock and bewilderment. As she followed the coffin down the middle aisle of the Episcopal church which she had attended only occasionally, Miles knew that she was not dramatizing herself. She was putting grief into action by following the body and she needed action. Those who watched her had thought more of her future than her bereavement—what would Sara Bayard do now? Marry again, of course. Miles had been as conscious of that silent speculation as if it had been shouted.

He turned on the air conditioner in the car, was annoyed by an unnatural wheeze in it and yearned for his own Jaguar. To which he should be flying directly today instead of making this lunatic stop. You wouldn't want it even if she would consider it, he said to himself. But she's never had a man who sees her as she is. First there was that insolent stableboy, then the British stick that her sister foisted on her, and Tom Bayard—he was the best of the lot but Tom had only one dimension. That's such a beautiful house. She should keep it. But living alone is not Sara's dish. She could have the spring and fall seasons in DeSoto—invite more interesting people—and keep an apartment in New York that would do her justice. Not ramble with anyone but learn to choose a group. Sara's never made the most of her money because she's had no guidance.

Absurd thoughts—Miles actually did not admit having them. He only admitted to himself that he had loathed that drinking, sexy cruise, and since he was not expected in Bar Harbor until two weeks from now and nobody was in New York this month, he might as well stop and see how Sara was getting on. For he was fond of Sara.

He stayed in the fast lane, passing all the lumbering trucks and the slick cars of salesmen whose coats were swinging from hangers beside the windows, and the cars of tourists whose rear-view windows were blocked by piles of clothes they might need and souvenirs and staring children. He passed them impatiently and with a built-in contempt, for none of these people belonged in the world he wanted to live in. But he saw them all nonetheless with the artist's eye because he could not help himself. He guessed at their thoughts and moods and habits as he did with the old ladies in DeSoto. He could have described very accurately several children with their mouths smeared with lollipops and he knew that the salesman in the Ford he passed was putting off—not much longer—a stop in a rest area and a drink from the fifth of bourbon that he undoubtedly had with him.

Miles could not help knowing about people, even those with whom he would never associate. That had given him his start as a writer. But it was part of his snobbishness that, when the critics had been unanimous in writing off his two books as amusing but lacking in depth, he was unwilling to settle for a possible popularity among people whose opinions he considered worthless. Fortunately he did not have to do that. He had money enough for the way he lived and there might be more when his aunt died.

It was a monotonous drive for eighty miles. The four cement lanes were bordered by the stubble of harvested fields and orchards stripped of fruit and withering in the heat. But finally the mountains, blue and misty, appeared in the distance. The road narrowed and began to curve, to mount little hills and dip into valleys. A sign promised that DeSoto was only ten miles away and curiosity stirred in Miles, raising his spirits. He wondered what the town was like in summer. He passed the estate that Gavin Bennett rented—to stow away his addled wife in safety, thought Miles. Horses with shaggy coats roamed in the long-grassed meadows, now not carefully groomed and ready for hunting or racing. He passed the five-barred white fences of Sara's estate. The main gate was open. It must be true that she was in residence. He would go to the Inn first, settle in and then telephone to make sure.

The town felt asleep. He drove along the streets where old, spacious Southern dwellings had become boardinghouses. Their windows were closed, the shades drawn. The old ladies are lying on their beds, waiting for sundown and supper, thought Miles. He saw the aging priest, Father Aberdeen—the name came to him—going slowly from the cottage toward the church. To hear confessions no doubt. Miles's well-furnished mind included the knowledge that Catholics confessed on Saturday. It would be very hot in the priest's little box.

The Grecian house on the hill came in sight and as always its beauty impressed and pleased Miles. It looked cool. Space and height and whiteness can do that, he said to himself, and it was fine planning not to clutter the front façade with shrubbery. The chestnut trees are magnificent and they give a feeling of shadow but do not obscure the house. In a good many ways the house would be quite right for Jennifer Cooper, if she could make herself believe that. He remembered that Corinne Miller had no liking for Jennifer. But Corinne would have contempt for any woman who did not make the seduction of men her chief business in life. Jennifer Cooper was shy of men—not socially skilled—but she thought well and talked well. If Corinne knew what she was talking about, the Coopers came here only because they needed to have a roof over their heads, because he lost his job. That explained a good deal about Jennifer.

At the entrance to the Cooper driveway Miles saw a car that was being driven very slowly and the man at the wheel was scanning the entrance closely as if he were interested in it or admiring its noble width. The man's face was familiar and their glances touched for an instant as Miles passed. The name shot into Miles's mind—Delaney—a cheap-seeming, pretentious character who had stayed at the Inn for a while last spring. He was evidently still hanging around DeSoto. Strange that he was prowling around the Cooper place on a hot summer afternoon.

Delaney thought the same thing. That was Halliday all right. Funny that he should be here in the middle of summer when all the swells were gone where it was cooler. But Halliday usually drove a Jaguar—that car he was in today looked like a rental job.

It was funny for sure—the people who stayed here in summer were mostly native North Carolinians. There were a few others, invalids like Martin down the road, and the one who used to be a college professor and had built that pink brick house. The Coopers stayed, probably because they couldn't afford to go away. And now Sara Bayard was back from Europe. One of the boys in the garage where she had her cars serviced said that she had told him she liked it here better than anywhere else in the world.

She usually picked up her mail about ten o'clock. She might be wearing shorts—she had the legs for them—or her hair might be wet and shining as if she'd just come out of the pool. Always a beauty. But she must be lonesome. A woman like that without a man. She wouldn't be able to live that way for long. She'll soon find someone, he told himself. But it's slim pickings here, especially in summer with her kind of people not around. The unexpected sight of Miles Halliday came back to Delaney. Maybe that was why. Maybe Halliday wanted to be in the running, that might be the reason he was here in DeSoto now. She'd never be

136

fool enough to take him on. What's he got to offer? Of course he thinks he's a big shot in high society, but he only had a bedroom at the Inn.

Delaney counted up his own assets in his mind. It was always a pleasure, a secret pleasure. There was so much more than anyone suspected. Because he used different men on his operations—and different bank accounts—that was the way to do it. He could write a check right now on any one of the three banks for over fifty thousand. And there were the safety deposit boxes. When this job was finished and the territory was pretty well mopped up, he could begin to enjoy life, get a horse of his own, take a few golf lessons, break in. He would have to go slow at first on account of the income tax snoopers, not flash a lot of cash. If he could buy the Cooper place, he'd make Joe Harris think it took every cent he had in the world.

But I'd just like Sara Bayard to know how I'm fixed, he said to himself. When the hunts start in the fall, I ought to be able to see a good deal of her. If I bought the Cooper place that would show her. Show her that I know class when I see it, that I'm going to live like class. She could do a whole lot worse. If Halliday is hanging around her, he's only after her money and that big place. I wouldn't want that house. This is better. I'd have to spend quite a lot to fix it up, but when it was done I'd have something.

He looked up at the mansion on the hill as he rounded the corner, his eyes greedy, his thoughts as grandiose as unscrupulous. When I get rid of the boys and through with that job on the mountain, I'll nudge Joe Harris about the Cooper place. Cooper and his wife may be fed up already—I'll bet she is, she's the New York type—and forty thousand—I'd even go to fifty if I had to—would look awful good to them.

II

JENNIFER SAID, "I can't this afternoon, Sara—there are some things I have to do."

Sara's voice could make her visible even in a telephone conversation. She was even more beautiful since she had come back from Ireland—the look of shock had gone.

"Don't do them," she said. "Not on a day like this. It's a day for lazy swimming, lazy drinking and something to eat when the sun has gone way down. That's the plan—all there is to it. Please come. What do you have to do? Write a book or something?"

"Nothing so easy. Our grapes are ripe and Aga picked them yesterday so Susie and I have to make jelly." That sounded absurd to Jennifer as she said it. To be making jelly.

"Let Susie trample the grapes," said Sara, "and make wine."

"She might just do that if I leave her alone. And there's another thing—I told Cicely Martin I might stop in there later."

"I like those two," said Sara. "I tell you what—I'll call up and ask them to come over too. That Martin man has charm."

Sara had met the Martins one afternoon when she had arrived at Chestnut Hill unexpectedly and Julius and Cicely happened to be there for a julep.

"But he doesn't go to parties," said Jennifer.

"This isn't one. All he would have to do is to settle down and put his feet up and let his charm float around. Anyway, I'll ask them."

You might even persuade them, thought Jennifer. If anyone could. And Cicely would love it for a change. She sees so few people and Sara dazzled her that day.

Sara was going on, "Steve is going to stop here after lunch and tell me what he thinks of the new hounds at Red Fox Farm. He's looking them over to see if we want any of them when our Hunt begins."

It will soon begin again, and without your husband. But the hunt must go on. Why shouldn't it?

"I'll tell Steve what's up and to come and fetch you."

"No, tell him not to, Sara. I've my car and can get myself over. He'll be hot—let him jump in your pool when he gets there."

Now I've agreed to go. I didn't mean to.

"Fine—we'll be waiting for you!"

Jennifer put the telephone down. That was how it was now. But there was nothing to worry about, nothing to be bitchy about, she told herself. Sara really wanted her to come, would be glad to see her. Steve would have been surprised if she had refused the invitation. If she had, he would have said that he didn't want to go either, that he would rather stay home with her, and she would have spent the evening not believing that. For what would any man like better on a summer day than the relaxed diversion at Sara's place, where there was the largest pool, plenty of service and Sara herself—never tired, never moody, tossing enjoyment about and catching it back. When she speaks of Tom and of how she misses him, it's true. She's remarkable in being sorry—even sad—

but not inflicting her grief on other people or making anyone pause for a heavy embarrassed minute if his name comes up. She doesn't ask for pity—actually she doesn't need it. She is happy in DeSoto. As she said when she came back from Ireland, "I've found out where I want to be and it's here. It's heaven to be here."

Everyone was glad when Sara came back, the people in the shops, the people who worked for her, as well as her friends. But it's not been the same for Steve and me since she came back. Those were such lovely weeks before she came. Half of May. All of June. Most of July. We found out that we could make this a year-round home. Steve found that he liked it here even when it wasn't the horsy season. I know that he did. If he missed Sara it was only an additive he missed—not what was necessary. We were happy by ourselves. We were happier in those weeks than we have ever been since we were married. I was beginning to feel so sure—and maybe to realize that I never have been completely sure about us before.

With the horses out to pasture and the season's important social and sporting events over, living had been quiet in the early summer. But it had not dragged for Jennifer and Stephen. They had time to keep up with what was happening in the world as well as in DeSoto. They listened to the morning news on the air, made a habit of the evening reports, talked them over.

"It's funny," Stephen had said one day, "but sometimes I feel more up on things—more in the midst of them now—than I ever did in New York. You get a kind of perspective here."

"In New York we were in a groove and couldn't see over the sides of it. I know what you mean. I feel like that too."

"It isn't," he said thoughtfully, "that I want to get in a hole and pull it in after me. And of course I suppose I am a dropout."

"No, you aren't. Or if you have dropped out, it's only out of something that wasn't right for you. And dropped into something that is right."

"Right for you too? You're looking awfully well these days. My very handsome wife."

Although it was quiet there was no apathy in those days of early summer. They had lunches that were cool or hot according to rain or shine, dinners that Jennifer planned carefully so that she wouldn't look hot and steamy when she served them. They lingered over cocktails while the mountains darkened and ate when they pleased.

They explored the country roads, almost always finding new ones that wandered through the back country. Stephen and Aga had filled the old stone pool that had been empty since Henry Cooper's death, and Stephen said it did not have to be expensively filtered because he and Jennifer were the only ones who used it. It was fun and rather magic to take dips late at night. But everything about the nights was wonderful.

They were like the ones in their first weeks of marriage when love was so astonishing to Jennifer. She was astonished all over again. She felt romantic and sometimes bawdy. Love was a secret, a treasure and sometimes a joke between them.

But that was before Sara had come back. Now it was different. Now they went to the Bayard place to swim. Sara always wanted company.

"She needs to have people around," Steve would say.

"I know. But we were there just yesterday."

"Sara doesn't think about that give-and-take stuff," Steve might answer. "Don't you want to go?"

"Of course—it's always fun there—"

"And she has all that staff. She wants to give them something to do."

It had happened so often, so naturally, so somehow irresistibly. Like the invitation for this evening. There was nothing Jennifer could do about it. Nothing to protest. She knew that Stephen was not having an affair with Sara. Sara did not like affairs. She liked to be with Stephen. It was as simple as that. In a group she would somehow choose him, with no rudeness to Jennifer. Jennifer was always included and almost always felt left out.

By midafternoon twenty-four glasses of jelly stood in a row on the shelf in the butler's pantry.

"Susie, we did a job."

"Sure did, Mis' Cooper. Never saw jell no more clear and sure."

Clear and sure is the way I wish all things were, Jennifer said to herself.

And aloud, "You'd better go home and rest now, Susie. And take a glass of jelly to Aga."

Susie gleamed. "That man has sweet tooth. I fix you biscuit batter for your supper before I go."

"Not tonight, thanks. We're going over to Mrs. Bayard's house for supper."

"I guess she lonely. I pray my God that he take Aga and me both same time. I don' wan' be no widda-woman."

"No woman does."

"She soon pick herself a man again. Miss Sara Langley, she pick any man she want. She young, she handsome, she rich."

That adds it up, thought Jennifer.

She dressed slowly, putting off joining the party as long as possible. I'll take a little ride by myself, she decided. A ride up the mountain will do me good, clear my mind. And I'll stop and see if there's any mail as I go by the post office.

The big office was almost empty when she went in— One stranger and one woman whose name she couldn't remember were opening boxes. In her own she found some magazines and under them two letters with airmail edges. She looked at the one with the return address to *Portfolio* with surprise—Geoffrey's initials were scrawled in ink over the address. What on earth was he writing her about? She hadn't heard from him since—

But now she read:

Dear Jenny,

How are you? I was going to telephone you and then decided to write instead because I was afraid you would make a snap judgment on the phone and turn me down. I want you to think this proposition over and try to see it from my angle as well as your own. This is it. Sally Lord is pregnant and her ass of a husband insists that she stop working now, and Sally weeps and says what can she do? I could tell her what to do but she's nuts about the guy. There isn't

142

anyone in sight to replace her and we are planning on the biggest Christmas issue ever—have promised it to the ad department. I can find another fiction editor but I'd have to break anyone in and haven't time to do it and Sally says she has to quit now. Will you step in and come up from your hamlet or forest for a few weeks until I can get someone? I know that you said you were through, but can't you give us a break? Don't write me that you are pregnant or I'll commit suicide. You'll get this begging letter on Tuesday at the latest and I'll call you Wednesday a.m. about ten. Be a good girl. Rally round old *Portfolio* and you can write your own ticket. More on phone Wednesday.

Love always,
Geoff

P.S. Sally is writing you. I have told her I'll take her back if she wants to come. And if he lets her. He will. Sooner or later the boys miss the money the girls bring home.

Tuesday. This is Tuesday. He would call tomorrow. Of course she couldn't do it. Jennifer opened the other letter, the one from Sally. After the preliminaries it read:

The last thing I expected or intended was to get pregnant. As far as I'm concerned I would be willing to go on working and have the baby in the train if necessary. But Mark is a demon about my working from now on and the doctor is in cahoots with him. Mark wants this child far more than I do—though I'm glad about it too—but I guess Mark has always wanted this to happen. Anyway he's a maniac and keeps telling me to lie down. You can imagine Geoffrey's reception of the news that I have to quit now—with the Christmas issue in work. But it's Mark or Geoff. Between you and me he could get May Fox back—she is footloose again—and that terrifies him. He's afraid she would fasten on him personally again if she gets in the office. So I suggested that maybe you would help out temporarily—just maybe because I know from what you wrote me that you love it down there—and I suppose Stephen will be as bad as Mark if you told him you were coming back. But perhaps he wouldn't mind for a few weeks and, if you can and will come, I and my heirs will bless you forever. I've never been so torn up about anything. I told Mark that with a baby we'd need my money but he's had a raise and says that he can afford a full-time wife now— he's always hated to have me work—

I Took My Love to the Country   *   143

Poor Sally—Jennifer said it aloud. But I can see what Geoffrey is up against. There must be someone he could get—the names of editors she knew ran through her mind. None of them fitted the situation. Of course it's out of the question as far as I'm concerned. There's the house here to look after. Though if I were on a salary I could pay for a cook, and at this season there's plenty of help available in DeSoto. But I'd be back where I started. I'd be earning and Steve wouldn't and that's the situation we came here to get away from. Of course it's different now. He's adjusted—he likes living here.

She put the letters into the big straw bag which held her bathing outfit and got into her car again, turning it in the direction of the mountains. Think this out before you go to that party, she told herself. Plan what to say to Geoffrey tomorrow. Anyway, it's a good feeling to know that he wants me back on *Portfolio*. Steve will think it's queer—perhaps I had better not tell him about this or he'll realize that I wasn't fired. Even if I only worked for a month, the money would be a windfall. I could have the sofas reupholstered. If I were in New York I could find exactly the right material for them. I could get a room at the Wilmington Hotel. That's close to the *Portfolio* office and it's not too expensive. The biggest issue they've ever had, Geoffrey says. No—I'm out of it and have to stay out.

She had come to love the mountain road, bordered with waterfalls, vineyards and forest. Today, warmed and excited by the letters from New York, she drove farther than she had intended. I must go back, she told herself, but instead went higher into the coolness. Just a little farther. Then I'll turn off the highway and find that old road back to town. There won't be any traffic on it and that will give me a chance to think.

She thought she turned off in the right place. There was a short stretch of cracked tar paving between the highway and woods which should lead to the disused, original road up the mountain. Jennifer slackened her speed and lit a cigarette. I couldn't do it, she told herself. I don't want to leave Steve. I'm afraid to leave him, for one thing. But perhaps that's why I should. Am I going to spend

144

the rest of my life being afraid of Sara Bayard? Living in her shadow?

She came to a fork in the battered old road and was not sure whether to go right or left. The left direction seemed most logical, but after she had driven several more miles she believed that she was driving away from DeSoto instead of toward it. She had not passed a cottage or a farm. The woods were thick and a snake slid across the road. She decided to go back to the fork but as she looked for a place to turn the car she heard the sound of hammering on metal not far away. Someone was working near here and so there must be a house down beyond that grass-grown driveway. She could inquire about the road and directions there. This was a grim place to be lost. Jennifer guided her car toward the noise.

She drove into an open space where there were sheds and the ruin of a burned house. Three men were working on an automobile and several other cars stood around. The men looked up and they all stared in something that seemed more than silence. They did not look friendly. They certainly did not welcome her appearance.

She had seen one of the men before, seen that green hat. At the steeplechase—the memory came back to her mind. And before that she had noticed him one day at the post office. She had asked Miles Halliday who he was.

"Can you tell me the way back to DeSoto?" she asked. "I seem to have lost my way, taken the wrong turn." She began to be frightened, felt danger as the man in the green hat approached her. He did not take it off as he spoke.

"You have to go back to the highway," he said. "Maybe three miles."

"I thought there was an old road down the mountain."

"The bridges are out on that," he said.

"Thank you," said Jennifer and began to swing her car around.

He put his hand on the fender and moved with it. She did not dare to put on speed. He might leap at her. He might have a gun. And there was no mistaking the menace in his face.

"It's Mrs. Cooper, isn't it?"

"Yes, I'm Mrs. Cooper."

"I've seen you in the village. Small place like this, you get to know people. By sight anyway."

She said yes again.

"My name is Delaney," he said. "I've met your husband at the hunts."

"You have?" She tried to make the words commonplace and civil, wondering if she should step on the accelerator. But she would have her back to the man if she did that, and the top of her car was down.

"Out for a drive all by yourself?"

"A little drive."

He was making up his mind about something, what to do or say. She could tell that.

He said, "These boys had a wreck and are trying to fix up their car." His grin was utterly false. "I was out for a spin myself and stopped by to help them."

She did not believe it. There were four cars in sight.

"Well, I hope they can get it fixed," said Jennifer.

"Oh, they will. They'll be out of here in no time." There was a threat in the explanation and his next words. "Don't give it a thought, Mrs. Cooper. And if I may be so bold as to give you a piece of advice, driving is dangerous in these mountains. I wouldn't get off that highway if I were you, Mrs. Cooper. There's a lake just over that cliff that they say has no bottom to it. Hoodoo Lake, they call it. Yes, it's a lonely place around here. Not safe for a lady, Mrs. Cooper."

Don't ever dare show up here again, that was what he meant.

"I'll take care," she said and stepped on the accelerator. She thought, they must be stolen cars. They are a gang of thieves. She was sure that he knew that she would figure that out. His glance was wicked as he let the fender slide away under his hand.

"Should you have let her go?" asked Todd doubtfully. "The dame might talk. Might spill the beans."

146

Delaney snarled at him, "There'll be nothing to talk about by morning. Get rid of these heaps in the lake. Do it quick. Then burn down these sheds and I want both of you out of here tonight. On your way."

"Could set fire to the mountain."

"Fire enough of it to make sure," said Delaney.

Jennifer drove fast over the ruts and hummocks, the man's malignant expression pursuing her. The undercurrent of secrecy and evil-doing and the menace she had felt in the encounter kept her nerves taut until she reached the highway, but once again in the current of traffic she relaxed. She would tell Steve about the place and the men and he would get the sheriff or highway police to investigate. She must ask him how a man like Delaney happened to hunt with his group. Then walking briskly along the shoulder of the road she saw the lean, weather-beaten figure of Mrs. Valiant. Jennifer braked her car and called, "Can I give you a lift?"

"I thank you kindly," said Mrs. Valiant and settled herself on the seat beside Jennifer with satisfaction. "I was going into town for a short spell."

"Do you live near here?"

"A piece back on the mountain. My folks been livin' there nigh a hundred years. My grandpa—he was in that old war that they fought over the nigras."

Jennifer remembered Miles Halliday telling her jocosely that Mrs. Valiant had seven sons.

"Have you a family?"

"Seven boys I raised," said Mrs. Valiant. "All grown—all spread out all over. They send me cards. My boy Jefferson, he done right well up North. He got him three autos and a ship."

"Do you visit him in the North?"

"Can't seem to leave the mountains," said Mrs. Valiant.

"You must know the whole country around here."

"Every crick and holler."

Jennifer said, "There's a place about ten miles back, off a side road near the old road. There's not much there but some sheds. It looked as if there once had been a fire there—not recently."

"Old Prentiss place," said Mrs. Valiant promptly. "Burned to the ground—could be thirty years ago. She were a hard-drinkin' woman. Burned her to bones right in it. Some said the boy that was working there set the fire and skipped with her silver things. You been there?"

"I happened on the place by accident. I was driving on the mountain and lost my way. And I saw some men there who said they'd been in a wreck and were working on their cars. It seemed funny—rather strange."

Mrs. Valiant gave a dry chuckle.

"I was wondering if I should say anything about it. Report it to the highway police or the sheriff," said Jennifer.

"Pay it no mind, ma'am. That place a hant. Bad place to wander."

"Is there a Hoodoo Lake?"

"That old Prentiss place sets right straight above Hoodoo Lake. Over the side of the mountain there, down below. It got no bottom to it. Nobody want to fish there. Nobody ever built a house there except that crazy, hard-drinkin' Mis' Prentiss. Them men you see there, they foreigners. Just as lief give you a bullet in the back."

She knew more than she was willing to tell—that was obvious. But she would not be drawn out further, and Jennifer's questions met with either monosyllables or the dry chuckle. She let Mrs. Valiant off at a grocery on the edge of the village, getting brief thanks and a flash of liking from the shrewd old eyes. Jennifer looked at her watch and saw that it was nearly seven o'clock. She sped through the sleepy streets of the town toward the estates of the hunting country. Glimpsing her own home, so serene on its hill, she had a now familiar feeling of affection and pride and wished she were going there instead of to Sara's house.

The front terraces were deserted when she arrived except for a couple of servants who were arranging a buffet table at one end.

The guests, the butler told Jennifer, were down at the pool and she made her way toward it. The pool was on a lower level than the big house, set in an expanse of tile which was bordered in turn by matched Lombardy poplars. It was reached by a descent of wide fieldstone steps. The sun was almost gone but its last glow suffused the stretches of green lawns, the fountain and statues which had been brought here from other beautiful places in the world and the lustrous blue of the pool. It was a picture in color of luxury. Jennifer paused at the top of the steps, struck by the contrast of all this to the lonely hidden roads on the mountain and the quiet streets of DeSoto. This too was DeSoto.

Sara's parties usually grew larger than she planned or promised, and there were about a dozen people either in the pool or lounging around it. Jennifer identified most of them as she stood there watching. Cicely Martin was there and Sara had beguiled Julius into coming too. He lay in a long chair just as Sara had planned. Jennifer had come to understand the situation of the Martins during the last months, to feel the depth of their love and their desperate fear of hurting each other. There was Anne Bennett, who seemed a little better lately. Gavin was not there. He is working. He likes work, likes earning, thought Jennifer. As I did. And I have a chance to get back to it. But I can't do that.

There were Sara's two handsome boys—and two girls who were strangers and had probably flown down with the boys for a weekend. And was that Miles Halliday? It couldn't be—he had left immediately after Tom Bayard's funeral and had said to Jennifer that he would see her next spring. But it was Miles—there was only one head like that. There were Steve and Sara coming out of the pool together. Sara was wearing a bikini—a couple of strips of black satin against her smoothly browned skin. I would feel exposed and embarrassed. She doesn't. Steve looks like a Greek athlete—he is like the ancient Greeks in his respect for physical skills. And in not being concerned about earning money. He wants to live, not just make a living. That's the aristocratic posture. I don't have it.

She went down the stone steps into the midst of greetings.

"Here she is at last!"

"Hi, Jenny!"

"We've been waiting for you—" that was Sara. "You know my kids, Bill and Jim. And this is Dotty Baker and Jane Lyman—"

The young boys and girls were beautifully polite, estimated her age and quickly went back to their own age enclosure. Julius gave Jennifer a cordial, welcoming hand—"No, don't get up," she said and sat on the end of his chair. She waved at Cicely in the pool, let Miles give her one of his meaningless kisses and said to Stephen, "I finally made it. I'm sorry to be late, Sara."

Stephen asked, "Where were you? I called the house twice and no one answered."

"I went to the post office and picked up the mail and—I'll tell you about it later—" She couldn't explain to all of them how she happened to be in a remote place in the mountains when she should have been at this party, so quickly she said, "Gin and tonic," to one of the colored waiters, and to Miles, "I couldn't believe my eyes. Am I dreaming you?"

Sara said, "He was on a yacht and it broke down."

"So I came to see Sara."

"I'm so glad," said Sara. "It's always more fun when you're around, Miles. One more dive, Steve, and then the refreshments. You're coming in, aren't you, Jenny?"

"Too lazy," said Jennifer.

She watched Sara make a perfect dive and Steve follow with as good a one. She herself loved to be in the water but she swam with the beginner's form she had learned in the high school gym. And Sara and the young goddesses who had come with Bill and Jim were doing water ballet.

"Was it serious trouble on your yacht?" she asked Miles.

"No—but the boat had a hole in it and the company had holes in their heads."

"How did you happen to be with people like that?"

"One of them was a friend of yours—Corinne Miller."

"Oh—Corinne—"

"Your tone is revealing. She spoke about you and Steve—"

"In different keys, I'll bet."

Miles grinned at her, not denying that.

"Corinne says you're a career woman," he said.

"I had a job, not a career. But Corinne wouldn't know the difference."

"She sounded a little wistful about Steve. As if she had a yen for him."

"She has a yen for all mankind. I mean malekind. I'm surprised you escaped unscathed. Or did you? Is she the reason you came here in a hot, slow month?"

"No, I came to see the Widow Bayard."

"Don't call her that—"

"I don't like the sound of it either," Miles said, and added ever so lightly, "I wish she'd marry me."

"Have you asked her?"

"No. Not yet."

"She just said she likes to have you around. That you bring fun. And you'd be a new experience for Sara."

"Will you build that up with Sara? Build me up?"

Jennifer laughed.

"I mean it. Will you?"

It sounded almost like a request, almost as if he were serious. She scanned his face but he wasn't smiling. And he said the same thing again, "Will you?"

"Why, it's none of my business, Miles."

"Isn't it?" he asked, looking toward the pool. His glance and question bracketed Stephen and Sara and flung the danger at her.

Cicely Martin, who was looking almost as young as the visiting girls, interrupted the taut moment as she ran over to speak to her husband.

"I'm going to get dressed. Are you all right, darling?"

"I'm fine. Having fun?"

"It's a heavenly party," Cicely exclaimed and turned to share her enthusiasm with Jennifer. "I do love you for letting us know

Sara! Isn't she wonderful? And the most beautiful thing you ever saw? She gives everyone such a good time!"

"Run along, dear," said Julius. "You're dripping all over me."

He was very quick and his swiftness in cutting off what his wife was saying made Jennifer sure that he too saw what Miles did. Perhaps he had heard what Miles had just said to her although he had not seemed to be listening. Jennifer felt cruelly exposed. In a flash of anger she wanted to tell Miles, tell Julius, tell Steve himself that she would not fight for possession of him. If he wanted Sara, he could have her. Jennifer's fury said speechlessly, I can take care of myself. They need me in New York. I won't stay here and watch this. I'll get out of their way and let Steve make up his mind about what he wants.

The anger was in her mind and heart, not visible in her face. She spoke to Miles, answering his question, giving a casual shrug as if it were not important.

"No—if Sara wants you—or anyone else—that's for her to decide. And anyway I won't be here to build you up. I'm going back to New York this week. The editor of *Portfolio* sent me an SOS. They need me on my old job for a while."

"Going back to work?" asked Miles incredulously. "What does Steve say about that? Doesn't he mind?"

"Actually I haven't had a chance to tell him yet. I only heard about the *Portfolio* problem this afternoon, just before I came over to the party. But no, I don't think he'll object. It will probably be a temporary thing."

Julius Martin had not moved a muscle, still lying there in apparent ease. But he had heard Miles's jibe and her cool answer. Julius had watched many people put up a good front when they were forced into a corner. He was helpless in this situation. He did not know either of the Coopers well enough to have any privilege or duty of mediation or advice. But he was painfully sorry for this woman who had attracted him from his first sight of her and whom he had come to admire more and more, who was too sensitive for her own good, and brave, and undoubtedly deeply passionate. She loved her husband—Julius had been aware of that when he saw them together—and she was in a bad spot, facing Sara Bayard's unusual endowments and dangerous availability. If Jennifer meant what she said about going to New York and went through with it, she might be doing a very wise thing or she might be playing a losing card.

Jennifer left both Miles and Julius and went over to the bar where her husband was with Sara. They had come out of the pool now and Stephen was mixing a drink.

"One for you too, Jennifer? On the rocks?"

"Straight up, Steve. And I must tell you my big news."

"What gives?"

"I had a letter from Geoffrey Clark this afternoon and he wants me to come back to *Portfolio* and take over my old job. For a month, more or less."

"Well, the nerve of the guy! After the way he dealt you out!"

"Oh, that shake-up wasn't really Geoff's fault. He was never for it but he had to go along. But the problem now is that Sally Lord is pregnant and her husband insists that she stop working and Geoff hasn't anyone in sight to take her place. So he wants me to pinch-hit until he finds somebody. He's going to call me about it tomorrow morning."

"I hope you'll turn him down with a thud he won't forget."

"I honestly don't see how I can do that. The biggest Christmas issue they've ever had is in the works and he did write me as if he was desperate for help."

"You mean you'd consider it!" Steve stared at her over the jigger in his hand.

"It's something I have to consider. There's such a thing as loyalty to the magazine."

"Loyalty to that rag!" he said contemptuously. "And what would I do if you went to New York?"

"You'd be all right. I'm sure I can find a woman—a cook-general who'd take over the house, do the things that Susie can't manage. You'll be busy with the hunter trials next month and with getting the hunts under way, now that you're Joint Master with Sara. And you have to see that Aga gets our stables in repair so perhaps they can be rented next season—you'll have so much to do you'll never miss me. And your friends will take care of you. Won't they, Sara?"

"Of course," said Sara, "if you have to be away—"

Stephen didn't like it. He did not give up without considerable argument. It started that evening when they were on their way home and went on intermittently even after Jennifer had told Geoffrey on the telephone that she'd come for at least a short time.

"I don't like the idea of my wife running around New York by herself," he protested.

"Steve, I did it for years before I was your wife."

"It's different today—gets worse all the time in New York."

"I think that's exaggerated— Anyway, I won't be running around. I can get a room at the Wilmington, which is very respectable and close to the office—and if I want to go anywhere at night there are always taxis."

"You have this all doped out, haven't you? Have you been planning it for some time?"

"Just since that letter came from Geoff. At first it did seem impossible, but when I began to think about it—"

"I thought we decided to come to DeSoto to live. Now you want to get out of it, to get away—"

"Oh no!" cried Jennifer. "It's not that at all. You don't understand. Maybe it will be good for both of us."

"I know it bored my mother," said Stephen, "but some women like it here. Sara says that nothing could pry her loose from DeSoto again."

"Yes, I know she feels that way."

"You really want to do this, don't you?" he said accusingly.

She might have broken down when he said that and told him the truth if he had not gone on, "I'd go up there with you if I could. But aside from the money angle, I'm involved with things here that I've taken on. It would be a tough break for Sara— Last year she had Tom for Joint Master and she sort of needs me to stand in."

"I know," said Jennifer again. Her resolve to go had hardened again at that mention of Sara.

Stephen gave in reluctantly in the end. "If you want to, of course I won't try to stop you. I suppose I couldn't anyway. But how long will you be gone?"

"I don't know—but I should know before too long. Know if I'm more needed there than here." She added the last words so quietly that Stephen read no special meaning into them.

12

IT WAS EXHILARATING to be living again in the dangerous, tolerant, demanding city. In the few months that Jennifer had been away from it many things had paled for her. She was caught up again in the indifference created by so much life, and at first it gave her a feeling of release, almost freedom.

She had not forgotten but she had not remembered sharply the beauty of millions of lights in the office buildings on Park Avenue at dusk, the drill of uncountable cars obeying the rule of lights. She had not forgotten but she was shocked all over again by the cost of food in the restaurant where Geoffrey took her on expense account to celebrate her return and to talk over the problems of the Christmas issue. In DeSoto artichokes cost only twenty-nine cents apiece.

She had forgotten the terrible noise of jackhammers and compressors building and destroying on the grand scale. She had

156

forgotten, in the recent ease of getting into her own car when she pleased, that the city was so dependent on dirty taxicabs and sullen or loquacious drivers. The feeling of crowds came back to her as she was part of the rush hours again, the touch of strange elbows, the faces very close which did not see her.

She had forgotten how it felt to be very important in the office and utterly and immediately unimportant when she was out of it. But she stepped into her job as she might have put on a dress which she formerly liked but had not had occasion to wear for some time, and was pleased to find that it still fitted and looked well on her.

"It's good to have you back," said Geoffrey and made the gesture of a toast with his glass. She had forgotten how tired and battered he could look at this time of day when the impetus of the morning pill had worn off and the first of the midday martinis had not yet picked him up. "You look wonderful. Blooming. Do you know I sometimes think that for two cents I'd chuck this rat race and get myself a place in the country."

"You won't," she said realistically.

"I suppose not. What do people do in a place like your De-Soto?"

"Eat, drink, make love, mind the weather, make a thing of getting the mail, go to the drugstore and pick up the Times or the Wall Street Journal and get yesterday's news. They may even buy Portfolio. They play golf. Prolong their lives. Build houses—some of them very handsome too. Train horses. Ride to hounds."

"Do you do that—ride to hounds?"

"No. But Steve does."

"What do you do?"

"I have a house to take care of, you know. Biggish. I do a lot of things. My last achievement was making jelly."

"Did you enjoy making jelly?"

"I had to. Our grapes were ripe. They couldn't wait another day."

"Sounds rather a peasant place, your town."

"In its own way it's rather sophisticated. Anyway it's another world and I'm back in this one for the time being. About that spread for the first page—the Merry Christmas message from the editors to our readers—I read it and it seems to me that it doesn't quite come off. Who did that piece?"

"Sally wrote it. After a staff conference."

"She'd write a different one next year," said Jennifer. "This is a typical staff piece—I might have written it myself last Christmas. It's all right. But not good enough."

"I didn't think so either. But what's wrong with it?"

"It lacks feeling. It's remote and rather too public, like the tree in Rockefeller Center. You look at it and admire it but it isn't for your home. This piece has to be for millions of women who are going to be trimming trees and filling stockings and worrying about what they are spending and dead on their feet. They need sympathy and a lot of praise."

"We're after the young audience, not hags."

"I know that," she said, "but they marry young and for a lot of twenty-year-olds Christmas is kids and bills and memories of the ways they used to celebrate before they were married. Another thing—this piece skips the religious angle. And a great many of our six million readers go to church."

"Think so?"

"In DeSoto practically everyone does—the riding and hunt colony, the halt and the lame who are retired, the shopkeepers and plumbers and certainly all the colored people."

"That's in a village, dear."

"There will be crowds at all the Masses here."

He motioned to the waiter to bring the second martinis.

"Christmas is tips and bonuses," he said, "as far as I'm concerned."

"And fur jackets," said Jennifer, remembering the mink one that Steve had given her, and that same year she had given him star sapphire cuff links. The mink was shabby now and he had lost one of the cuff links— "And a drinking party on Christmas Eve and another one on Christmas Day. I can tie that in to the piece too and be realistic."

"Well, see what you can do to tone it up," he told her. "Now tell me—should we begin that two-parter by Corey Bates in the holiday issue? It's a tough war story—doesn't pull any punches."

"The war is tough, Christmas included. I certainly would run it. To give your readers the belief that you don't want to evade anything, that you want them to know what's going on in the world. How bad it is, if it is."

"For a girl who removed herself from what's going on in the world that's an interesting point of view."

"But I didn't remove myself from the world."

He said, "I think you're glad to be back on the job."

That was true, as far as it went. It went through the working hours. She had taken a room at the Wilmington Hotel—an adequate room and bath which startled her when she woke for the first mornings, because it was all she had to live in instead of the tall, spacious rooms of Chestnut Hill. Breakfast in the coffee shop was a duty and that was adequate also but nothing more. But then the excitements and problems of the job took hold. Lunch always went along with shop talk and because there were so many interruptions and demands she worked for some nights, after the rest of the staff went home, on the Christmas message which was to begin the issue. The rewrite was a harder job than she had anticipated. She had thought she could excite a mood in herself that would carry over to the readers, but the first drafts went flat. It was almost a week before she satisfied herself, and her wastebasket was full of discards one night. She tossed in one more and thought—what do people want for Christmas? What would it be like in DeSoto? Her mind slid back to the town and the people.

Aga and Susie would be reverent—they are sure that Christ was born exactly like the pictures—they believe in the manger and the star and the shepherds. And they'll be gay—kill a goose—and have candy for Aga's sweet tooth.

The estates where people are in residence will be decorated—

they still talk of what a superb job Sara and Tom did at their place—with lighted electric candles all along their fences that people came from miles to see. Will Sara do that again this year with Tom dead? Yes, she will.

But at our house we should have two matched trees in the marble urns and a great branch of holly on the door—not a wreath with ribbons but a branch cut from our own holly tree on the side hill. There's mistletoe in the top branches of some of the oaks— we could hang a clump in the hall and it wouldn't cost a cent. Tinsel things don't belong in our house, but it should have a smell of Christmas— In our house you could really deck halls and there would be the smell of fresh pine and maybe I could try making mincemeat. Christmas is what people are—they show through the celebration. That's why it lasts—it's never quite the same in one house or flat or hotel as in any other— It's rowdy and religious and greedy and profound—

She began to write again and this time she didn't tear it up.

She and Stephen had never made a habit of letter writing. Since they had both been in New York when they met, there had been neither the occasion nor necessity for writing to each other. The cards that came to her from Stephen along with flowers or gifts would have exclamations of love written on them. But for the most part they communicated by telephone if there was something to say when they were not together, or if, after they were married, Stephen might be away from New York on a business trip. These were often long and luxurious conversations but the cost had not mattered. It was included in expenses.

For the first week after she had come to New York from De-Soto, Stephen had telephoned almost every day to ask how she was getting on. But after that the calls thinned out and what they said became repetitive. Jennifer always said that she was fine and that it wasn't too hot and that everything was air-conditioned anyway, and asked how he was and if the cook was doing her job. Stephen invariably told her that he was fine and might mention a hunt or the weather. He did not ask about her work on the magazine but he had never taken much interest in that routine. Jennifer prevented herself from asking if he was seeing Sara often and if this separation was making Sara—or herself—dearer to him. The rambling telephone talks often parted them instead of bringing them together. They ended when one of them said, "This is running into money," and left Jennifer feeling empty and unsatisfied. She wrote Stephen a few letters but they seemed contrived to her. And she knew why. They avoided depth and truth.

She had soon found that she knew very few people well in New York who were not connected with *Portfolio*. She had many acquaintances and formerly some of these had counted as friends. It was possible to call them, explain that she was in New York and suggest a meeting. But as a name or a person came to mind she always rejected it. The group with which she had been connected during the time she was married to Stephen and when he was with the corporation in New York would have no interest in her now, and she had no claim on the time or the pleasures of those people.

At first the magic variations of the city were enough, the sights, the freedom to stop by herself in some cocktail room at the end of the working day—which in DeSoto was impossible. There were foreign-made motion pictures and the new plays to see. But after the shows were over she would be coldly alone and never more conscious that other people were not alone. Women had men or other women for companions. Jennifer had not realized that for years she had grown very used to the escort of a man. Now she was alone, waving for a taxi on a corner. Before long she began to be sated with the theaters and even more sated with her own company after she left the *Portfolio* office.

She had been in New York for sixteen days—the Sundays were the interminable ones—when her secretary said from the telephone in the outer office, "There's a Gavin Bennett on the telephone. Do you want to speak to him?"

"Why yes, put him through."

"Jennifer?"

"Gavin—how are you!"

"Pretty angry—no, not when I hear your voice. But aggrieved. Why didn't you let me know that you were in New York?"

"I was going to—" and it was true that several times she had thought of calling him but shied away from doing it. For when he had suggested it in DeSoto there had seemed no possibility of her being here—this might be the wrong time, be an inconvenience, seem a presumption—or had she not done it because she was afraid that Gavin Bennett would see through the surface of her return to work to the feelings and failures beneath it? She asked, "How did you find out I was here?"

"I was in DeSoto last weekend to see how Anne was doing. And I met your husband one night at Sara's house and he told me that some editor had shanghaied you. How's it seem to be back? Fun or slavery?"

Steve at the Bayard house—of course—naturally—where else—why not?

"Something of both," she said.

"When am I going to see you?"

"When do you want to?"

"Right away. But I can wait until evening. Will you have dinner with me?"

"Nothing would be nicer."

"Wonderful. Where can I call for you? Where are you staying?"

"At the Wilmington. A faceless hotel near Third and Fifty-eighth—you've probably never noticed it. I think I'd rather meet you some place than have you come there."

"Well, if you'd rather," he said doubtfully, and there was a tiny pause as he chose "How about the Maisonette?"

"Lovely."

"At eight? Or can it be seven thirty?"

"Seven thirty just as easily."

She put down the phone, already feeling the lift of gaiety. Tonight she would not have to walk down the streets past so many places where a woman was not welcome without an escort and firally settle for an inconspicuous table at a Longchamps with a book beside her plate.

Jennifer was handsome. Her bones had settled that. But her beauty was not always in use. She could be so indifferent to it that other people sometimes overlooked it too. At other times men who saw her would think that they had once believed women were really like that, refreshing and not greedy or scheming. She never worked hard at her looks nor expected them to work hard for her. But she always wore clothes that pleased her in color or mood, clothes that were friendly or loved. Happiness could make her radiant. She did not realize that, but of course Stephen knew it.

When she came into the foyer of the restaurant Gavin Bennett knew that he had made no mistake. This woman who had charmed him by her manner at a dinner table before he had even spoken to her was as rare as lovely. She wore black chiffon, a soft but confident dress, right for an evening of pleasure, seductive without effort or exposure. Her arms were bare except for short white gloves and she carried a small glittering jacket. Her not quite yellow hair was piled high but not starkly. And she was glad to see him without pose or caution. He felt instantly that she was glad to see him as a person, not as a dinner or a good time.

Gavin Bennett was a very successful, very disappointed man, and the pleasure he felt now rather startled him. He knew the techniques of enjoyment and he practiced them but he knew they were techniques. Why he had not made his wife happy, why she had withdrawn was inexplicable to him in spite of the explanations of the experts. From her childhood, perhaps because of her heredity, her retreat from reality had been inevitable. That was what they told him and what he would not believe for years, as he tried new environments, new stimuli of people and amusements, new drugs. There had been innumerable hopes, always coming to nothing as the veil was drawn over her mind again. And, no matter what the doctors said, they did not destroy the consciousness— almost a deep sense of culpability—in him that he had failed to give Anne health and happiness. He never talked about it. He never allowed it to show. With his money, his position and his charm he could always create enough well-being around him to cover up any appearance of failure and drug the pain of it in himself.

His pleasure at seeing Jennifer delighted him. His instinct, liking, guesswork and insistence on seeing her, which could hardly be called that, were all justified. He released her hand and they followed the headwaiter to the table that Gavin had chosen—and been given, though other reservations had to be adroitly changed to make it available.

"Don't hurry us," he said quietly, and the headwaiter signaled his subordinates into slow motion.

Across the beautifully appointed table Gavin said first, "Thank you so much for coming."

"I'm thanking you from the bottom of my heart for asking me. New York after sundown is pretty grim when you're alone."

"But you must have a great many friends in the city."

"That's the funny thing I've been finding out. I suppose I knew it but it never mattered. The people I work with all have their own lives after work—their husbands, wives, mistresses—their own patterns—and I don't fit into any of them. I never did. And the pattern that Steve and I used to have doesn't exist any more. We knew a great many people but we didn't really know them well even when we saw a lot of them. They were some of the fringe benefits of Steve's job—except a few—"she thought of Corinne— "and they were more Steve's friends than mine. I've no reason to see them now. Do you know what I mean, how it is in New York?"

"Yes, I know how it is. How transient people can be. But a lovely girl—"

She smiled and said, "A woman over thirty. There are so many lovelier and younger. And with rights and proper claims, legal or otherwise. Anyway, it's fun and really wonderful to be here with you tonight."

"Wonderful for me."

"I can't quite believe that. From the way you have the headwaiter eating out of your hand, you must come here often. And feed him well."

"But this is a very special occasion."

She said, not arguing it, obviously not believing it, "I know."

"Listen," said Gavin, "for a man and a woman to have dinner together may seem one of the most commonplace things in the world. But it isn't. It's always an experience in relationship— maybe something is fading, something being endured or something beginning. It's like a fingerprint, it can't be duplicated. And this is our dinner, not like any other one of the millions that men and women are sharing in New York tonight. It's something I imagined when I asked you at your house that night after the steeplechase to let me know if you were in New York. I've been looking forward to it this afternoon as if I never took a woman to dinner before. I have a feeling of something like triumph, of being in tremendous luck. And I'm going to enjoy every minute of being with you."

"So shall I."

"You're very beautiful tonight. New York becomes you. But DeSoto looked well on you too. You didn't find the humming-bird's nest, I gather."

"How do you know that I didn't?"

"Somehow I don't think you'd be here if you had found it."

"They put the pressure on. They said they needed me here."

"So your husband told me. But didn't DeSoto try to keep you there?"

He did not mean DeSoto and she knew it. He meant Steve. She said, "I thought I should come. Try it."

"I see. What shall we drink first? A very dry martini?"

"Yes—but not with vodka. No beating about the bush."

He laughed, stipulated that the gin be imported, and after their second cocktail had been finished they considered the magnificent menus. What he said is true, thought Jennifer. I have never had—never felt the mood of a dinner like this. This is quite by itself.

"You order," she said, laying the menu aside. "If two people order different things they might as well eat by themselves— Make it a symphony."

"All right—then the overture will be little oysters with a few clams—"

The most delicious thing about it, she was thinking, is that he really wants me to be here. I've been hungry for being wanted and it tastes so good. I will not mention Anne. This dinner is a detachable thing, like a color page that can be taken out of a book without destroying the binding. A page that I can keep if I want to, look at again, that I could frame if I should like it well enough.

"How does the editor's chair feel now that you're back in it?" he asked.

"It has the same old hollows. But in some ways it was rather hard to fit into it."

"Why? You haven't been out of it very long."

"I know. I was surprised myself. But DeSoto seems to have done something to me—given me a new slant on things—even on the magazine."

"Tell me about the new slant."

"I'm not sure that I can. It's subtle. It creeps up on me. When I was working on the magazine before I went to DeSoto I thought I knew what the people who buy it wanted to read. It's our job to tie in with their interests, of course, if we expect to sell. I had—you know that dreadful word 'image'—well, I had an image of our readers: they were a conglomerate lot interested most of all in sex—and all the trimmings of sex—they were without any illusions and they didn't trust each other—they'd better not, we told them. I lumped them as people who wanted to be startled—and seduced —mentally, since we had no other equipment to do it—even the older ones. We have plenty of older readers, the surveys show, even if we try to play up to the younger ones."

She stopped, frowned and said, "The wretched image was something like that anyhow."

"I can visualize it. And it's different now?"

Jennifer said, "Well, I'll tell you. Every once in a while since

I've been back, in my mind I see a copy of *Portfolio* in the DeSoto drugstore—on the shelf in the window—and I see the people coming in to pick it up and look it over, maybe buy it—real people, not our image—and sometimes I feel that we aren't getting through. There was a Christmas piece I had to rewrite—it was a tough assignment because I kept seeing these people—some of them were pretty profound and some backwater—rich and skilled—some of them knew they were going to die before long— what could you say to all those people who weren't the glassy image?"

"What did you write for them?"

"I hardly know. I just tried to remember what they were like—that Christmas is big enough to go around—and I thought about homes. You see the first time that I had ever had an owned home of my own was in DeSoto, so I began to understand that it's not just interior decoration and recipes and gadgets—it's something you feel when you walk into your front hall or your kitchen. My God, am I going to say that there's dignity in walking into a kitchen?"

"You seem to be on the verge of it."

Her laugh was a sound of delight. "It is so good to talk out loud instead of to myself! Gavin, I'm having such a good time!"

He thought, I'm still capable of it. I can fall in love with her.

"You know," she went on thoughtfully and a little dreamily as she looked backward, "I suppose I never did get accustomed to the luxury I had in New York after I was married to Steve. It always seemed a little unreal."

"What was real?"

"My job always was." She paused and then said with frank sweetness, "And so was Steve. But the trimmings, no. When I was growing up, I always had to get along without them. I didn't mind. I didn't covet things except once in a while." She laughed suddenly. "But there was a yellow wool sweater I did want once—for some reason I wanted it awfully, incredibly! That was during my last year in college."

"Did you get it?"

"Oh no, it was much too expensive."

A waiter finished stirring the wine sauce over the flame of a chafing dish and another waiter poured it over the boned partridge and set it before her. The orchestra was playing something muted and almost melodious.

"But I was lucky after I got on *Portfolio*. At first I had to manage pretty carefully but I was used to that. I had quite a pleasant little apartment—and sometimes a hyacinth to feed the soul. That was before Steve and I were married."

"After that you had everything you wanted."

"We had a nice place. Quite close to the river, a good address. We needed that because we entertained so many people. It cost a ridiculous lot but Steve said it was worth it. The architect and decorator had done a good job—the apartment was quite new when we moved into it so we didn't have to do much to it. There was an artificial magnolia on the wall that looked real—almost. We have magnolia *grandiflora* trees at Chestnut Hill that are real and they bloomed this spring, so now I wouldn't be fooled by that wall. The other day I walked past that apartment house and I could hardly believe that I had lived there for such a long time, and been so gay there."

"It must have been a wrench to leave it."

"No—by the time we did that it had become just a worry and more than we could afford. I sold some things I might have liked to keep—at the time I thought so—but they wouldn't have looked right in the DeSoto house. I wouldn't want to spoil that house—or divert it."

"You like it better than the charming apartment?"

"It was strange—when I walked into Chestnut Hill the first night I felt as if I had always known the house. Or that it had known me. It was home immediately."

"It has great charm."

"More than charm for me. Something was built into the house.

168

Is it the wine that makes me so garrulous? I'm not usually a compulsive talker."

"I'm not usually a compulsive listener. But I want to know all about you."

"Why?"

"Because when I sat across the table from you at Sara's house you instantly were interesting."

"At Sara's house— I didn't want to go to that party. But Steve did. When Sara says come, people come. Even I do. That's one thing I got away from."

"Let's not have Sara dine with us tonight. I want you to myself. Let's not have anyone interfere."

He said it quietly but it was not casual. This is what they write about, thought Jennifer. This is the way it goes. I have read about thousands of love affairs—I can even tell whether they are true stories or phony when I read them. And I'm living this, not reading it. What will he ask—how soon? What shall I do about it? Be frightened by inhibitions? There's probably not a woman in this room who doesn't or hasn't except me—

Gavin was talking about the wine, about vineyards in France. She felt herself travel with him, see and learn. He said, "About sixty-five miles south you come into the country where wine is a way of life."

It would not be tawdry with him, no matter what, she thought.

He asked, "What would you like to do tonight?"

"Is there more of tonight?"

"A great deal more, I hope."

"It's too late for theater."

"All I want is to have the curtain go up on us," he said. "How about coming to my house for a brandy? I'd like to show you some pictures of my children."

"You don't carry them with you?"

"Not these. They are portraits. You see, Jennifer, I also want you to know about me. It works both ways."

"I want to know. I'd like to see your house and the pictures."

It was a tall house, old and noble, very private with the closing of its thick front door. He opened it with his key, after ringing a couple of times. "Eaton's evidently having one of his rare evenings out," he said. "Do you mind?"

"Of course not." Inside, this house was quiet and handsome and well cared for. The crystal chandeliers were bright, the mahogany dustless.

"Did you grow up here?"

"Oh no—I bought it—let's see, twelve years ago. It gave me a great deal of satisfaction at the time—it's so exactly what it is."

"Certainly a fine gentleman's house—with fine gentleman's furniture."

"Perhaps—or maybe just fine craftsmen. When you collect things," he said, lighting a drawing room and leading her through it, "you don't feel complete ownership. At least I don't. It's only temporary possession, relating yourself to history. No, I didn't grow up in the environment that I've tried to recapture. I was raised in a small mining town in Pennsylvania. With my parents and a brother and sister in a very commonplace workman's house with a front stoop. My parents are both dead—they didn't have money or knowledge enough to see that my mother had a necessary operation in time, and my father was killed with six other men in a mining accident which gave shudder headlines to the news for a few days and then was forgotten. My sister was killed in a car accident when she was trying out for a beauty contest—she was very pretty but she wouldn't have won, I imagine. We were an accident-prone family. My brother lives in Mexico. He married a girl or woman down there. He will probably drink himself to death. That's my very ordinary frame."

"And you did all this by yourself?"

"I had considerable help. My father's death gave me a start I wouldn't have had otherwise— The company was generous in its settlement to his children—that was why my sister got the beauty contest bug and why my brother had a little money to let him drift. Korea got him too. By then I was married and didn't have to go. I had the breaks—good advice and a push here and there. I went to Harvard Business School and that practically guarantees a job."

"And then—"

"Then I met Anne. The way ambitious young men do meet girls who are cuts above them socially—well-placed—Anne has always had money of her own. Seeing her now you'd hardly realize what she was like at nineteen."

"Yes, I would. I do. It's still apparent."

"Come in here," he said. "The pictures I want to show you are in this room."

It was a library with two walls free for the paintings. They were oil paintings in gold matching frames—of a boy holding a tennis racket, of a girl in a sleeveless blue dress that might be gingham.

"Tennis is Pete's game," said Gavin Bennett, pausing in front of his son's picture.

"He doesn't look like you," said Jennifer.

"No, he wouldn't want to. He happens to hold that racket, but a few hundred years ago he might have had a hawk on his wrist. Pete is very polite to me but we have very little in common. Pete is—well you can call it a snob, an aristocrat, a cynic, a contemporary youth. However, he's not stupid and he's not mean."

"But—remote?"

"The gap's tremendous. And the fellow who painted this got it, didn't he?"

There was a resemblance to Anne Bennett in the boy's face, a doubt or disbelief beyond what looked at first like contempt in his expression. Jennifer twinged with pity for his father and turned to study the painting of the girl.

"What is her name?"

"Veronica. Everyone calls her Ronny."

"She's a beautiful girl."

"Look more closely. What else?"

"I don't know. Is she happy?"

"For a long time it didn't occur to me that she wasn't," said Gavin Bennett. "You see it at once."

"She's very young. At that age girls are secret."

"She was. She was sent to Foxcroft—it's a school with an accent on riding, you know."

"I've heard about it."

"She did very well—rides very competently. She's been in a number of shows—got ribbons—and then, a couple of months ago I went down to visit her. I try to do that because visiting schools is too hard for Anne—they seem to scare her. As always, Ronny was polite—it's hard to penetrate that terrible politeness of the kids—and I was praising her and saying I was proud of her and that I'd like to give her another horse—a thoroughbred hunter—I had my eye on one—and that she could take him with her to Vassar next year. I said we could make arrangements about the stabling. Well, when I got through with all that—she thanked me very much—never had a break in the politeness—but she said that, if I didn't mind, she would rather not have a horse. And she said—if I didn't mind—she would rather go to Europe next year than to Vassar. She wants to live in Madrid and study primitive paintings. Primitive paintings! She said she was interested in the early Catholic Church. At first I thought she was beginning to retreat—like Anne—but apparently that isn't it. She's latched on to something that really interests her."

"Does that disturb you? It shows she's an individual."

"No, it doesn't disturb me. It just shows me that I didn't know anything about her. Let me tell you the rest of it, it may interest you. I said all right and began to talk about Spanish horses, trying to tie that in, and Ronny said, 'I don't think I'll be riding. Would you mind awfully if I didn't ride for this coming year?' "

"I asked her if she wouldn't miss it and she said, 'No, you see I hate riding. I hate horses. I'm frightened every time I get on a horse.' That's what she said in so many words. After all the shows and blue ribbons."

"And you didn't know? You had no idea of that?"

"I thought she loved it. I especially wanted to tell you the story because this has happened since I saw you at the steeplechase in DeSoto. You told me that horses scared you too—you see you aren't alone in that."

Jennifer was still intent on the painting of Veronica Bennett.

"But she did it. Without a whimper," she said.

"She didn't have much choice. She had to fall in line. I stuck her in that school—I suppose to get rid of her safely. I did the same thing with Pete. I thought they both were in storage in a way and that when I had time I could take them out again. But it doesn't work out that way. Ronny is under the influence of things I don't know about—ancient art, an ancient church. It may be all to the good—Europe may be good for her if she doesn't pick up some tramp. She'll at least be detached from Anne."

"Does she worry about her mother?"

"Modern kids are pretty realistic. They all have a smattering of psychology—they are used to homes going haywire. Things a lot worse than mental breakdowns happen in the families of some of their friends and they must hear about them. Ronny and Peter both inquire about their mother and then change the subject."

"How old is Peter?"

"Almost eighteen. And I am almost forty-three. That picture was done about a year ago."

"Is he like you? I don't mean in looks—his features are more like Anne—but in other ways?"

Gavin laughed and looked with a kind of challenge at the portrait of the boy.

"He's so unlike me that if I didn't know that he was, I wouldn't believe he was mine. Maybe it's natural—maybe I used up certain ambitions. Ran through them so there was none left for him."

"What ambitions?"

"There's nothing that interests Peter less than earning a living. He doesn't see why he should—doesn't get the point. He knows of course that he doesn't have to—there's a fairly substantial trust for each of the children that was set up by Anne's father aside from what he presumably will get from me. Peter doesn't see why he should earn and I can't understand that instinct being left out of a normal boy. He believes in skills—in that tennis racket, in polo—he likes sailboat racing and is good with a gun—that might come in handy if this war strings along until he's called up. But try to talk to him about the causes of war and you get nowhere. Try to interest him in politics or the state of the nation and even if he looks as if he were listening he doesn't hear you. He doesn't throw money around—in fact he takes money rather seriously, the way rich people without earning capacity often do. Sometimes he almost makes me feel I'm the naïve one."

"I won't go along with that. But it's too bad if you can't get closer to him."

"Inevitable maybe. Common enough from what you see and read. And the kids may be right. Maybe Ronny's smart to run to primitives and the Catholic Church—virgins and miracles. Girls seem to be overinformed on the practical aspects of sex and the Catholic Church is about the only institution left that offers any protection or respect to women. And Pete—he may not want to earn money but he'll hang on to what comes to him, probably marry some more of it—he wouldn't be apt to become interested in a working girl."

"I can believe that," said Jennifer, watching the boy's picture.

Gavin said, "I try to think it through—to be fair. Pete doesn't want a job with a bank or corporation, but I didn't want the kind of job my father had in a mine. My father's job is obsolete now and my kind of work may go down the drain next. Working for a living could get that way. Maybe my brother has got a point, sprawled out with a bottle in some Mexican bungalow. Your husband may be making sense, building a life out of fox hunts."

"It's not just that he's doing."

"Sorry. I'm talking out of turn—and we decided to ignore DeSoto."

"Oh, please—if we are talking let's not be afraid of what we say. Or apologize for saying it. But Steve was let out of his job here in

New York and the reason he was let out was basically because he was a misfit in it. I've been looking at this picture of Peter and thinking about Steve as a boy—he may have had that doubt in his face. His father placed him in storage too, I think—but both his mother and father wanted him to follow them—each of them wanted to be mirrored in him and continued by him. Then I came along and was not much help. The only good thing I ever did for Steve was to put the possibility of living in DeSoto in his mind—it was a desperate notion, utterly selfish actually—I was afraid of losing him, of having him begin to hate me. I was thinking mostly of myself."

"I doubt that."

"It doesn't matter now. One thing I have found out is that you can lose a person no matter where you are—just as easily in the country as in the city. It's not place that holds people together— whatever does hold them. Anyway, it turned out all right for Steve. He isn't a misfit in DeSoto—you saw that, didn't you?"

"Yes, I saw that. And I didn't mean to belittle his adjustment."

She didn't want to be interrupted. She went on, "And you must have seen that I was the misfit there. I told you. You know that's why I came away. Why I'm here."

"It's not so simple as that, I think."

"No—beautiful, fascinating women who share a man's habits and tastes don't grow on bushes. They may not be available. Nor suddenly widowed. Gavin, there are so many times when I want to break through to generosity, to clarity, to bravery. I can feel those things just out of my reach."

"Look," he said, "I'm not going to pretend that I had no intimation of this—but I tell you again that it's not simple. Too many people are involved—too much decency. I think that there are things you don't understand about yourself. Or about Steve. Or Sara. Or me. For I'm involved too, you know."

"You mustn't be—"

"No one can beg off in a situation like this. I can't. I don't want to. No matter what we are talking about—my kids, your husband, your work, food—it's happiness to be with you. I had almost forgotten the feeling of such happiness. It's a man-woman relationship that takes over everything within sight and hearing and feeling. The sparkles on your jacket—the chime on the clock a minute ago—what you tell me and the truth of your face as you speak. A long while ago—with Anne—I used to have that. Not after Ronny was born. Never after that."

"Early this summer," Jennifer began but she did not finish. She had been sitting on a bench covered with white velvet, facing the girl's picture. Her black chiffon dress drifted along the white velvet. As she stood up she moved toward him, her hands out until he took them in his own. She said again, "It's good to get things out of your system." The words were lame and evasive but her hands were grateful, almost tender.

"We were going to have a brandy. I must get it."

"No, I'd rather go without it. I don't need any more to drink tonight nor any more to think about. I've had all I can handle in both departments. Will you take me back to my shelter?"

"If you want that. And if we can plan what we'll do tomorrow night on the way."

"Not tomorrow night. That's too soon."

"Let me have all your free time. All your nights after work."

"That's impossible. You must have other engagements."

"If there are any, I'll cancel them. I've no present personal obligations. Ronny is spending this month in Maine with the family of a girl who's also going to Europe in the fall—Pete's sailing at Martha's Vineyard or thereabouts—and that last visit of mine to DeSoto this time didn't do Anne much good. It can't be helped and I'm on call if I'm needed. The doctor says there's a psychiatrist in Austria—" He put that thought aside and Jennifer felt him come back to her.

He said, "What I was afraid of was that you'd be bogged down with dates and people. But you say you aren't, and think of all the things we can do—must do. You must have a flight with me—let me show you the city from on top—and do you like ballet? The Russians are going to be here."

"I saw that in the paper. I was hoping—I thought I might go alone."

"Not a chance of that. And we'll dine—I suggested the Maisonette tonight because I wasn't certain—of us—and it's a safe take-off, but there are places with more flavor. We'll try them all—and some night wander down Broadway and be crowded and commonplace and stop at Nedick's. And we'll have dinner here. I must present Eaton to you. Shall we skip El Morocco?"

"Willingly—Steve had an expense account there. But—"

"Don't begin resisting. You're not a person to go through a lot of motions. Let's just decide to be together every night after work—why not? Why not?"

"Yes," said Jennifer, as his question hung over her, "why not? Until you get tired of me. I don't suppose it will be very long—it can't be. So why not?"

"Lovely girl—"

He did not like her hotel. He surveyed it as he took her to the elevator and said, "You described it. Faceless. When you get out of the elevator you always have to think again whether to go left or right."

"How did you know?"

"I know what your room is like. You've moved the bed closer to the window and if you have a meal sent up there's not quite enough space to get the cart past the bureau."

"You've been snooping."

"You should get out of here. You know I have a friend who has a suite at the St. Regis—he keeps it for the use of people who come to town. If that happens to be available—I can find out in the morning—it's a very attractive apartment. This friend of mine furnished it himself."

"But that's not for me," said Jennifer. "Don't ask about it on my account."

He was holding the door of the self-service elevator open, not allowing it to start, covering her with his glance.

"I suppose not," he said slowly.

She held the door open a second longer. "I go to the left when I get there," she said. "I remember. Good night, Gavin. How can I thank you?"

"I'll call you about five tomorrow."

He telephoned shortly after five and suggested taking a short flight in his plane. The weather was perfect and he knew a good seafood place up the shore. They could make it in less than two hours. "Don't dress," he told her, "but take a wrap of some sort. I'll pick you up at the hotel at half past six."

She hurried back to it and found a box from Bergdorf's lying on her bed. A mistake of course—and then she saw her name and address on the label.

Hesitantly she opened the box, folding back the crisp, clean tissue paper and saw a cardigan, the yellow sweater she had told him she had wanted long ago and not been able to buy then, a very soft, very plain sweater of finest wool.

The card said, *It's high time you had that sweater. You don't want it to be the odd sixpence you never get out of the world. Thank you for last night. And tonight. And tomorrow. Gavin.*

She lifted it happily—it would be ridiculous not to accept it—this was something woven out of memory and conversation. She would wear it tonight.

Flying between the stars and the surf that would appear in white rolls and then vanish, alone in the plane with its pilot, was strange and exciting and curiously unfrightening. Jennifer had flown in commercial planes fairly often and once taken a chartered flight with business friends of Steve's. On that one she had some qualms of fear. But tonight there was none. Gavin Bennett's confidence, his obvious experience and skill, his rapport with his machine and with the elements, freed her to enjoy the beauty and speed. He did not talk very much, only now and then explaining some device in the plane or identifying some landmark so that she would know what lay below. There was no trace of sentiment in his manner and he did not act as if they were doing anything out of the ordinary.

But it went on and she felt it—that happiness of which he had spoken the night before when everything that was felt or heard or seen—the sudden flight of some dark birds, the turning signal of a lighthouse, the unknown voice on the radio—was absorbed in the relationship between them, never to be shared by anyone else, never to be released by one of them because it also belonged to the other.

Their dinner was late and simple, lobsters caught an hour before, greens, brown bread. Gavin urged Jennifer to have the three drinks, his second plus her two. He had only one cocktail because he was the pilot, but he said that flight to him was a stronger stimulant than alcohol. On the way back to the city he talked more than he had at first, putting into words what flying did for him. He told her that he could fly out of disappointment or worry because those things had no power after a person reached high altitudes— Such things, he said, were earthbound.

"Do you know what I mean?"

"I never have until tonight," said Jennifer, "but I know now. I feel that too. My doubts—the should I or shouldn't I?—the insecurity and the loneliness too—they are earthbound. I left a lot of things thousands of feet below me tonight. I've never felt more secure—here where I suppose anything could happen to us."

"Lean this way," he said. "Give me your hand—the other—take hold here—now you have the controls—doesn't it feel safe?"

It was after midnight when he settled the plane in its hangar at the airfield and they walked to the parking lot where he had left the car he was using tonight. Last night he had driven a polished and elegant coupe. This one was open, its windows and top sliding into grooves at a touch.

"Would you like to drive?" he asked.

"Will you trust me with your beautiful machine?"

"You've been trusting me. I wish you would take over the car."

She put it in gear and said, "I love to drive. But I've never had my hands on a Jaguar before."

"I've had bad luck with them. The last Jag I had was stolen."

"Nothing's safe in New York any more."

"Believe it or not my car was stolen in our holy little village, DeSoto."

"I didn't hear anything about that. When?"

"At the time it didn't seem important. It was on the day of the steeplechase. When Tom Bayard was thrown. I was told by someone that a car was stolen from the Bayard garage on that same day. I suppose some gang was operating. But Sara had her mind on other things, poor girl—she may not even have known it. I meant to ask her about it the other night when I was at her house but I forgot. They never did catch up with the thief who got away with my car. It was insured, of course, but that's not a satisfying answer."

She was on the point of fitting something she knew to the fact of the car theft. She was reminded of something, but a vivid picture of Sara as she must have looked the other night blotted out the half-emergent memory.

She asked, "Was Miles Halliday there at Sara's the night you were there?"

"Oh no, Miles only comes to DeSoto in the season, when things are social enough to be worth it."

"He was there in August. He came to see Sara. He said so. Do you know that he would like to marry Sara?"

"Is that his latest quip?"

"I didn't take it seriously either at first. Then he said something to me that made me sure that he was really thinking about it, wishing he could. And Sara is special with Miles—I've felt that before when he talks about her. It may not be soft or kind talk but there's no mockery."

"She'd never take Miles. She couldn't live with his snobbery."

"I suppose not."

"Sara will marry of course. That's in the cards. She's realistic about marriage. In fact she's one of the few women I've ever known who is."

"You mean that she doesn't take it seriously?"

"Seriously, yes. But if a marriage is no good—or if it's over for good, as it was in Tom's case—she accepts that. As many people can't—or don't."

"Maybe too many people do."

"I don't think that's true, Jenny."

"It's a contract for life—at least that's what people agree when they take it on."

"It's a contract that people wouldn't let themselves in for in any other phase of their lives." Gavin spoke almost with anger. He said, "I know a lot about contracts—for life insurance, real estate, contracts for selling things or employment— Have you any idea how much there is in the fine print, the outs that are offered if circumstances alter or get out of control? Do you know that fools and incompetent people and children are prevented from signing contracts? Because they might cheat on them? Or default? But when it's a question of marriage any boy or girl in a highly emotional, maybe hysterical state of mind can rattle off, 'For richer, for poorer, till death do us part.' When they are thinking of almost anything except poverty or sickness or death—more likely of how they look and the wedding breakfast and the presents. Most people who get married don't realize what they're promising. Half of them probably aren't competent to make promises or to keep them."

"How bitter you are!"

"Just trying to be honest. Take me. I've looked at my own marriage pretty squarely for what it was. I was twenty-four, ambitious, full of sap—and there was Anne, lovely as a girl could seem, wanting to be married like all her friends. I wasn't after her money—I was too sure of myself for that—but it was a pretty glamorous break for a young fellow who had come out of a miner's cottage. So I said, 'For richer, for poorer,' but believe me I was thinking it was going to be for richer. I was going to see to that. And I said, 'In sickness and in health'—what did I know about sickness? I'd never had anything but measles and mumps and I thought that Anne might have a bad cold or a baby and if she did you bet I'd take care of her."

He said after a minute, "I learned. I learned that a woman can turn on her own child, resent it the way Anne did Ronny. I found out that health isn't a matter of having a cold in the head. It's still a mystery, even to the doctors. I did the best I could."

"I know that."

"How can you know?"

"Doing your best has left its mark on you," she said. "Suffering—trying—"

"The worst of it is that those two kids of mine have to fight it out by themselves. And I realize that they must have been fighting it out for years."

"Let them fight it."

"As you had to do," he said with sudden gentleness.

"And that left its mark on me."

"Take your own marriage," said Gavin, coming back to his argument. "Steve came along and wanted you. You had a job that you liked, but marrying is a better dish for a girl than a job—at least that's what girls think, isn't it?"

"It's true," said Jennifer. "I could get another job or keep mine, but Steve wouldn't come along again. If I'd had to make a choice, I'd have taken him—but I didn't have to choose. And I was still afraid—"

"You still are. But you made the contract with Steve."

"In the chapel of a New York church where neither of us had ever been before. I went back there only once. Yes, I made the contract—I said all those things. I meant them when I repeated them after the minister. They sounded beautiful—I remember that too."

"But you weren't realizing what they let you in for. You said, 'Till death do us part,' but you weren't thinking of death."

"I was thinking of life. I was frightened and ignorant. A virgin. And I could hardly wait."

He said, as if he hadn't heard that, "If you turn left at the next stop light there won't be so much traffic."

182

He seemed to have decided that they had reached the end of what had to be discussed tonight.

"Wasn't that Gavin Bennett with you in the bar at Twenty One last night?" asked Geoffrey Clark.

The question was like the prick of an electric shock. She said, "Yes, he's a neighbor of ours in DeSoto."

"DeSoto must be quite a place."

"It's a country village," said Jennifer.

"Where big shots like Bennett go."

"Down there we don't think of people as big shots."

"Just as neighbors," said Geoffrey.

"That's right."

She couldn't openly resent what he said or the slight implication that went along with it. But she did not repeat it to Gavin. She was sorry that they had gone to Twenty One last night while they were deciding how to spend the rest of the evening. It had been a restless one—first those drinks—then viewing a French motion picture dealing adroitly with passion that had to be transferred to themselves, clarified, cleaned and rejected—then the long loiter in a night club, eating without hunger, watching the show and thinking of themselves.

This can't go on, she told herself after Geoffrey had gone out of her office. It's been wonderful and I'll never forget it, but I must go back to where I belong. Do I belong anywhere? Gavin talked about the contract I made. I'll keep it. I'll call Steve—I'll tell him I'm coming back—I'll do better when I get home.

She put through the call. The voice that answered was strange, the voice of the servant she had hired to take care of Steve's needs.

"Mr. Cooper's residence."

His residence, not mine.

"No, ma'am, he's not at home."

"Do you know where I can reach him?"

The drawling voice had not recognized Jennifer's nor that the call came from New York. It answered, "If you call Mrs. Sara Bayard's house you reach him there. The number am—"

"I know the number," said Jennifer and put down the phone. But she did not call Sara's house. She sat for a while in the silent office, accepting rejection. For that was what it was. Stephen had not called her for days. He did not want to talk to her and he did not want to have her come back. He was with Sara and perhaps Sara was already closer to him than his wife. So Sara was the one who should be Steve's wife. Face up to it, Jennifer told herself. Everyone else has, except you.

The telephone rang. "You're working too late," said Gavin.

"I'm leaving now."

"When can I come for you?"

"Give me an hour and I'll be ready," Jennifer said.

It was like coming into light and warmth to hear his voice tonight, to know that he loved her, wanted to be with her, understood the person she was as no one ever had before. Stephen never had, nor ever would. She told herself that as she dressed, bathed, hurried, running from something and toward something.

"What shall we do tonight?" asked Gavin.

"What would you like to do?"

He said, his hands idle on the wheel of the car, "Surely you know."

"I know."

"Isn't it time?"

"Perhaps—yes—I think so, Gavin."

He had made plans for this. In case of this. She was conscious of that, for there was no wavering or indecision about where they were going. It was on Long Island—she remembered the crossing and the sweet mixture of smells of wind and water. The inn was beautiful and quiet—"Don't worry, darling, I own the place," he said at one point. But it wouldn't have mattered to Jennifer. The important thing was to have it over—to commit herself—all through the hours she met the surprises and the turbulence and the duty to comfort him as they came in turn.

"Are you all right?"

Gavin looked happy and boyishly nervous as he asked. Jennifer had worked all day in occasional astonishment that she could work so well.

"I'm fine."

"Not sorry—never be sorry, Jennifer."

"No," she said hesitantly. "All I feel is that I am no longer quite I. Probably that's all to the good, but I must get used to it."

Tonight he had been waiting for her in the lobby of her hotel.

"How soon will you be ready?" he asked.

"Where are we going?"

"I've ordered dinner. For eight o'clock. We haven't eaten there before."

"Shall I dress up?"

"A little."

She wore the black chiffon again. Tonight he was driving the polished town car and they did not talk, nor need to talk.

"But not here," said Jennifer, as he stopped the car. "This is—"

"Yes, here tonight."

"In your own house?"

"I wish to God it were yours. I wish I could give it to you. Come, they're expecting us."

The butler opened the door with formality.

"Eaton, I want to introduce you to Mrs. Cooper. Mrs. Cooper is one of our friends from DeSoto."

Eaton bowed and said that was a beautiful part of the country. A maid was in the dressing room where Jennifer left her scarf, and drinks were served before dinner in the room where the portraits of Peter and Ronny hung. Jennifer knew what Gavin was trying to do. It was to restore any dignity and self-respect that she might have lost.

"I love you for this," she told him when they were alone.

"I love you for all reasons."

Dinner was served. Gavin had not put her across from him in what must have been Anne's place but at his right. He talked of light matters, touched on serious but impersonal things, and Jennifer found answers. But she did not know what she was eating or drinking or whether she was coherent. She was only aware of a sadness, a sorrow that was rising in her, aware that this should not have been done, must never be done again. She must tell him that they had come to the barrier of the impossible—for her and for himself.

Somewhere a telephone was ringing. Then Eaton came into the room, at a little faster pace than previously, and said something to Gavin in an undertone. Gavin frowned.

"I'm sorry—will you excuse me, Jennifer—I have to take this call."

"Of course." She lit a cigarette and made it last, smoking lightly. He was gone for some minutes and when he returned his face was bleak, disturbed and distant, charged with unhappy news.

He did not sit down. "This is awful."

She pushed back her chair.

"If something has happened, Gavin, don't bother with dinner. Or me."

He said, "That call was from DeSoto. I'm afraid I'll have to go down. Anne's in a bad way."

"Something unexpected?"

"No. They warned me," he said drearily. "The despondency— it's been like this before—she gets almost impossible to control and then I'm the only one who can—unless I put her in an institution and I don't want to do that."

"Don't do that," said Jennifer. "Never if you can help it."

"I asked the nurse if tomorrow would be soon enough. But they're all rather hysterical."

"You can fly down tonight, can't you?"

186

"Oh God," he said. "Oh Jenny, my love—" and stopped as Eaton came back into the room.

Jennifer said, "Will you call me a cab, Eaton?"

"I'll drive you back to the hotel," said Gavin quickly.

"No—it takes time and you'll want to get to the airport quickly. Please, Eaton, at once."

The butler looked at her with respect and left. Gavin moved and Jennifer said, "No!"

"But," he sounded bewildered, "if we hadn't come here tonight—"

"It was the sweetest mistake a man ever made," said Jennifer gently. "I'm glad you made it, Gavin."

"Our plans—tomorrow night we were going to see the ballet."

"That doesn't matter—"

"I have the tickets in my wallet—my secretary picked them up today." He pulled the leather case out of his pocket and took the tickets out of it as if he needed to prove something to himself.

"I must go now—you must go—you'll be all right—fly safely— Thank you, Eaton, I'll be there immediately."

"Take these anyway— Oh Jennifer—"

"Thank you," she said and took the tickets he was offering her in a helpless gesture of what she knew had to be farewell.

13

ALL DAY it rained and the steady weeping of the skies was what the weather should be on that day of misery for Jennifer—bad news from Asia, confusion in Washington and a taxicab strike in New York that was called with no warning to the public. With delay and extra efforts, things that had to be done were accomplished, and the business of putting together copy for future issues of *Portfolio*, calculating its increase in circulation and boasting about it in advertising, went on as if it were important too. Jennifer had little time to think about herself, not that she wanted to, but she carried around a weight of futility and mistakes. Aggravated by the sleeplessness of the last two nights, it left her exhausted to the point of being lightheaded when at last the curtain came down on the working day. Her companions disappeared as quickly as they always did in various directions. She organized her desk and faced the evening alone.

After ten evenings spent with Gavin Bennett—no, it was eleven she found when she began to count them up—they had formed in her a habit of anticipation, of happiness spiced with daring. She had not known from day to day what would happen—only the direction, only that she would not be alone. Tonight she could not even go back to the pattern in which she had been living until Gavin had telephoned her the first time. Then, lonely as she had been, she at least had a decision to make and a problem before her. She hadn't burned her bridges completely. She possibly could return to DeSoto, Sara might marry Miles or someone else, Steve might— The things that probably would not happen could have happened two weeks ago. Not now. The sick distaste she felt for herself included what she had done to Gavin. It had been a happy interlude with him—the fine restaurants, the posing in his expensive cars and his plane, but the gaiety had evaporated as if it had never existed. Perhaps, she thought, it never did exist. He wanted me to be his mistress—he wanted it very much. He believed that it could be arranged with delicacy and without coarseness— He tried so hard. But I should have known better. Since I was a child, since Selma had her men around, I've known how it goes. The other night when that telephone call came I didn't yell or fight, but I suppose I felt pretty much as Selma did when a man who belonged to someone else had to tell her so.

I shan't stay on *Portfolio*, she thought, tearing today's sheet off her calendar, dropping the record of that horrid bit of time into her wastebasket. Because Geoffrey will guess—his whole personal life is made up of affairs with women and he would see no difference between his and mine. Is there a difference? She snapped off the desk light which had trudged through the dark day with her, put on the jacket of her linen suit and went out to meet the streets.

They were strangely empty at this hour when automobiles should have been darting by on the avenues and cross streets, wangling for every possible space. Several crowded buses rolled by, ignoring the clusters of people on the corners, and private cars, seeming almost intolerably privileged, sped by proudly. It was growing dark and people were hurrying on foot as if racing with darkness. No yellow cabs, no lighted tops requesting passengers were visible.

The helplessness of so many confronted by distance and the general emergency made Jennifer feel sorry for them instead of herself as she watched and was glad that her own hotel was only six blocks away. She decided to cross to Lexington Avenue and have something to eat—there was a steak house which would not be crowded on the night of a taxi strike and a double martini might make her hungry. She thought—we were eating that soufflé last night, it was the second course and—since then—I had some coffee this morning but only that Coke at the desk after that. I couldn't face food today.

She stopped for a newspaper at a corner kiosk and took it to the steak house to read while she had supper.

"Very dry—make it a double one, please. A boneless sirloin—rare, very rare."

Gavin would not have chosen this place for dinner certainly, she thought, trying hard to make the thought amusing. But it was not. Tonight he was in DeSoto, doing what he could and must. When his wife was calmed and sleeping, what would he do? Ask Sara if he could come in for a drink? Gavin and Sara—and no doubt Steve—would be in that beautiful place, where they all belonged—and here I am. Jennifer rubbed that contrast into her mind—wiping probable grease off a steel knife with a paper napkin.

She became a little dizzy after the large cocktail but she ordered a second one with the steak, and was hungry when it was served. She read about the strike, the dangers of it, the inconveniences, the reasons. She read about deaths in Vietnam. She tried to make herself not matter, seem of no account. Finally the waiter said, "Anything more, madam?" and she said no, gave him a dollar and took her bill to the cashier, waiting in line behind a man who enjoyed staring at her.

There was more money in her purse than she usually carried

with her but she had spent very little lately. Gavin had been doing the spending. As she opened her bag she saw in it the little black satin purse that she had carried last night and must have tossed absently or angrily into the larger one when she went back to the hotel from Gavin's house. She couldn't remember doing that. To avoid the stare of the man waiting in line with her, she opened the evening purse as if she were looking for something. There were dollar bills, the new lipstick, a still folded handkerchief and two pieces of pasteboard. She remembered—those ballet tickets. Lifting one of them she read that the performance was at the Modjeska Theater, West on 55th. Quite close. Why don't you go, she asked her spinning mind? Why waste the tickets? Get hard, face up to facts. Tickets are tickets, and cost money.

She was glad that she had done it. When she slid into the seat in the theater, which was already darkened, she had the first moments of peace that she had known in hours. The music gave her the release from herself that she had failed to find in work, or in the newspaper or in alcohol. The dancers took her into their world. She went along with the fantasy, the delicate romance, the pursuit, resistance and yielding— She thought, that was the way Steve looked one night last summer—I remember how beautiful his shape was in the shadows of the room.

But the lights came on, exposing her. It was the entr'acte and people were rising all around her to make their way to the foyer. The dancers were gone, might not have been. Jennifer felt the nausea of loneliness close to desertion. The seat next to her seemed very conspicuously, mockingly empty. She left the theater by the first possible exit, behind one of the boxes. On the curb she stopped from habit to look for a cruising taxi and the empty street reminded her that there probably would be none. This was 55th Street and her hotel was near the corner of 58th and Third Avenue. It's not much of a walk, she told herself. When you first came to New York you always walked home from the theater and much farther than you will tonight.

From Broadway she would cross to the Avenue of the Americas

and walk one block up that street, then cross to Fifth. It was probably best to stagger the distance by going along lighted and wide streets when she could. Not so desolate, she told herself. But the familiar area was eerie tonight. The theaters were not out and it was misty enough to be almost raining, so that the usual crowd of Broadway strays was under cover instead of on parade. On Fifth Avenue she walked to 58th, with only mannequins in the shop-windows for company. But now she felt almost carelessly sure of herself. There were less than four blocks to go, to Madison, to Park, then toward Lexington until her own hotel would be in sight. She stopped and looked both ways on Fifth once more, just in case a taxi might come along. There was none, but a handsome, polished car like Gavin's town one raced by her. The memory drove her quickly on her way again. She reached Madison and crossed with the green light to the east side.

She was between Park and Lexington when the two men—who sounded more like boys whose voices had only recently become heavy—came out from the shadows beside one of the flights of brownstone steps. Unlighted steps. Each of them took one of her arms in a hard, practiced way and a hand came over her mouth. They pulled her back from the center of the sidewalk silently.

Jennifer remembered what she had been told would work if she were attacked and said through the covering hand, "Twenty dollars—let me go."

One of the boys said softly, "The girl's loaded—" and her bag was snatched away, its straps tearing her hand.

"A swell—one of them debutantys—"

"Look for her dimons—"

"Better down the stairs—they're clear—dimons and what else you got to give us, girlie?"

The low vicious voices were like their movements. There was an unlighted area below the street level. She remembered that Stephen had said it was dangerous—he had said— Jennifer saw the dark steps. If they pulled her down there—she let herself go limp, then suddenly jerked back with a strength and violence she did not know she had. She flung the hand off her mouth long enough for a scream—it came out wildly, "Steve! Steve!"

Incredibly a police car had rounded the corner. The boys threw her down and ran. She was flat on the sidewalk, stars flew before her eyes.

"You all right, lady?"

There were two policemen. For a second she wasn't aware that it still wasn't attack. One of the officers was running down the street after the boys—the other lifted and propped her against his shoulder.

She straightened her body. "I'm all right," she said breathlessly. "You were just in time."

"They hurt you?"

"No—they got my bag—it doesn't matter—I don't care."

"You shouldn't be out alone like this," said the officer more reprovingly than with sympathy.

"I couldn't get a taxi."

"Don't you know there's a strike on?"

"Yes—"

"And then they blame us," he said in a kind of disgust. "Look, a girl ain't safe on the streets alone, don't you know that much?"

"I couldn't help it—"

"You could of stayed home," he said. "Or were you coming home from work?"

"From the theater—"

"You should of had a man with you."

"Yes—I should—"

"Get in the car now and you can rest up at the station."

"No—I live right near here. I live at the Wilmington Hotel—next block—"

"You ought to make a complaint."

"I couldn't see them—I'm all right—"

The other policeman came back. He said, "No sign of them."

"Girl says they didn't hurt her. Just got her purse."

"Much in it?"

"Not very much," said Jennifer.

"Sure you're all right? Nothing happened to you tonight?"

"Nothing happened to me tonight," she repeated. "I'll get back by myself now—to the hotel."

"She says she lives at the Wilmington."

"I better go with you," said the policeman who had picked her up. He was still disapproving, and evidently he didn't quite believe her. He walked by her side to the hotel, the other officer cruising watchfully in the car behind them. The policeman lectured, "These kids got no sense of right or wrong, they do anything— they got no more morals than animals—you got to take that in, you got to play it safe—this world ain't moral any more—that's a fact."

"I know."

"You want me to come in with you?"

"I'd rather you didn't—"

"Well," he said, looking at the Wilmington with respect and at Jennifer in the light of the doorway. "You really got a room here?"

"Yes. And thank you—"

He wasn't satisfied. But she didn't look like a tough girl. And if she didn't want to come to the station and make a complaint— "Well," he decided, "you got a room in a beautiful hotel like this, you stay safe in it. Better get to bed. You look shook up. Of course it's enough to shake anyone up, to have those bums jump you."

She managed the elevator, sent it to her floor—went to the left, closed her door and bolted it. The policeman's homily rang in her head. "It's enough to shake anyone up—this world ain't moral!"

Then she fainted across the bed and did not hear the telephone when it rang persistently.

14

OFTEN in DeSoto the temper of the day would change very suddenly. Usually about noon or soon afterward. The morning might be sunny and brilliant but at midday clouds would gather hastily, thrusting up from behind the mountains, and the short but violent tempests which the natives called showers would drive humans and beasts to the nearest cover until they passed over, sometimes leaving a broad rainbow as a kind of apology.

There was a shower during the hunter trials in September, which were being held, as they usually were, at the Loomis place. Most of the annual sporting events which had some social flavor were divided up among the residents who had estates large enough to allow generous hospitality. The Pipers always had open house after the horse show and the Altons were hosts during the Thanksgiving season, giving a barbecue for all the country people who allowed horsemen to ride over their lands.

Archer and Bee Loomis managed their affair very well. Their estate was like them, carefully correct in its chosen way, almost to faultlessness. Not especially historic in itself, their property had acquired history as it was developed. The Loomises had bought ancient houses in the region and wrecked them to get old bricks and rare paneling and fireplaces once built laboriously by the hands of slaves. They took great pride in the hand-hewn timbers of their rooms and the locust pegs which held them together. They had achieved a large and very comfortable establishment, where a dozen horses could be stabled, married children and their friends well entertained and an occasional community festivity set up in the meadow near their private riding ring.

Practically everyone for miles around who took any interest in riding was almost sure to be at the hunter trials, along with a good many onlookers who did not know exactly what was going on. Hearty sandwiches and soft drinks were served at long trestle tables on the grounds, and in the house, after word-of-mouth or telephone invitations, thirty or forty chosen people were offered stronger drinks and provided with lunch from a row of English silver-covered dishes set out on the authentic cherry hunt board in the dining room.

Steve Cooper had no entries of his own in the trials, but he was greatly interested in the performance of Dark Melody, a young hunter that Ross Painter had trained. Steve coveted Dark Melody. He had not analyzed a growing reluctance to ride Sara's horses, but since Tom Bayard's death the reluctance had existed, confused with the desire to have a mount of his own. Today he stayed out on the Loomis grounds, mixing with the general crowd, though he had been told that lunch was now being served in the house.

"Looks like a shower," said Joe Harris, coming up with a paper cup of well-spiked Coca-Cola in one hand. Joe went to all local events because a real estate sale often began with an unexpected or unplanned contact.

"It may go around the mountain," said Steve. "Aga says you never need to worry about rain down here until it falls on you."

"Can I do anything for you?" asked Joe, indicating his cup. "I got a pint with me."

"Not right now."

"I've been waiting to have a talk with you, Steve. Called you yesterday."

"I haven't been home much."

"That's what the girl said. And that Mrs. Cooper is away."

"She had to go to New York."

"You alone up there then?"

It was none of Harris' business and the remark annoyed Steve more than was natural, rubbed him the wrong way. He said yes abruptly and was moving away when Harris put a hand on his arm.

"What I wanted to talk to you about," said Joe Harris, "was your house. That's why I called."

"What about it?"

"There's someone who's interested in it. Wants to know if you'd consider selling it."

"Too bad he wasn't around a year ago," said Steve. "I'm living in the house now. You'll have to find him some other place."

"The thing is that he doesn't want any other place. He's got his eye on yours."

"Who is this?"

"He's a man called Dave Delaney. You must have seen him around. He rides, so he told me."

"Oh, that fellow—yes, I know who he is. You're crazy, Joe—he's kidding you—he's never been inside our house, so far as I know. He doesn't really want it."

"Maybe he hasn't been inside it but he's got a fixation."

"Just talk—"

"I was inclined to think that. But you know what? He made an offer of forty-five thousand."

The figure halted Steve. He repeated, "Forty-five thousand— He hasn't got that kind of money, has he?"

"I think he has. He deals in second-hand cars or auto parts—or he used to. He says he's thinking of retiring. That's where the money comes from, and a rough customer like him can build it up in autos. He's a bit secretive, doesn't brag—rather the other way, unassuming. But he came down here last spring, took a liking to what he saw and means to stay apparently. If he can find what he wants. You know how it is—I do anyway, for it often happens in my line of business—when somebody takes a fancy to a place you can't budge them. You know what I think? I believe I could get this nut up to fifty thousand. And you know it's not a place that most people would be willing to take on. This is the first offer I ever had for that house of yours, the first that sounded halfway firm. You know how it hung on the market ever since your father died until you thought I wasn't making any effort. But it's not so easy, believe you me, to find a buyer for a big place that looks like a lot of upkeep. If anyone wants a job of that size, they build to suit themselves."

"I still think it's a lot of conversation, Joe. Anyway, we're settled in. In a way you might say we've burned our bridges. I severed connections with New York." But Jennifer hasn't, he thought. He finished, "This is home now for my wife and myself."

"You could build something modern for a lot less than what he offers. Take that place of the Martins' just below you. I know that cost under thirty—and it's got all the new features. They're crazy about it."

"Jennifer likes Chestnut Hill." She did at first, thought Steve as he said that.

"Well," said Joe Harris, "I had to put it up to you. And it's a proposition that, if I were you, I'd give very serious consideration to. There was a time last year when you said you'd take forty— remember? If I could get forty."

"I remember. But the picture's changed. Not that I don't appreciate your keeping it in mind, Joe."

"That's my business. Anyway if you want to think it over I can keep this character dangling for a bit. It's often a good way to build up a price—play it cool. There comes the rain—"

It had suddenly torn rips in the skies. There was sharp thunder and the less privileged of the groups on the grounds began to scurry to their cars, the others toward the refuge of the big house.

"See you," said Joe Harris and moved off with his hand over his paper cup to prevent too much dilution.

Steve went in the other direction with the astonishing offer rumbling in his mind, even though he did not fully credit it. Fifty thousand dollars—Joe was dreaming. He was letting himself be taken in by that man Delaney. There would be a six percent commission for Joe—forty-seven thousand clear. The property is worth a lot more than that, Steve said to himself with a seller's reaction. You couldn't build it today for twice the money. But nobody would build it. This would certainly surprise Jenny—but she wouldn't want to sell—or would she? I couldn't get her on the phone last night— She must be having herself a blast. She doesn't want to be called at the magazine because she thinks it's bad for discipline for her to get personal calls there, and I haven't been able to reach her at the hotel for a week. She never seems to be there. But that doesn't mean anything. That's the way it is in New York.

"You should learn to come in out of the rain," said Sara when he went into the dining room. In the mess of sweaters and plaid jackets she stood out, different and defined in a cherry-colored suit of corduroy with deep pockets. He had never seen her wear it before.

"I like your outfit," he told her.

"Then I shall like wearing it," she said simply. "Ross says that Dark Melody is going to do very well."

Steve thought, forty-seven thousand—I could buy Dark Melody for eighteen hundred. I can buy him anyway if I arrange a small loan at the bank here and I could pay it off in six months the way things are now—because Jennifer— It's a hell of a note for me to be able to buy a horse because my wife is working.

"Kidneys and mushrooms," said Bee Loomis to him, lifting the cover of a silver dish, "one of the specialities of the house. What do you hear from Jennifer?"

"Not much. She's pretty busy, I guess."

"Gavin Bennett came down last week," said Bee, "he took Anne back to New York. Did you know that Anne isn't in good shape? She was all right for a while—seemed so much better—then slipped back. Desperate melancholy. They finally sent for Gavin again. I thought they should. I told the nurse so. While he was here, Gavin was very low in his mind. I asked him if he'd seen anything of Jennifer in New York—that night when we were all at Sara's you remember he said he was going to look her up."

"Did he?"

"Yes, he said they had dinner together. I wanted him to stay over for the trials today. I thought he should, that it would take his mind off things. But he didn't feel like seeing a lot of people, he said. I'm so sorry for him. Oh, take more than that. There are vats of it in the kitchen."

Steve took more.

Sara came back to stand beside him. "Do you think it's going to clear up?" she asked. "Ross doesn't. He says it's going to rain all afternoon."

"It could. Those clouds looked as if they meant business."

"Then we'll have to postpone the trials."

He said absently, "That's right."

"What's the matter, Steve? What's on your mind?"

"Nothing. Why?"

"You sound as if you're not here."

"Sorry. I was thinking of a proposition that sort of took me by surprise."

"Propositions can do that," said Sara. "I've had a couple lately that knocked me for a loop."

"Good ones?"

"Not just what I wanted," she said, "but what can you do?"

"Do about what?"

"The weather," said Sara. "And people. What can you do about either? It's better to face up to that."

"You always do."

"Well, I like all kinds of weather," said Sara.

"And all kinds of people?"

"I won't go that far."

Archer Loomis came in, his face red, moist and deliberately cheerful. He said, "It's really coming down now. Even if it lets up it would be chancy for green hunters. Everybody wants the trials postponed. So I said, until Friday, if we get a good day then. This looks like an afternoon for a little drinking and a little gambling."

Steve did not want to stay for either amusement. As soon as he could break away he left the house and went first to have another look at Dark Melody, who was now back in the van.

"Too bad," he told the horse, "but you'll have your big day coming."

"Say that to me too," said Sara.

She had followed him out and now stood beside the horse van—it was her van. Her red suit was a splash of brilliant color against the dripping green of trees and grass.

"You'll ruin your suit."

"It's water-resistant," she said, "like me. Why are you running away?"

"I'm not. But I have some things on my mind and since they've called off the trials—"

"Will you come over tonight?"

"It's a mean night for a party."

"There won't be any party. I thought we might talk over propositions—yours and mine."

"Sara, at the moment I'm a little bothered. There are some things I have to talk over with Jenny and I haven't been able to get in touch with her."

"Is Jennifer coming back?"

She asked it outright, with no softening. She didn't ask when Jennifer was coming back.

Steve said, "She hasn't said that she wasn't. Jenny would tell me. But there's an outside chance that something might change the picture for both of us. I don't know."

"Why don't you find out?"

"That's what I'm going to do. I'm going up to New York tomorrow if I can't reach her by phone."

"Yes, you must." Sara took a few steps toward the house and turned again. She said, "Let's talk it out tonight, Steve. Or we'll always wonder, always be mixed up. Please come. But after dinner. I want to talk with you, not eat with you tonight. And I never want to see kidneys and mushrooms again!"

"I'll come along, Sara. After eight."

He had no plans for the broken afternoon ahead of him. He wasn't sure of what he would do with it. But he knew that he did not want to be part of the company at the Loomis house, paired with Sara, subtly committed to a situation that he knew he must look at with honesty from all the angles.

Today he was driving Jennifer's little open car, and as he slid into the seat behind the wheel he wondered if she ever missed it. Or missed DeSoto. Or himself. She had been reluctant for them to buy the car but it had delighted her to own it. When she went away she had said that she couldn't take it to New York, that it would be a nuisance and an unnecessary expense. Jennifer always considered expense. She always had to, Steve thought, until we were married. And she did afterward. She never seemed to be quite sure that I could take care of everything. Of her. I suppose I knew that. All the time.

Sara never has to think of what things cost. If she wants a new house or a new horse or a red suit, she gets it. Or a husband. There it is. You may have come through the back door to face it, Steve told himself, but there it is. Sara wants a husband and I have a wife. But for Sara I'm in the field.

As he drove toward his own home he passed the Martins' house on the road below the hill. There were lights in the living room and he could see Julius Martin sitting by an open fire, evidently alone. Steve slowed his car, remembering what Joe Harris had told him about that house, that it had cost less than thirty thousand dollars and was very satisfactory for the Martins. They are nice people, thought Steve. Jenny likes them both.

Yielding to an impulse he backed his car to their entrance. Why not drop in and have a visit with Martin? He had often intended to do that but the right occasion had never come.

He said truthfully, as he shook hands with Julius Martin, "You looked so comfortable in here that I thought I'd stop in and see if some of that would rub off on me. Am I interrupting?"

"There's nothing to interrupt. Very glad you stopped," said Julius. "My wife is out doing some errands and I'm doing nothing. My customary occupation."

"It's one of the leading industries around here."

"Can I get you a drink?"

"No, thanks. I've just come away from one. The hunter trials were cancelled because of the weather, and at the Loomis house a lot of our friends are drinking to their frustration."

"It's one way to drown it. Not one I can indulge in myself."

"You probably aren't frustrated."

Julius Martin smiled without irony.

"I try not to be. It's the one thing I can do for my dear wife."

"Aren't you both very happy in DeSoto?"

"We'd better be. But Cicely does miss your wife. Is she still in New York?"

"Yes. They seem to be holding on to her up there."

"That's not surprising. I'm sure that she's as competent as she is charming."

"Jenny felt obligated to help them out on the magazine. It was her old job that was temporarily vacant."

"A person can feel a personal responsibility for that. If you've been valuable to an organization."

"That was about the size of it."

"There are a good many people," said Julius, "who feel guilty anyway when they aren't in the earning world. Men and women both. And there will be a lot more unless we revise the American tradition."

"Revise it how?"

"You may have made a mistake in stopping in here," said Julius with a smile, "and giving me a chance to shoot off my mouth."

"I wish you would."

"Well, stop me if you've heard it," said Julius, "or if I bore you. But in the shape I'm in, all I can do is sit here and try to figure the score. What I mean is that the respectable accepted tradition of America always has been work. No politician used to be respectable unless he said that once a week or more. Work as hard as you can—for as much as you can earn—as long as you hold out. If you didn't you were an idler, a loafer and so an outcast. A few people didn't go along with that but they were exceptions. Filthy rich. Dilettantes. Or unfortunately incapacitated. But now the entire tradition is being questioned. Resisted too."

"Because of earlier retirement?"

"That's part of it of course. But there's also the personal question of whether work in itself is always desirable and synonymous with virtue and good sense. A good many quite young men have that in mind. They want to know not how long a time but how short a time they have to earn. What else they're giving up. If the tradition is obsolete. Maybe we're developing a country that will be built on leisure as well as work. A balance. Naturally I'm defensive. In a mood to believe that. Because I couldn't go on with my profession when I became ill."

"I'm in a mood to believe it too," said Steve with a grin, "because I was let out. I know what you mean by being defensive. I felt disgraced."

"I suppose you did."

"But when I came down here to live, I more or less got over that feeling. I think it's true that some men, even young ones, wonder if the old game is worth the candle. But that doesn't mean that they're going back to the farms. All the statistics show that they're flocking to the cities more and more."

"And in the cities crime and crowding and nervous breakdowns are on the increase," Julius said, "also in the cities the individual has less and less individuality."

"That's why it seemed such a good life down here once we made the break."

"Seemed? Doesn't it stand up?"

"It has for me. I don't know about Jenny, whether or not it did for her. This spring I thought that it did—she seemed very happy. But when this chance to go back to New York came along, she snapped it up."

Julius Martin thought, he must be either blind or bewildered. She didn't want to go. She made herself do it. And he recalled that bright defiance of Jennifer in the twilight around the swimming pool at the Bayard house, when he had listened to Miles Halliday knifing her with insinuations.

He said, "I wonder why she wanted to go."

"She wanted to get back into the mainstream."

"Your wife would never be out of the mainstream, no matter where she is."

"We didn't feel that we were, here in DeSoto. We talked about that more than once. We thought that it's possible to get more perspective on what goes on in the world if you are in a place like this."

"You know, Steve, your house did that for me."

"My house?"

"It's in my line of vision when I lie out on the porch and I do that a good deal of the time. I've wondered why your father—it was your father, wasn't it?—built it. Why he chose the Greek style."

"He was interested in Greece—everything Greek—something of a scholar in that field, I believe."

"I decided that it must be that. Greece has always excited the imaginations of some men—I happen to be one of them. And the more I thought about it the more I convinced myself that I knew what he had in mind. The similarities began to amuse me. Then they rather startled me."

"I'm way behind you," said Steve. "You'll have to make that clearer."

"I figured your father was perhaps a man who came here by accident—"

"It was an accident," said Steve. "It just happened that he came to test the climate, I think. He wasn't too well at the time."

"So he looked about him," Julius Martin said, "and he saw not only better health and a new pattern for himself maybe, but a classic setup. A place for men of leisure, active in sports and outdoor pursuits in the Greek tradition. Where respect might be equal for mental and physical prowess—please remember this is just guessing, just the useless reflection of an invalid."

"Not useless to me. What else did you figure out?"

"He knew the way the Grecian aristocrats had lived—they were accustomed to country life, they developed the skills demanded by life in a small community—you know the city-state was small but it included the lands around it. It was the meeting place of people who lived inside and outside its walls."

"That's certainly DeSoto for you."

"Sure it is. Your father may have seen that, commended it, wanted to mix in it. He saw a place where farmers, craftsmen, tradesmen mingled—a place where there was free time—the mountaineers rocked on their porches and your father reflected in his library. Do you know of many places where the individual gets a better break than in DeSoto? With less criticism?"

"I never thought of it that way."

"I think your father did. And that was why he built a Greek-type house on a hill where the chestnut trees that Greece loved had grown. From his hill he saw fertile pockets between the mountains—you can see similar ones from the mountains on many Greek islands. And grain grew here and grapes for wine—even if we don't produce olives. I'm garrulous—I hope that I haven't offended you. Not knowing your father I have presumptuously built up a character that may not have had any existence."

"I didn't know my father very well," said Steve. "I wish I had."

"You live in his house. It's not an ordinary dwelling."

"No. I used to wish that it were more commonplace—when it was on the market after father's death. But it kind of grows on you. I may as well tell you that my mother never liked it here and, though I came as a boy for school vacations, sometimes I doubt if

206

the place was ever lived in as he wanted it to be. And of course if it doesn't satisfy Jennifer—"

Julius said at a tangent or perhaps it wasn't one, "Living here was hard on Cicely at first. Very hard for months, all last winter. The peace preyed on her. She thought in terms of other environments. The proportions of this little house cramped her—she had always lived with space. But she was incredibly gallant. We have never discussed any lack of satisfaction or regrets. There may have been a great deal of pretense and withholding in Cicely, but she has had a bravery that came—is coming, I think—to contentment. She misses your wife though."

"I miss her," said Steve, and the talk paused, then picked up small coverings like weather and local needs for a while, until at length Steve said, "I must go along. I can't tell you how much I've enjoyed our talk. How I appreciate it."

"Then come again and often. We feel very fortunate that you and Jennifer are our neighbors."

"We feel the same way," said Steve. But shall we be neighbors for long he wondered, depression clutching him suddenly as he went out of the pleasant room.

Where his private drive branched from the highway there were old cypresses on either side, and Steve thought today as he went between them, those were little trees when I first came here—Father must have planted them. Cypresses are Greek trees too. There was a faded green sign reading PRIVATE in an inconspicuous way, and across from that was a marble slab backed by a post with the lettering CHESTNUT HILL carved deeply in it. Years of weather had dulled the letters but they were very legible and looked as if they would always be so.

Father did a job, thought Steve. What Julius Martin has figured out is probably more or less the truth. The longer I've been living here the more I've been conscious of something like that. This isn't an ordinary house and it wasn't built without a big idea back of it.

For he was so determined to have the house, to live here. He used to urge her to come and stay, in spite of the way she felt about it. The memory of one thing his mother had said came back clearly in this moment. Stephen had never allowed his parents' arguments to affect him deeply— He thought now, I used to dodge them. I didn't want to share them. But he recalled that his mother had once said to his father—it must have been bitterly said but a boy would be impervious to that—"Everyone who lives here would rather be someplace else except you!"

And the reason I remember that, Steve said to himself, was because it was one of the few remarks I overheard that bothered me. Because at the time I didn't want to be in any other place. I didn't want to be under an umbrella on a fashionable beach in Florida or on an ocean liner or sitting on the front seat with a chauffeur in somebody's car being driven to some strange big house. I wanted to be here where I could go out to the stables and see the horse that was mine, and come back into the house when I wanted to, where there was the faint sweet smell of years of cooking in the kitchen—that was as close to the smell of home as I ever got when I was a kid. And it was here when I'd come back from a hunt this spring and Jenny was in the kitchen or up in that little room she took such a fancy to. But I suppose she feels just the way my mother did—that she'd rather be anywhere else.

He went into the house with mixed relief and dread today. It was so completely quiet that the silence almost had texture. The temporary cook had gone. Stephen had told her that she need not stay after the morning housework was done, for the day of the hunter trials was always a very social one and he did not want to commit himself to being here for dinner. Susie was not here, but she came and went like a gray drift of wind anyway, so that was not unusual. Nor was Agamemnon around. He was usually puttering within or without the house on some small job of plumbing or carpentering or raking. It was a very empty house. Stephen went through the hall and drawing room and library, thinking again that it couldn't be built today for twice fifty thousand dollars.

208

When he went into the kitchen—and he was tramping through all the rooms to use up his restlessness—he saw that there was a note lying on one of the big work tables. It was not a modern kitchen. There were no slick counters and the oilcloth on the tables had been scrubbed so long that the pattern was gone. But it was a big, able kitchen.

The shapeless, ragged handwriting of the note was Aga's. It read—*Mr. Steve—cannot work on driveway today—my son from New York here on visit. Aga.*

Father named him Agamemnon, Steve remembered. That was when social security began and Aga had to apply for a card. He used to be called Crikey before that, but father thought it wasn't dignified enough for a government record and Aga was very proud of his long, new, Greek name—when he got used to pronouncing it. Father used to roll out all the syllables—the rest of us settled for Aga. Father wanted everyone to be treated with dignity. Julius Martin would say that was his feeling for Greek tradition, for the dignity of the individual. The Greeks never carried it as far as Father did, not so far as to give dignity to servants or slaves. They'd have to today. And Steve thought of Jennifer again, for they had often talked of the problems of Negroes and what they could do to solve them locally, and it would be interesting to bring up this Greek business in that connection. Hell, thought Steve, what I think I miss more than anything is just talking to Jenny.

Martin says that he and his wife miss her. Of course anyone would. What will Jenny say if forty-seven thousand dollars comes out of the blue? Jenny takes money very seriously—but there's no one more generous. She made me raise Aga's wages. And she'll spend money on flowers but not on bottles of perfume and things most women want.

He was back in the library and paused to look at the fireplace. Jennifer said that marble facing was worth a lot of money. She'd found an account book that told what his father paid for it. It was probably still here on the desk. Stephen looked over the row of books between two jasper weights and saw the brown leather notebook. That must be the one. He thumbed through the pages, found the notation—yes, it had cost more than three thousand dollars and that inscription meant, "Be it soon or be it late, men find that sweet turns to bitter and again to love."

Turns to bitter. You bet it can, Steve thought, and was angered. He thought it was anger at the prospect that these valuable marble facings might pass into the possession of a man like Delaney. Steve had always ignored him as much as possible when he turned up at a hunt. Steve always bypassed things and people that were annoying or not worth attention, and this Delaney—he rode well enough but he had very bad manners in the field.

There is probably nothing to it anyway, Steve told himself, and was both reassured and depressed by the thought that Delaney was unlikely to have enough money to buy the house. It was a real estate man's pipe dream, that was all it amounted to. I myself might check on Delaney, he thought. I could drop in at the bank this afternoon—talk with Ed Woolsey, who may be only a country banker but he certainly knows what goes on around here. I'll do that—it will kill the rest of the afternoon and then I'll come back and call Jennifer. She should be at the hotel around six o'clock. Sara said to come over there after dinner. To talk, not to eat, she said. What is she going to talk about? What does she expect me to say? Because even if Jenny doesn't come back, even if I should get rid of this house, even then—

He left the thought unfinished, torn off there. He went out of the house, got in his car and went to the town to see if he could find the banker, Ed Woolsey.

Whatever Sara wore was always right for the hour and the occasion. But the effect never seemed overplanned or contrived. She had chosen the soft blue hostess gown almost carelessly tonight, knowing that it would meet her mood and her intention. It was high-necked and slim and the firelight and lamps played with the color, giving it elusive, changing hues of blue.

"You didn't mind coming?" she asked.

"Of course not. I wanted to. You know that."

"Did you talk to Jenny?"

"No. They are very dumb at that switchboard in her hotel. I left word for her to call back. I tried the magazine office too but that was closed—New York can be so incompetent."

"I suppose she has a great many friends to take up her time."

"She knows a lot of people. I never knew the literary ones—the ones she worked with—except very casually."

Sara moved her face out of the firelight. She said, "They probably wouldn't interest you. I've often wondered—how did you happen to meet Jenny?"

"Happen is right," said Steve. "That was a strange thing. Why, it was this way. I was in public relations with Atlantis, you know, and in that kind of work you get some funny assignments. This magazine *Portfolio*—the one Jenny was with—has a terrific circulation. And they were running some profiles of important people— the idea was that if six million people got acquainted with the name of the president of a big company and saw his picture and found out that he was married and had four kids, they might buy the product of his company. Atlantis makes a lot of aluminum gadgets and so somebody had the bright notion that we should move in on the *Portfolio* profiles. I was detailed to go to their business office and find out how the deal worked. So I did, and we were talking it over when Jenny came into the office—and the man I was talking with said, 'Here's someone who can tell you whether this is worth while for your company or not—' and that was how I met Jenny."

"And you liked her—"

"I was so surprised," said Stephen and sounded that way. "You see so many of those brisk, handsome girls around offices—and they're always just a little too brisk and too handsome—and here was Jenny, so sort of shy—well, innocent. Not that she didn't catch on to the job we were talking about right off—she did—but personally she was so honest. Well, I knew after we'd been talking five minutes that she was a girl I could trust."

"With the job—"

"With more than that," he said thoughtfully and let it rest. So did Sara, until Stephen himself went on. "I was in sort of a queer state of mind at the time," he said. "I was alone in New York—no family—my mother had died some years before and my father had settled down here in DeSoto for good. I had a good enough job—my father had a friend who had planted me in Atlantis and I was making some money, had all my teeth and you know—I was asked out weekends, and week nights too. I had some experiences that didn't make me exactly idealize women and girls. I had become sort of suspicious—you know what I mean?"

"I know what you mean and why," said Sara.

"There's no point in going into it. I was only trying to explain why Jenny was so different. Here was a girl—and the more I saw of her the more I realized it—who was decent and sweet and good and could stay that way right in the middle of New York. When I say she was innocent I don't mean that she was anybody's fool, you know."

"I'm sure she wasn't."

"She knew her way about—what went on—but it hadn't hardened or coarsened her. To come on a girl like that—"

"Pretty nice," said Sara softly. "Very, very lucky."

"It was."

He thought about it, watching the fire, not wanting to say more, then began to realize that this wasn't much fun for Sara. To have him sit there, sucking memories of his own, wondering why what had begun with so much delight hadn't come off quite as it should. He glanced at Sara in her blue robe and said, "You're looking especially lovely tonight."

She did not thank him. She didn't seem to have heard. He tried again.

"You shouldn't start me talking about myself."

"That's why we're here. Why you came."

"I thought that we were going to talk about you. Those propositions you mentioned this morning—aren't you going to tell me about them?"

"If you like. You see, Steve, it gets down to the fact that I don't want to live alone. I'm no good at it."

"Of course you shouldn't."

"It's so very alone. If I'd been a different kind of mother—if I'd had the chance to be and could have had the boys when they were small—perhaps they would be closer. But they were taken away from me. Now they're very friendly—they're fine—but I don't share their lives. They have girls who are closer to them, will have wives. I'm like an older sister—or a second cousin—they like me. But that's not enough to fill the spaces. And besides, being me, I want a man—I'm used to having a man."

"You could have almost anyone you want, Sara."

"Oh no. For one thing I want to live here. This is where I feel safe. And who is there here? Do I shock you by being frank about it? Do you think I'm not being a decent widow—not being willing to live in mourning?"

"You can't do that."

"I won't."

"Sara—there's Jenny—but you know I'm very fond of you. And I think you are of me. If you want it to be more—carry it farther—in the only way I could now—"

"You can't help that way. Once I tried it out when my first marriage became intolerable and it was the most horrible experience I ever had. It was the loneliest time in my life. With me—with you and me—it would have to be marriage to be any good. If you and Jenny were breaking up—but you don't want that! You love her. I heard it in your voice just now."

"That may not mean we won't break up," he said almost violently. "I don't know, Sara. I don't know what Jenny wants."

"As I told you this morning, you should find out. But what I found out tonight—or maybe this morning when I first was sure—is that you're not for me. You're not available, Steve—and wouldn't be even if you were divorced. You'd still have Jenny deep in your mind. I would never again marry a man who wouldn't completely belong to me. My second husband never did. He belonged to a social establishment. The first man I married never belonged to anyone except himself. But Tom was mine. And after we came here to the country, it was very good. For him and for me."

"I know it was."

"But he's dead. You were wonderful when that awful thing happened. And since then I've thought that perhaps—sometimes Jenny seemed so remote from both of us—we could make the transfer. Decently. Not hurting anyone. But I know better. I know you're fond of me but you don't want me. Not even as much as Miles Halliday does."

"Miles!"

"Oh yes, that was one of the propositions. I don't mind telling you because after a while Miles will make dinner conversation about it almost certainly. And we'll all laugh. Yes, Miles asked me to marry him. And I considered it too. For in his way Miles cares for me, as much as he can care for any woman. I've known that for a long time, and it's why, in spite of his cruelties, I have a tenderness for him. But it would be no good with Miles. He belongs to an establishment too. This place here, which is my safety and my love, is a season and a fine house to him. A little bit of a joke. Something to enjoy and analyze. Miles was superbly frank. He laid out the advantages for me and for himself, if we married, in a neat row, and it was quite impressive. But I didn't want advantages. I just wanted to be here to have what Tom almost could give me. What I almost gave him. What he thought I did."

She might almost have been talking to herself. Her voice was low, the flow of words interrupted here and there by a thought coming through fearlessly. Suddenly she laughed.

"There is also that man called Delaney—"

"Delaney—what about him? Do you know that man?"

"Not really. To speak to. But he watches me. He waits in the post office. He covets me."

"Sara, you're upset—you're imagining—"

"No, it's not a thing a woman imagines when she sees it in a man's eyes. Lurking around his mouth. I could have Mr. Delaney. Once in a while he makes an excuse to talk to me—when will the

214

Hunt start?—he hopes to be here for the season—he's thinking of settling here—he'll hold the door open at the post office and make a delay— Once when I was riding alone I met him on one of the trails—he knew somehow that I was going to ride that day and where—probably from one of the stableboys."

"I don't like this at all. Why, that character— He's evidently got a little money and he's—"

"Don't worry," said Sara, "I'm not losing my head. Or my mind. I have no intention of marrying Mr. Delaney. As a matter of fact, I'm going to marry Ross. Ross Painter. I shall tell him so very soon probably."

"Ross—why, Sara, he's your—"

"I know—he trains my horses. He was a groom. And before that he was a livery stable hand, sweeping out those rank barns that fortunately burned down. He's always lived in this county—I can remember him as a ragged boy always hanging around horses—he was on the edge of the picture, from a desperately poor family. But he hasn't done badly with his life. He's stuck to what he wanted to do. He knows horses. He has good form in the field. He's handsome and he's healthy."

"That's all true enough. But you can't throw yourself away on a man like that."

She stood up and the long blue robe rippled to the floor. She looked very tall and fearless and Stephen could feel the vitality, the eagerness for life coming from her as she spoke again.

"I won't throw myself away. You know I might if it were to be you and I. Ross loves this place—the mountains, the little town—so do you. But also Ross loves me. He always has, through all those marriages of mine. He told me so not long ago. It was terribly hard for him to tell me, but finally—as he said—he had to take the high jump even if he couldn't make it. I told him I had to think, that I didn't know—I was still wondering about you and me. But I didn't humiliate Ross by making him feel that it was impossible. I won't let anyone else humiliate him. Never. It will be all right. I think it will be good."

The admiration and the flash of jealousy Steve felt went almost to the point of breaking into love at that moment. As Sara seemed to know, for she pulled emotion back, brought it under control.

She said, "We'll all be hunting together soon. Steve, if you left word for Jenny to call you back tonight, maybe you should go home. She might be trying to reach you."

15

THE TELEPHONE RANG shortly after ten o'clock and Steve answered it quickly. But it was not Jennifer calling. He heard a man's voice, a Southern drawl.

"You there Steve? This is Clint Allen. I been trying to get you on the phone."

"I just came in."

"Well, I must apologize for calling at this late hour. But there's a little excitement going around the town and I didn't know if you was aware of it or not."

"What's the excitement about?"

"Well, I tell you," drawled Allen, who ran the politics of the village without ever hurrying a syllable, "it concerns the colored that works for you. Old Aga. His boy Mailer seems to have come back to town."

"Yes. He left me word about that. I didn't see Aga today but he left a note to tell me his boy was here."

"You know about Mailer?"

"Not too much. He's the one in New York?"

"He's one of the nigras just been in that riot in Harlem, New York. You read about that—saw on TV what they did?"

"I didn't connect Mailer with it."

"He was right in it. Maybe his name didn't come out in the papers but the colored here all know about it. I understand Mailer's some firebrand. They tell me he came back here all cut up. Now this is it, Steve. We don't want no nigra troublemaker around here. This little town's been peaceful. It's had no part in the things been going on elsewhere. This town's highly Christian in its attitude to the colored but—"

"But what?" asked Steve, impatient with the drawl.

"Well, there's considerable feeling that this boy Mailer better not stay around here. Nobody knows what he's got in mind—but the colored gather around a character like that—and they been looking at TV, ain't one of them not got a set—they can get highly emotional. There's citizens around here talking about getting out sheets—we don't want none of that in DeSoto."

"Good God, no!"

"That's what I said to them. I said there won't be no disturbance. I said I'd call you and ask you to see that Aga gets his boy out of town quietly but right smart."

"I suppose he has a right to visit his father."

"We don't want no trouble," the lagging voice repeated. "It's kind of up to you, Steve. That family been attached to your place a long time. They your people."

The final statement went back through generations to an old responsibility and an old power. It came strangely to Steve's ears.

He said, "I'll look into it first thing in the morning, Clint. I must fly up to New York tomorrow but I'll find out what the situation is before I go. And call you."

"Be very grateful to you, Steve. Keep in touch. Because we don't want no commotion around here."

There was commotion in Steve's mind. Too much for sleep. He tried his bed after a while but the problems and questions which had been flung at him marched through his mind in an incongruous procession. He got up again and had a drink, but that did not quiet them. Why didn't Jennifer call back? Could she be ill? Could she be caught up in one of those riots in New York? I'll fly up there tomorrow, why didn't I do it before, I was waiting until after the hunter trials— Sara is going to marry Ross Painter, she's making a fool of herself, it might work out all right at that. I liked it as it was, but I knew all the time— Why the hell doesn't Jenny call, she can call collect—I told her to do that before she left here because she always takes the cost of toll calls so seriously. If Agamemnon's boy is a troublemaker what can I do about it—it's not up to me—this is a hundred years after the Civil War, and Clint Allen sounded as if it were still going on.

He put down the drink and went out on the terrace. It was cool and there were a lot of fireflies winking at him. Jenny was crazy about the fireflies—I thought she liked it here—Sara said that she could hear that I loved Jenny and that I wouldn't get over her. I do love her.

Finally he fell asleep on one of the long, precise sofas. The dawn woke him before the cook arrived. Steve shook his thoughts out and put the things that he had to do in the order that they must be done. He called the airport and made a reservation on the two o'clock plane, because the one which left at ten wouldn't give him a chance to see Agamemnon and report to Clint Allen.

As he was eating an early and brief breakfast, the telephone rang again, giving him a shiver of hope that this was Jenny and all was well.

It was Joe Harris with a chuckle. "Steve, I've got some news for you. You know that customer we talked about? Well, he was in to see me again. I played it very cool, said you weren't interested. He asked if you'd be interested if he would go to—hold your hat, Steve—fifty thousand."

Steve said flatly, "Did he—"

"He's got the money, Steve. And I said you'd want all cash, so there's no risk."

"Yes, I guess he has the cash. I had a talk with Ed Woolsey and apparently Delaney is well enough fixed. But Joe, I don't know that I want to sell to that fellow. I don't know that he's the type we want around DeSoto."

The thought of Delaney affronted Stephen this morning. Delaney leering at Sara, watching for her in the post office, having the insolence to even imagine that—unless it was Sara's imagination. But Sara wasn't the kind of woman who saw desire in every man's eyes. She had written him off last night because there wasn't enough. She had stood there and decided that she would marry Ross Painter.

Harris was saying, "As far as that goes, DeSoto already has about all the types there are—and this is a big deal, Steve."

"I don't know. You couldn't build the house today for twice that, to say nothing of the property. Anyway I haven't talked it over with Mrs. Cooper. I'm flying up to New York today and I'll tell her about the proposition and see how she feels about it."

"You do that. When will you be back?"

"In a couple of days, I expect."

"I'll keep it on the fire that long—tell him that you're out of town and will be ready to talk when you get back. But I wouldn't let this slip through my fingers, Steve. There aren't many people who would put up that amount of cash or could—"

The local banker, Ed Woolsey, had been reassuring about that. He had told Steve yesterday, "Of course I can't tell the amount of his bank balance to you or anyone else. But Mr. Delaney's credit is very good. He hasn't been here long but he gave me the impression that he was likely to settle in DeSoto— Well, I can tell you this much, he has certificates of deposit with us that run into five figures and I suppose he banks elsewhere too. It's an amazing thing, that automobile business—"

Harris said, "You might tell Mrs. Cooper that if you consider building, there's a beautiful piece of land on the Ledge—"

"I'll let you know, Joe."

Stephen had not been inside Agamemnon's house since he was a boy. But he knew where it was, of course, and often rode past the rambling, shabby, still substantial frame house where the grapevines were now red over the fretwork on the slanting porch. He felt out of place and intrusive as he knocked on the door.

Aga opened it and gave the odd little nod that was not quite a bow.

"Mr. Steve," he said, "I lef' a note."

"I found it," said Steve. "So your son is here."

"My son is here." Aga's voice was somber, unnatural.

"I thought I'd drop by and meet him."

"He am ill, Mr. Steve."

Suddenly Susie appeared in a doorway which apparently led from the kitchen, and tears streamed down her face as if they were in constant flow. She did not try to check them and Steve looked away from her in embarrassed pity. His glance went to the wall where the motto hung. EVIL IS NOT SPOKEN IN THIS HOUSE.

"Ill?" asked Steve. "You and Susie are worried about him?"

"My son, Mailer, he been in a accident."

"What kind of accident was it, Aga?"

Agamemnon's face was utterly sad but his dignity held firm. "No need burden you with our trouble, Mr. Steve. No need talk of it."

"I think we'll have to, Aga. As I understand it, Mailer was mixed up in a riot in Harlem a day or two ago."

"It am his work to help his people, Mr. Steve."

Susie wailed, "He going to lose him his eye, Mr. Steve! Him all cut wiv them bottles an' knifes!"

Aga said, his voice trembling, "He druv bleeding through all the night."

"Will you let me see him?" asked Steve with quiet authority. Aga led him up the stairs and Susie tumbled along behind them.

A big man lay under a coverlet on an old-fashioned maple bed. He was inert but obviously conscious. He stared up at Steve with the one eye that was not bandaged. His chin and forehead had been gashed, for strips of adhesive were plastered on them. But the eye was clear and wise. Mailer said, "Mr. Stephen Cooper. I recall you."

Aga spoke in easygoing dialect and Susie picked up the nearest word when she talked. But their son had the voice of an orator and used an educated vocabulary.

"I recall you, now that I see you, Mailer. You've grown a bit."

"You too, Mr. Cooper. Mr. Cooper, I hope I don't make you any trouble. I don't want to be the cause of trouble for my folks here."

"You've been in plenty of it yourself obviously," said Steve.

"There was trouble and grief and destruction. And I was unable to make it cease."

"Are the police looking for you, Mailer?"

"No, Mr. Cooper. I am not a criminal."

"Your father says you drove all night in this bad shape. Why didn't you go to the nearest hospital? Why did you come all the way down here?"

"For peace, Mr. Cooper. The feel of the sweet peace of this place. If I die, I wish to see my parents first."

"You're not going to die, Mailer."

"This morning I do not think so. Yesterday I was not so sure." There was almost a smile on the broken lips, but it hurt too much and was withdrawn.

"Too bad you got into a thing like that Harlem riot, Mailer."

"It is my work," said Mailer. "I told them to march quietly. But they roused into terrible anger. Reason goes. Hatred comes. I saw my failure. I wished to come to my old home to die or to heal my failure."

Like a lot of other people, thought Steve grimly, I came to heal my failure. He said, "I can understand that. You grew up here."

"But I am not welcome in this community today," said the Negro leader with terrible perception.

"They don't want any trouble here," said Steve. "They're afraid of having that uncontrollable hatred you speak of being stirred up in DeSoto. It's a good town, you know that."

"There will be no stirring up," said Mailer.

"I have your word for that?"

"You have," said Mailer very wearily. He did not end his sentences with "sir" but spoke as man to man. And as Stephen held out his hand Mailer took it and released it with the words, "I remember your father, Mr. Cooper. When I was a little boy I was in some childish trouble and your father found me behind the stables. I was weeping over some small injustice. He talked to me about the individual and I did not understand that word. But it had the sound of something big and fine and I stopped my crying. Now I have learned what the word means. And I remember your father with respect."

"Thank you," said Stephen. "I'd like to talk to you about him at some other time. But now you are in no condition to talk or even move. I'm going to make it clear, Mailer, to anyone who might be disturbed about your connection with the Harlem riots or your presence here that you are here as your father's guest and a friend of my family. You have seen a doctor?"

"Yes. We have a doctor."

"You must see a specialist about that eye. I'll arrange that with the hospital when you are stronger. Today I have to go to New York to see my wife."

Susie said, "She be lonely for you. In that sad city. I hope she come home."

"Perhaps," said Steve. "Maybe she will, Susie. In any case I'm going to ask some neighbors of ours, Mr. Julius Martin and his wife, to keep in touch with all of you while I'm in New York. You know Mr. Martin, Aga?"

"Some days I stop by on his porch to greet him," said Aga. "He very frail."

"Not frail here," said Steve, touching his forehead. He said to the man in the bed, "Mr. Martin is a very distinguished lawyer. A famous arbitrator too. He can take care of any question that might arise."

He understood what I meant, thought Steve as he drove away. How quickly and instinctively they all understand the situation. Without resentment. With that motto on the wall. I'll stop and see Julius first. From his bed he could be legal enough to scare the daylights out of anyone who tried to start any bullying. I'll tell him that Father talked about the Greeks to little bawling Mailer behind the stables. That will interest him.

And then I'll call Clint Allen. No—I'll see him and talk turkey. He wanted me to do the dirty work but he didn't like it any better than I did. This is a good town, but we can't let anyone begin to push other people around. People who have homes and belong here. Who come back to heal, like Mailer.

Tonight I'll tell Jenny all about this. And that Susie thinks New York is a sad city and that she'd better come home.

16

Mrs. Stephen Cooper?" The clerk at the registration desk of the Wilmington Hotel repeated the name. "I don't think Mrs. Cooper is still with us. Just a moment, please." He consulted his file of cards and said pleasantly, "No, Mrs. Cooper checked out on the nineteenth, a week ago."

"But I've been calling her here. They didn't tell me that. I've been leaving messages and they took them."

"I wouldn't know about that," said the clerk with the same impervious gloss of courtesy. "That would go through the switchboard."

It was completely baffling. The girl at the switchboard told Stephen that she had just come on duty today. The other girl— she was only temporary help, said the operator with an unsatisfied look—must have taken the calls. She looked for records but could not find any. Had the calls been completed? Finally Steve went to the house telephone himself and called room 629, which was the number of the room that Jennifer had lived in. A man's voice answered and became rather angry at the inquiry. "Yes, this is six-twenty-nine. No, there is no Mrs. Cooper here. This is my room."

By the time the fact that Jennifer was not living in the hotel had been established against Stephen's will, along with the realization that for some nights a careless girl had jotted down his request for a return call, found no person registered to receive the requests and probably thrown away the memorandum, it was almost seven o'clock. Stephen called the offices of *Portfolio*. A janitor finally answered and told him that everyone had gone home. Stephen looked for the name of Geoffrey Clark in the telephone book. It was not listed. Of course it wouldn't be, thought Stephen. Clark would not leave himself wide open to calls from disappointed writers or pursuing women.

He must wait until morning. Stephen walked from the Wilmington to a big familiar hotel, registered, had a couple of drinks at the bar and forced a tasteless dinner on himself in the grillroom. He knew this hotel well but tonight it seemed strange. In a small room, closeted with a television set, which held his attention as little when he turned it on as when the screen was blank, he spent a night in which exhaustion and restless speculation took turns on his mind and body. He would sleep heavily and then wake to the fact that Jennifer had for some reason cut off communication with him. She had left the Wilmington without letting him know, and the clerk insisted that she had given no forwarding address. But perhaps that was another stupid blunder of someone at the hotel. Something may have annoyed her at the Wilmington—all this may be completely explainable. I'll go down to her office in the morning and probably find that I've been a fool to begin to panic. She will be there by half past nine. She always made a point of that.

The *Portfolio* offices began with a lavish foyer and went down corridors of glass-fronted rooms. Stephen told the receptionist that he knew his way and brushed past her desk, leaving her frowning. He went to the office that had been Jennifer's and opened the door without formality. Jennifer was not there. A handsome blonde woman was talking into a dictaphone.

"I'm looking for Mrs. Cooper."

"Mrs. Cooper? She's not with *Portfolio* now," said the blonde.

"She's not working here?"

"No. I am Miss Fox. Is there something—"

"Where do I find Geoffrey Clark?" asked Stephen abruptly.

"Mr. Clark is not in yet. Have you an appointment?"

"When will he be in?"

May Fox hesitated. This man was attractive and he might be important. She said, "He usually comes in about ten o'clock. You might ask his secretary. Mr. Clark's office is on the right at the end of the hall. But unless you have an appointment—"

"I'll take care of that," said Stephen. "The end of the hall?" He looked at the woman again and asked, "You are replacing Mrs. Cooper?"

"Yes."

"When did she leave the magazine?"

"Very recently."

"Thank you," said Stephen. He went down the carpeted corridor and found the room with Geoffrey Clark's name on the door. The secretary asked him if he had an appointment and he said no, but that Mr. Clark would see him. The girl was puzzled, as the receptionist and May Fox had been, but it did not seem feasible to get rid of Stephen. Doubtfully the secretary allowed him to wait in the small room outside Clark's private office.

Stephen had never liked Geoffrey Clark. Jennifer said that Clark was a brilliant editor and the magazine's success seemed to bear that out. But when, and it happened only very occasionally, he and Jennifer and Geoffrey had a drink together, it seemed to Stephen that the editor's cynicism reeked of tawdry experiences. He hated to wait for Clark and to question him, but there was nothing else to do. So for more than half an hour he sat there, chain-smoking, until finally Geoffrey Clark came down the hall, wearing his usual morning pallor.

Stephen stood up and Clark recognized him.

"Well—how are you, Steve? I thought you were settled in the country. How's Jennifer?"

"I'd like to speak to you alone," said Steve.

"Why sure. Come in." He nodded a dismissal to the secretary and closed the door of the inner office.

"Well—anything wrong with Jennifer?"

"A woman out there said she was no longer working on the magazine."

"No—but surely— You didn't know?"

"There's been some mix-up—letters went astray."

Clark's eyes grew cautious.

"Oh, too bad. Well, there was nothing I could do about it. Jenny said she was leaving and she did."

"She never should have come back after the way you treated her."

"I treated her?"

"Letting her out last winter—that was beastly."

"My dear Cooper, I never let Jenny out! I begged her to stay. But I couldn't make her change her mind. She said that you were going to this place you have down South and that she had to go along. Good Lord, Jenny's the best fiction editor we ever had. What makes you think I let her go?"

"That was my understanding."

"Of course I don't know what she told you—"

"It doesn't matter—that's all over the dam. But I want Jenny's present address if you have it."

"I haven't it myself. I'll see if someone at the desk—" He pushed a buzzer, asked a question, waited, asked another question and said to Stephen, "Nobody seems to have it."

Steve sat there disbelieving, then slowly got up. He was conscious of the way Clark was looking at him, knew what the other man was thinking and felt stripped of privacy.

Geoffrey Clark said, "Gavin Bennett might know."

"Bennett?"

"Jenny and he were seeing a good deal of each other. She said that he was—a neighbor—of yours."

"He is," said Stephen stiffly, "occasionally."

"Sorry I can't be of more help."

"That's all right," said Stephen mechanically.

He walked out of the editor's office, down the long corridor, into the elevator, out to the street. He walked without choosing a direction, trying to fit the facts together, to believe them. Jennifer had disappeared deliberately. She had left her work as well as the hotel where she had been living. She had done it of her own free will. And from what Clark had said— What reason would he have to lie about it and he had sounded as if he weren't lying, he had seemed astonished. That was what she had done last winter. She had not been fired. She had given up her job on his account, because if neither of them had a job they would be forced to go to DeSoto. She had stayed there as long as she could stand it. Until she couldn't stand it any longer.

She did all that for me, he marveled, and kept it to herself. Never threw it in my face even when I was playing King Cophetua. Nor when I was ugly, as I was when she began to pay the rent of the apartment. She took that too without telling me what I was. All this time she's let me accept her generosity and not had a word of thanks. She will be thanked when I catch up with her now. It was my stupid pride—she's a better woman than I am a man.

But why had she left *Portfolio* this time? Why had she run out on everything? Where was she now? Clark had said that Gavin Bennett might know. He was insinuating—of course Clark had that kind of a mind. We only know the Bennetts casually, Stephen said to himself. He's been at our house—Stephen remembered it—it was the night of the steeplechase and when I left Sara and came home, Gavin Bennett was there. Why not? He told me that he was going to look her up in New York. Why shouldn't he?

They were seeing a lot of each other, Clark said. I couldn't knock him down for saying that. I have to find out. I have to talk to Jenny. But I can't go to Gavin Bennett and ask him where my wife is. Tell him that I don't know. Perhaps he knows that I don't know.

In midafternoon he stood gaunt-faced in the anteroom of Gavin Bennett's suite of offices.

"I'm sorry. Mr. Bennett is not available."

"It's very important that I see him."

The quiet, middle-aged secretary measured him with her glance.

"I'm sorry. It is not possible."

"My name is Stephen Cooper. I live in DeSoto."

"Do you—such a lovely place." The mention of DeSoto changed her manner and made her more responsive. She said, "Mr. Bennett will be so sorry. He always likes to see friends from DeSoto. But he isn't in New York at present."

"Where can I get in touch with him?"

"That would be difficult. And frankly, we aren't bothering him except with very important matters."

"This is important."

"Perhaps when he returns I can make an appointment for you."

"When is he coming back?"

"It's indefinite. He's traveling abroad."

With Jenny?

"Traveling abroad," Stephen repeated.

"Yes, he and Mrs. Bennett left for Austria only a few days ago. You know Mrs. Bennett?"

"Yes, I do."

"Then you probably know that she's not in the best of health. That is why we're not troubling Mr. Bennett with business matters."

"I quite understand," said Stephen, "and I'm sorry to have bothered you."

Jenny is not with him. He has taken his wife to Austria, probably to see some doctor or try some sanitarium. No matter how much she may have seen him, Jenny is not with Bennett. The fact exhilarated Stephen. He was suddenly hungry and thirsty and found a nearby taproom. He ordered whiskey and a sandwich and sat in the dim, almost empty room, patching the pieces of information together, trying to figure it out. If she left the Wilmington and cut off all the people she worked with professionally, where would she be likely to go? In this mad city? In this city that old Susie called sad? Jenny would not seek out any of the people they used to entertain when he was with the corporation. It would be more like her— He thought, anyway that might be worth a try. I have to do something.

He finished his drink and went out to signal a taxi. Cabs were moving again today.

"Drop me off at Fourteenth and Fifth," he said. "I'm not sure of the exact address and I'll walk from there."

It was a long time since he had been on this street but it had not changed very much. The apartment Jenny had when he first knew her was in one of these old houses with stained glass in the front doors and bare broad stairways. This was the one. He looked up at it, told himself that it would be a miracle and went in. He read the names in the slots by the bells. He read 3A JENNIFER COOPER on a piece of clean white pasteboard. Staring at the name as if it might disappear if he took his eyes off it, he pressed the bell and waited. There was no answer. Stephen climbed the stairs to the third floor and knocked on the door of apartment 3A. There was no sound from within so he sat down on the stairs to wait for her.

17

Tʜɪs was ᴛʜᴇ ᴅᴀʏ when Jennifer saw the material that was right for the sofas in the drawing room at Chestnut Hill. Since she had left *Portfolio* she walked for hours every day to tire herself enough so that she might sleep at night. But after dark she stayed in her apartment with the door locked, for the memory of the assault on her in the street was still terrifying.

She had given up her room at the hotel on the day after that happened, careful to leave no forwarding address, and then immediately faced Geoffrey Clark's angry disappointment when she told him she was giving up her job. She was in a state of shock but it gave a superficial effect of cool decisiveness.

"No, not another week," she said, "not even another day. You knew all along I could only be here temporarily."

"But why leave all of a sudden?"

"Things have come up," she said.

"You're putting me up against the ax."

"Don't call May that. She's a good editor. And one day Sally will be back."

"I thought you were getting a bang out of New York lately."

"Did you?"

"Do you really like those grim hills better?"

"Yes. I like them better."

"It's a damned waste," said Geoffrey, "and I guess maybe I'm not the only man in New York who thinks so."

Jennifer ignored that insinuation. She asked, "Shall I call May and tell her? Or will you?"

He groaned and said, "You do it."

So she had done it. And, desperate for a lodging, she had wondered if there might be anything vacant in the apartment building where she used to live. She had little hope of it but was told that there was one very small, sparsely furnished apartment which could be sublet for a few months. Jennifer moved into it that same evening with a sense of having found refuge.

She had wanted to be sure that Gavin would not be able to find her when he came back to New York from DeSoto. She knew that he would try and that he must fail. She sent him no message because her action was enough to tell him all that need be told. She did not let herself think of him because that could rouse such pity in herself, pity that was very close to love.

It was Stephen to whom she must write, and as she walked the streets she wrote that letter over and over again in her mind. It always began simply enough— She would write—*Dear Stephen, as you probably guess*—(no, as you must know)—*I am not coming back to DeSoto. I think it would be a good thing*—(no, I think it is sensible)—*for you to start divorce proceedings. For a long time I have known how you feel about Sara and I have come to the conclusion*—(no, not conclusion, it sounds so stupid and so hard)—

She wrote the letter as she walked and as she lay in bed. But it was still not on paper or in the mails. When the letter was written and sent, she would look for a job. It was not necessary yet for she had cashed one of her bonds. She had brought it to New York to reinvest because it was soon to be called, and the other day she had cashed it and added it to the small account she carried in a New York bank. She told herself that she would find work when the money ran out, but she had an indifference to money that was new to her. Once she wondered if it was because Gavin had introduced her to so much luxury that was worth so little. But she did not really believe that. It was because other things were obviously much more important.

Tonight, she told herself, walking along a street where fine furnishings were displayed in narrow windows, I shall write to Steve. I'll begin, *Dear Steve, By this time you realize*—no, sounds like a come-to-realize story. I'll write—

She stopped in front of a shopwindow to rephrase the sentence, absently regarding lengths of damask and silk on easels behind the glass. That was when she saw it. The house on the hill was suddenly in front of her. She thought, that white textured stuff would be perfect for the sofas. It is firm without being harsh. It looks as if it would last forever. That beautiful room— I was so happy—

The material was twenty-seven dollars a yard, the salesman told her. Jennifer felt it with her fingers and under her touch it was as it looked, soft but indestructible.

"Of course it's handwoven. It's a Grecian design—the pattern is hardly noticeable—" He began to explain and praise.

"The sofas—there are two—will need sixteen yards," said Jennifer, at length.

"There are twenty yards in the piece. I would give you the whole piece for the price of the sixteen yards you say you need."

"That will be fine," said Jennifer.

"Shall I charge it, Madam?"

"No, I'll pay for it. And take it with me."

Now I know that I have lost my mind, she told herself, carrying the bulky bundle down the street. What am I going to do with it?

But it was so right that I couldn't leave it there. Four hundred and thirty-two dollars! How Steve would laugh. She herself laughed aloud at that idea and a man passing her looked to see if she was drunk.

None the less, it was a pleasure. Her first pleasure in days. She wanted to get back to the apartment with the material, open the big bundle, look at the stuff again, imagine the sofas—

She pushed open the front door of the apartment building, climbed the stairs, came upon him sitting there, then starting up to catch her arm as she went backward.

"Look out—steady—"

"Steve?"

"In person," he said.

"How did you know I was here?"

"I guessed," he said. "I figured it. Why didn't you let me know?"

"I've been going to write you. I was going to write you tonight."

"You can save yourself that trouble. Are you going to ask me in?"

She took the key from her purse and opened the door. Steve flipped on a light switch and then stood looking at her for a long minute.

"You look tired," he said.

"I'm all right."

"Sit down," he said, taking the coat from her shoulders and almost placing her in the largest chair. "What's been going on? Who are you hiding from? Me?"

"No. I told you I was going to write to you. Tonight. I really was."

"What were you going to write?"

Jennifer said, stumbling over it as her thoughts had done so often, "That I'm not coming back to DeSoto. That you can divorce me. And that I want you to be happy with Sara. I really do, Steve."

"Happy with Sara?" It was hardly a question.

"I've seen it for a long time. I knew before I came to New York. I don't blame you. You and Sara are suited, belong together. You like the same things."

"Sara," he said, "is going to marry Ross Painter."

Jennifer stared at him. She said, "No—why—"

"Because she thinks he will be the right man for her."

"Oh Steve, she doesn't mean it!"

"She's the best judge of that."

"But you want—you must have wanted Sara."

"Let me be the judge of what I want. And whom," he said. "But I didn't come to New York to discuss Sara. I came to find out what was wrong with you, why I couldn't get in touch with you, to find out if you were ill. And you'd disappeared—without a word. I've had a hell of a time. Running around to other men's offices, forcing my way in. What's this about you and Gavin Bennett? Is he the reason you're talking about divorce?"

She moved her head in denial but did not speak.

"You've been playing around with him? That's what your boss at the magazine intimated in his nasty way. Tell me!"

That was a demand and she met it, not immediately but after it had hung in the air for a couple of minutes. She seemed to be thinking, then met Stephen's eyes and said, "It wasn't just playing around. It was different—so much better than that. Gavin was wonderful to me. I was lonely—I was bereft—there wasn't anything except the work, doing the best I could at that. You didn't call. I called you and you were with Sara. And Gavin came. He really wanted to be with me and that was like having a light turned on when you've been groping around, trying to find something you've lost."

She stopped and he did not hurry her with questions. He watched her face as she finally went on.

"He made me gay. And there was the luxury. And being taken care of and being important. Very important to him. He made me feel that I was beautiful. One night we went flying and everything stupid and worrying was left miles below. Steve, he was very good

236

to me—good for me. He opened things up, not just the doors of restaurants, you understand?"

"I believe you. And I didn't do very well by you, did I?"

"Oh yes, you did—but this was different. And then—"

"Yes, sure—then—" he said in a hardened voice.

She lifted her hands and let them fall in a gesture of emptiness.

"Then—after that—the gaiety was gone—the happiness was gone—you know, those are real things. But—dear God, what I began to understand! Things I have been pretending to understand—editing and criticizing and bystanding for years—and I never really knew what it was all about."

"He let you down."

"No—no," she said. "He did everything he could to keep me from being let down. But he couldn't change what was in him—long years of loyalty—and he couldn't change what was in me."

"What was that?"

"I'd belonged to you for a long while," she said. "Steve, you asked what I was running from. From Gavin partly. I didn't want Gavin to find me. But if you want to know, I think I was running from myself. I was running from my own jealousy, from the danger of taking a lover for comfort, or vanity, or revenge—not for love."

The words tumbled out, stopped, fell into his silence. He did not answer them or argue what she had said. After a moment or two he asked in an almost matter-of-fact way, "This is finished with Bennett—over?"

"Completely. As soon as it began."

"And what are your plans now?"

"I haven't planned yet. I'll stay here—get a job of some kind. I can get a job of some kind. I can take care of myself."

"How about me? Have you thought about that at all?"

"You have Chestnut Hill. You're happy in the country, much better off than you ever were here. And without me you'll have income enough to live quite comfortably there."

"I am going to sell Chestnut Hill, Jenny."

"Sell it? But why? And that wouldn't be easy."

"As a matter of fact it will be. I've had a very good offer from a man who's very much interested. Of fifty thousand dollars."

"Fifty thousand dollars!"

"That's one of the things I came here to talk to you about. Maybe I'll keep enough—it will be forty-seven thousand after Joe Harris gets his cut—I'll keep enough to buy myself a horse. But you can have the rest."

"I don't want it! I wouldn't take it!"

"It's coming to you. You should look at it as compensation for giving up your job at *Portfolio* and taking me to the country."

"I—"

"Clark told me the facts. I admit they came as kind of a shock," said Stephen, "and made me ashamed of myself."

"But you were never sorry. You were much happier in De-Soto—"

"I thought that you were too."

"I was. I loved Chestnut Hill— Who is this person who wants to buy the house, Steve?"

"You wouldn't know him. A man called Delaney."

"Delaney—the man with a green hat and sort of pointed face and cautious eyes—"

"I've only seen him at a couple of hunt meets. He'll have to learn manners if he means to live in DeSoto."

"But you can't sell Chestnut Hill to him!" she exclaimed.

"I don't know why not if he has the cash."

"Because he's a thief!" said Jennifer. "I thought he'd probably disappeared long ago. I was going to tell you this before I came back to New York. But things happened so fast to me then and it went out of my mind. Listen—I saw him in a strange place on the mountain that day when I was late at Sara's pool party. He and some other men were dismantling cars. He looked as if he would have liked to kill me for driving in there and he told me the most obvious lies about the men being in a wreck. Then later on I heard that cars had been stolen around DeSoto—Gavin told me that one of his and one of Sara's had been stolen. That's the man. I'm dead sure of it, Steve. It all fits together, time and place. You couldn't sell your father's beautiful house—it's your own beautiful house—to him! You'd better go back to DeSoto and put him in jail if he's still there!"

"Do you know what you're talking about?"

"This is how it happened," Jennifer said, and told the story in greater detail. She finished, "Mrs. Valiant could tell you something about it if she would. Talk to her. Go look at that place."

"I heard about cars being stolen," said Stephen, "but it was at the time of the steeplechase accident and just then—"

"At the time you had to take care of Sara," said Jennifer. "Do you really mean she is serious about marrying Ross Painter?"

"Quite serious. She'll do it."

"But—if you should sell Chestnut Hill what would you do? Come back to New York?"

Stephen shook his head slowly. "No, this city's not for me. Just since I've been here this day or two I've felt that. Maybe that's strange, because I was born here and it was more or less head-quarters when I was a boy. And I was with Atlantis for a long time—the only job I ever had was here. But there's no pull at all—I wouldn't come back. I don't know what I will do. If you're right about Delaney I can't sell to him anyhow. I'll just go back to DeSoto and try to live. I feel as if I belong there. If I belong anywhere."

"It's a wonderful house to live in."

"You didn't seem to think so."

"But I did. I can see every room in it now. I'll never forget—Look—" She went to the table where she had put her bundle and unwrapped it. The folds of white fabric fell loose.

"You must take this back with you," said Jennifer. "It's stuff to re-cover the two long sofas. I bought it because it's so exactly right for them. It cost a fortune but it will last forever, and go to Davis—not McCarthy—to have them upholstered. Davis is the best workman there. Tell him—"

"Good God!" he exclaimed and fingered the fabric in a kind of wonder. "Jenny darling—" he began to laugh and when he could speak he managed to say—"you leave me, we both go through hell and all the time you're thinking about a couple of old sofas."

"Thinking about the only place that was ever a home for me—or for you," said Jennifer.

"Then we'd better go back, hadn't we, Jenny?" he asked her—quietly now—"You'll come with me?"

18

IT WAS LATE on a Saturday afternoon in December and in his room at the Tulip Inn Miles Halliday was writing a letter to Maud Patton. As he began it he thought with satisfaction that Palm Beach would be better in January anyway. In December all those children from colleges were there underfoot, masquerading as adults, and their parents were either lost in admiration of them or quarreling with them. But he wrote nothing about that to his friend.

As always he wrote fluently—

Dear Maud,

It will be a joy to see you in Palm Beach in January but I have impulsively decided to spend the holydays—I insist on the ancient spelling, misnomer though it has become—in this extraordinary little village of DeSoto. There is a curious merging of civilizations here at this season. All the many—so many—churches are dusting their altars for celebration of the mythical birthday, and the more sophisticated of the community are giving fine parties in their extremely modern houses, while the mansion which seems somewhat like a Greek temple from my window looks more B.C. than ever between its magnificent leafless chestnut trees. One can reflect and be amused and also be very well wined and dined here at this season.

The post office is bursting with packages—all distant sons and daughters send gifts to their aged parents who are wintering here (and whom they are very glad to have put out to pasture). The old ladies stagger out with their arthritic arms around boxes with the labels of Saks and Bergdorf Goodman. At night shapely little Christmas trees all up and down the main street sparkle with lights. This is a traditional Christmas decoration here and far more tasteful than the extravaganzas one sees along Fifth Avenue or the dismal red wreaths that most towns of this size hang on the lampposts. DeSoto may be limited to about 2,500 pop. (including black and white, mountaineers and retired capitalists, widows, horsemen and even one criminal racketeer who was recently up for trial), but it has a style that is all its own—this DeSoto.

It is the first time I have been here in midwinter and I am surprised at the number of people worth one's time who are in residence. Every year more houses are opened or kept open. I dine tonight with Sara Langley (legally she is Sara Painter, having married her groom and added one more handsome animal to the number she beds down on her estate). Do you know Sara—a sister of Lady Sukeforth's and a faultlessly beautiful woman? This is her fourth marriage. Her previous husband was killed in a steeplechase accident last spring and there was considerable speculation as to who the next one would be, for Sara is not a girl to be left unwed. I would have married her myself to prevent that and even told her so, but fortunately she did not feel it was necessary.

One day you must see this place. Why don't you come down in the spring and take a house for a month? There are some charming ones—Gavin Bennett, whom I'm sure you must know, had one here which is now up for lease. He married Anne McCutcheon but her mind clouded, to put it delicately, and I think he has tucked her away in some place in Austria with a retinue of psychiatrists. In any case that house is available. If you are interested in the lease I could inquire into it. I think I shall come here to live when I dodder —perhaps before that's quite the case. Don't you find that cities become more and more crude? Full of escapists? I except Philadelphia, because anywhere you live will never be crude. And I wait for the fifteenth of January.

He finished the page and folded the letter into an envelope. He wondered who else would be at Sara's dinner party. The Pipers were here and would have to be asked, as well as two generations of Loomises. Possibly Julius Martin and his wife—they have become very well-liked, thought Miles, but of course he had a very distinguished career. Too bad that his days of adroit mediation are over—there is certainly nothing of importance for him to do here. I hope that Steve and Jennifer Cooper will be at Sara's party. They seem to be getting along all right together now, but I wonder if she would have come back to him if Sara hadn't settled for her groom.

At the bus station a tall, handsome Negro with a patch over one eye bent to kiss the old man and woman.

"It's about to leave. I thank you from my heart for all you have done."

"It is a sad day when you leave us," said Agamemnon.

"Sad day," said Susie with a sob.

Mailer patted her shoulder. "I must do my work again," he said. "I wish to go. It is time for me to go. Mr. Martin agrees. Julius Martin taught me many things I shall not forget, that will be very useful in my work. I must get in the bus now." He smiled and the good eye gleamed at the old people. He said, "I shall take a front seat."

Father Aberdeen had absolved many of his parishioners in the course of the last two hours. It was no longer necessary to confess before each Communion, but the Christmas Mass was a special one and it seemed to him that the people who entered his confessional this afternoon had more need and desire than usual to rid themselves of fault and sin.

He had told Mrs. Piper—knowing who she was of course—very gently that Thomas a Kempis wrote that temptation must be resisted in the beginning, for first the thought comes to the mind, and then the imagination lessens resistance.

He had told Mrs. Joe Smith that she must not take the pill.

"No, it is still forbidden. These problems are being studied by the Church but the pill is not allowed." He absolved her, though he knew she would take another contraceptive pill before very long. But the poor woman might stay in a state of grace for a few days.

He had absolved the boys whose sins of the flesh were muttered with such embarrassment and reluctance. Now he was listening to a man's voice. He had heard it before. The priest frowned. How could this man be here? He had been jailed. What kind of mock confession was this?

"Bless me, Father, for I have sinned."

"Continue."

"Father, I've had a lot of bad breaks. I came here to get straightened out and then I was going to settle down and go straight."

"But you did not go straight?"

"Well, Father, I was in a complicated situation. It takes time. But I was going to make friends and I intended to contribute to the Church—"

"The priests of the Synagogue did not want the money that Judas offered them," said Father Aberdeen sternly. "Are you not a man under arrest?"

The breathing of the man on the other side of the curtain was rapid. "I'm out on bail, Father. I tell you it was my intention—"

"Hell is paved with such intentions. Have you made restitution for your sins?"

"It's not practical right now. It wasn't my fault—"

"Perhaps not your fault. But it is your sin. I cannot loose it until you do make restitution. I cannot absolve you. I shall pray for you. You may leave the confessional but do not dare to approach the altar rail until you have atoned, for that will be sacrilege."

Delaney said a foul word. He slunk out of the box, lifting the curtain cautiously. He was not out on bail. He had broken out of the jail, leaving a dummy under the gray cotton blanket on his cot. He had taken refuge in the church until it would grow dark, for he did not think they would look for him there. But Mrs. Piper had risen from her knees in a front pew and in fear that she would recognize him, for she had seen him once or twice at the Hunt, he had gone into the confessional as one of the small boys came out. Now he darted out of the church.

It was getting darker every minute and that helped. He had no car and they would watch the trains and buses as soon as they discovered he was gone. As they might have found out already. But if he could get to the four-lane highway, be lucky enough to hitch a ride and get over the border to Georgia, where he knew the woods so well, he might have a chance.

He walked on the far edge of the road, his hat pulled down over his forehead. But suddenly a switch was pulled somewhere and all the little Christmas trees which decorated the streets became illuminated with colored lights, as if they were trying to find him, expose him, one after another. He dodged around them, passed the last one finally. He was almost at the gates of the Cooper house. Now that the leaves were gone from the chestnut trees it was quite visible from the road, very white and handsome. He looked at it with hatred. He said to himself, I should have done for that woman that day in the woods when she was snooping around. She was the one who set the whole pack of hounds after me.

While Dave Delaney was cursing her and Miles Halliday was hoping that he would see her at Sara's dinner, Jennifer was cutting boughs of holly from a tree on the slope just below her house. She cut them carefully for she did not want to destroy the perfectly rounded shape of the tree. One more would be enough. She snipped it off with her garden shears and in the space which she bared she saw a tiny, beautifully made, empty nest, like none she had seen before in the grounds. The hummingbird's nest.

It was set on a branch of mountain laurel close to the holly tree, firmly built there. It was so small that she knew it must have been made for the two tiny eggs of a hummingbird. Woven of grasses and decorated with bits of gray fungus, it looked as if the bird, which winged so swiftly that sight could not keep up with its movements, had been diligently conscious of pattern. There was nothing ragged or careless about its construction and, looking closer, she saw with wonder that it was lined with spider webs. As Gavin had told her, it was a piece of beautiful architecture.

And you were supposed to find it for yourself. She remembered that Gavin had said that too. It seemed to Jennifer that there was a symbolism in that bit of superstition or old wives' tale. You had to discover some things for yourself, the most rare and beautiful things. She touched the nest gently, wishing that she could tell Gavin that she had found this and other delights because of him. Memories of Gavin came back, tender, grateful, pitying ones. She was entering a restaurant with him, they were flying above the clouds, they were looking at the portraits of his children, he was denouncing the contract he would never break. Jennifer did not often allow him to come into her mind but in this moment he had a right to be there.

Dear Gavin. She knew him better now than she had when they were gay companions and thwarted lovers. He could and would take his flights above the things he called earthbound. But he would always come back to disappointment and futility and responsibility. Jennifer looked again at the deserted nest of the hummingbird and then gathered up the cut holly from the ground at her feet. The spines of the glossy leaves pricked her fingers but it was a small penalty to pay for the pleasure of decking her own rooms with her own holly. She called aloud and the two beagles that Stephen had given her on her birthday came rushing through the deeply piled crisp fallen leaves to follow her through the woods path back to the house. The two beagles and Stephen's horse, Dark Melody, made a family for them now.

Stephen had borrowed money at the local bank to buy the horse, though Jennifer had wanted to sell two of her few remaining bonds to pay for Dark Melody.

He had said with authority, "No, I'll take care of it. I'll pay for

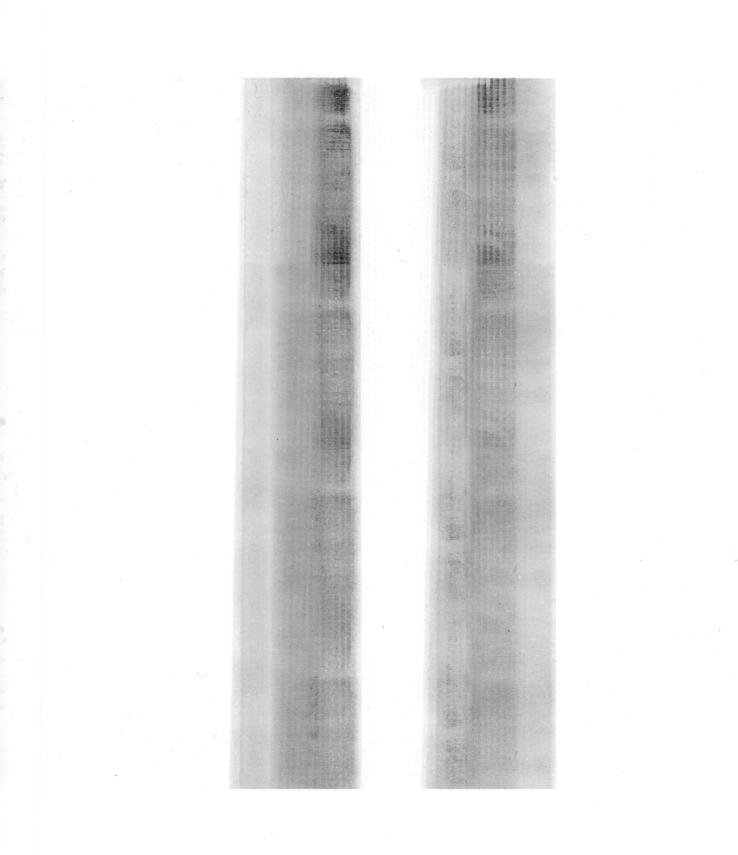

that hunter within a year." And he had told her the other day that he already owned Dark Melody's hind legs. "And I could sell him any day at twice what I paid for him."

She herself was less concerned about money since she had come back from New York and sometimes she wondered why. They had no more income than before. But Stephen had been renovating his stables, largely with his own labor, and if they could be rented in the spring, as seemed probable, that would bring in enough money to ease things. Stephen talked of giving riding lessons. And he would say, "If we get too hard up we can always rip out the marble on the fireplace." Or he would laugh. "We'll get by all right if you don't start recovering the furniture!"

Going up the stone steps she saw a visitor on the terrace before the front door. Mrs. Valiant stood there. Hearing Jennifer's step she turned and it was a handsome picture. Mrs. Valiant wore an almost colorless beret and woolen wrap that fell to her ankles. Her face, which had never known cosmetics, and her figure, shaped by work and movement, looked carved and vigorous. And her arms were stacked with foliage.

"I brought you some pretties for Christmas," she said. "There's laurel and rhododendron and mistletoe and some balsam—that's rare and from high up the mountain. I thought maybe you could put the boughs in them big jugs either side your door here."

They were clean, large branches, clipped to symmetry, and the leaves had been washed and oiled until they shone.

"That's wonderful," said Jennifer. "They're perfect for the jugs. Thank you so much. What do I owe you?"

"No price," said Mrs. Valiant. " 'Tis a gift."

Jennifer thanked her again and asked her to come inside the house. She wrapped a fruitcake in silver foil and brought it to Mrs. Valiant, who nodded her appreciation.

"Big, bare house you got," she said, "but it's right nice."

"My husband and I like it," said Jennifer. "His father built it."

"I mind his father," said Mrs. Valiant. "He was a fine figure in these parts. Your husband came to see me about them foreigners on the mountain. He set with me a spell and I told him some. I read in the *Crier* that they caught the main one. Seems he used to be the same boy was working on the Prentiss place when that drinking woman got herself burned up."

"He's in jail now."

"They better watch him close to keep him there," said Mrs. Valiant. "Well, you'll be wanting to get your dinner. I won't keep you longer."

"We're going out for dinner," said Jennifer. "Can't I drive you home?"

"No, I like to walk amid them little Christmas trees all lit up," said Mrs. Valiant lyrically.

She was swift in departure. The beagles rushed after her but she hissed them back on the terrace and they obeyed. Jennifer brought a pail of water and poured it into the marble vases. She began to arrange the branches in them. There was time enough, for Stephen was not home yet. She found herself wishing that they were not going to Sara's house for dinner and then tossed the thought away impatiently. Are you always going to be a little jealous of Sara, she asked herself? Or of someone? For there will always be someone, like the beautiful daughter-in-law of the Loomises who looks like the Blessed Damosel and rides like Diana and took Steve's breath away at the hunt breakfast the other day. And why not? Who doesn't have a flash of desire, a need for the extra relationship? Steve has never mentioned Gavin's name, not since that day in New York.

Not since we came home. She put a sprig of laurel in front of the rhododendron and then changed it to feature the balsam. With a branch in hand she paused to listen. There was the sound of a horse cantering up the drive, the lovely sound in motion of Steve coming home. He would put Melody into his stall, rub him down and come in to change for dinner. The mistletoe here—she went on fixing her decoration.

"Hi!" said Steve, "what have you been up to? Cutting down the woods?"

"Your friend Mrs. Valiant brought them. As a gift."

"I like that mountain girl. Does she know that Delaney broke jail?"

"She has second sight! She said he might! Did he really get out?"

"Yes, but they'll catch up with him. I met Clint Allen on the road and they're organizing a posse. They're sure he'll take off for Georgia and they'll get bloodhounds after him if they have to. And this time they'll clap him in state prison for years. All that money he seemed to have won't be a lot of use to him for a long while."

He opened the front door and a shaft of light rose from the inlaid floor to the noble ceiling.

"Mrs. Valiant says we have a nice, bare house," said Jennifer.

"Bare?" Stephen laughed. "Well, it suits us." He gave Jennifer the untroubled kiss of routine. He said, "When I think that criminal had his eye on this house!"

"It was probably the most decent desire he ever had. Maybe the only one."

"That's one way to look at it. But when I heard that he had broken out of jail and thought of what he might have done to you that day on the mountain, I wanted to join the posse that's going after him. I thought I'd skip the party tonight. Clint Allen talked me out of it. He said that it will take people who know the Georgia woods to do the job. So I came along home. Am I late? I stopped in for a drink with Julius as I went by their house and we got to talking."

"There's time enough. Are the Martins coming to Sara's?"

"I said we'd pick up Cicely. Julius doesn't feel up to going, but he wants Cicely to go."

"She should. Cicely's having a very good time these days, though of course she worries about Julius. There's nothing more than usual wrong with him?"

"No, he says he's just hoarding his strength. It seems to have given him a new lease on life to handle that business about Aga's son last summer. He's kept in touch with Mailer, advises him. He

I Took My Love to the Country * 249

told me tonight that he had never arbitrated anything that he enjoyed doing more or thought was more important. He says that arbitration between people of different colors is the big job in the world today."

"He's probably right."

"He's apt to be right," said Stephen, "and they are beginning to know that around here. Clint Allen says that Julius is the best addition to this town in a long while."

"Clint thinks you're quite an addition too."

"That remains to be seen," said Stephen thoughtfully. "Julius and I were talking today about DeSoto and how it fits into what so many people are talking about—getting a better balance between the city and the country, encouraging people to stay in the country and to come to live there. You've read about it, you know what I mean."

"Yes, I've read about it. But I believe it's one of the things you have to discover for yourself. There are things like that."

"Anyway DeSoto is bound to grow."

"I love it the way it is," said Jennifer, on her way upstairs. "Sara said eight o'clock."